SINNERS ON SUNSET

DEBRA DUNBAR

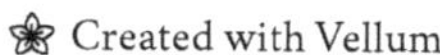 Created with Vellum

Jagged metal sliced the back of my shirt as I slid under the gate and into the yard. A high-pitched scream was quickly followed by the sound of gunfire—from behind me as well as to my left. Thankfully, the woman in a bikini on her back deck looked to be aiming more at the rooftop next door than at me, and the fuckers chasing me had the aim of kindergarteners.

But even kindergarteners occasionally got lucky. Rolling away from the fence, I felt dirt spray up beside me, then the sharp stab of pain in my side.

I sprang to my feet, threw my backpack over one shoulder, and ran. It never crossed my mind to ditch the thing. I needed every bit of salvage I could find, so I wasn't about to lose a morning's work to some assholes who thought I was poaching on their territory.

Admittedly, my license had been suspended, so technically I *was* always poaching at this time. But Karen and Chad were dicks. They would most likely have shot me even if I'd been in good standing and within legal rights to salvage anywhere in the greater Los Angeles area.

"Get off my lawn," the woman screamed, shooting the downspout off her neighbor's gutter.

"I'm trying," I shouted back, pressing a hand to my side and running for the opposite fence. Wow, her yard was big. It hadn't seemed this big when I'd first stood up, but weird spatial distortions apparently happened when you were shot and going into shock.

"Stay out of Sherman Oaks!"

I glanced back and saw Karen waving her revolver wildly. The woman had no sense of muzzle or trigger safety. It was a wonder she hadn't shot her husband. Not that Chad knew what he was doing with that semi-automatic .338 he'd outfitted to look like a fucking machine gun. It was bad enough they dressed like suburban yuppies, the least they could do is learn how to safely use a weapon.

That's what happened when Vulture licenses went to anyone with the money to buy one. They were supposed to be restricted to a certain number per area, but money talked, and Karen and Chad clearly had more money than sense.

I finally reached the end of the yard and jumped, catching the top of the chain link and nearly passing out as I pulled myself over the top. Blood decorated both sides of the fence as I slid down the other side and held on a few seconds to catch my breath. Neither Chad nor Karen were in any shape to climb, or even run more than half a block, and the home-owner had stopped shooting now that I was out of her yard. It felt as if I were out of immediate danger, but I didn't want to linger, so, gritting my teeth, I slowly jogged across a few more unfenced yards and got a few blocks away before pausing under the shelter of an overpass to evaluate my injuries.

I couldn't really see much of the bullet wound on my side, but it hurt like hell. It was low and enough on the side of my waist that I didn't think the bullet had hit anything vital.

Yanking a bandana out of my backpack, I wadded it up and pressed it to the wound. Then I took off my belt and used it to hold the makeshift bandage in place.

Fuckers. I wasn't surprised that Karen and Chad came after me, but the odds that they'd actually hit me with one of their poorly aimed shots had been slim. With the amount of bullets they'd been shooting, they were bound to hit something occasionally. It sucked that their luck hit on the one day they were shooting at me. I'd need to clean this wound up, put some sterile gauze on it, and maybe throw down some of the antibiotics I'd bought for Sadie. I didn't need a raging infection right now.

Despite getting shot, the haul had been worth the risk. The dead guy must have been flush from some big drug deal because I'd scored at least seven hundred in cash. I'd also grabbed both his guns along with a fully loaded second magazine for one of them. I'd been about to grab the gaudy-ass gold chain sporting a ruby-eyed dragon pendant he'd been wearing, but the arrival of Chad and Karen had prematurely ended my scavenging.

Cash. Guns. A handful of bullets and a spare mag. Normally that wouldn't have been that great of a haul, but the cash had me nearly giddy with excitement. Cash meant I didn't have to risk going to a pawnshop and hoping the broker would deal with me under the table and not turn me in for a bounty. The surveillance at Bags's place was no longer 24x7, but I knew the taxing authority was auditing his books regularly, and I didn't want to put him in danger by running stuff through his store right now.

I needed my license reinstated, but to do that I'd need to get that crooked cop to revise her report that pegged me for salvaging a haul I didn't take and put me in the crosshairs of the demons who ran the tax office. That wasn't likely to happen without pointing a gun at her head, and I wasn't sure

I wanted the entire LAPD after me for threatening and assaulting one of their own.

Not that I *could* threaten or assault her. I didn't even know the cop's name or where she could be found. Finding that out was quickly moving up my priority list—just as soon as I threw some cash at Bishop. It had been over two weeks since I'd brought Nevarra home. I wasn't sure what Bishop's expectations were as far as a payment plan or even exactly what I owed him, but I wasn't willing to test his patience by letting too much time go by without some effort at repayment.

Smoothing my shirt back down, I turned to leave and barely missed getting punched in the face. As I dodged a second punch, another assailant grabbed me and slammed me against the bridge abutment. Pain bloomed through me and I gasped.

"Don't kill her," the initial guy said.

"More worried about her killing me," the other replied, pinning my arms against the concrete.

I kicked out, nailing the one guy's shin, then squirmed in an attempt to get free.

He swore. "Little help here? Grab her gun."

The other guy hesitated.

"Five thousand, Jeff," the guy who held me said. "Five fucking grand. Ten if we get her to tell us where the loot is."

That motivated Jeff, who tried to grab my pistol from the shoulder holster. I twisted, blocking him with my shoulder as I kicked my attacker once more. He stepped closer, trying to pin my legs with his own, which put him close enough for me to head butt him as hard as I could.

The guy yelped and jumped back, his grip loosening enough for me to get an arm free. I spun, punching Jeff in the nose. Then I kept turning, bringing my elbow up and slamming the other guy in the face with it.

They both stepped back. I pulled my pistol at the exact same time they pulled theirs.

"Drop—"

I fired, not waiting for the guy to finish his sentence. I'd been aiming for his shoulder but missed and hit the bicep of his gun-arm instead.

He screamed, the pistol falling from his hand. I hopped to the side and swung my gun around, hearing a gunshot and feeling the spray of concrete chips less than a foot from my head. I unloaded in a wide pattern, hoping at least one of my shots hit something vital. Small groupings were impressive as hell on a target at a range, but I'd learned long ago that in an adrenaline-filled situation, shooting a broad pattern was what got the job done.

Four in Jeff. Pivot and duck, then put three more in the other guy, who'd picked up the pistol with his non-dominant hand and was seconds away from plugging me. I ran over to Jeff, kicking his gun away before doing the same to the other guy. Then I spun in a slow circle, looking for other assailants and walking backward to park my rear against the bridge abutment and catch my breath.

Thank the Lord for a twelve-round magazine that had been illegal in California up until the demons came. With the traffic noise and the pain from my gunshot wound, I hadn't even heard these guys until they were attacking me. I'd been lucky. If the one guy had knocked me out, or if Jeff had been able to get my pistol free, this might have ended very differently.

No one else came for me, but I wasn't taking any chances, so I switched out my magazine for a full one, kept my pistol in hand, and tried to decide if I should linger and see if these guys had anything worth stealing, or get the hell out of here.

Five grand. My hands shook as what the two had said sank in. The typical bounty on someone was anywhere from five hundred to a thousand, depending on what they'd done and what sort of risk a mercenary might have to take to bring them in.

Somehow I'd gone from an easy job to one requiring a large bounty. No doubt that had something to do with the fact that I'd been leaving a trail of bodies in my wake for the last month. A bounty that big meant I was going to have a whole lot more people gunning for me. Five grand would bring out the big guns, the experienced and highly skilled mercenaries who didn't bother with the little jobs. And if that wasn't bad enough, I was evidently worth ten grand if someone could bring me in along with the loot.

My life just got a fucking whole lot more dangerous. I'd need to be looking over my shoulder every second. Bea and the girls would be in even more danger, from mercenaries trying to pump them for information to those who would use my family as leverage to get me to come in on my own.

This needed to stop. It wasn't just about getting my license reinstated anymore. I needed to get my name cleared. I needed to get this bounty off my head. There was only one person I could think of who might be able to help me, and luckily I had a meeting with her this afternoon.

Quickly rooting through the dead men's pockets, I grabbed what little cash and bullets they had, leaving their guns behind. Then I settled my backpack on my shoulders, made my way to my bike, and headed east to the mountains. I had a bit of time before my meeting and I didn't like the idea of walking around with this much cash on me. The quicker I got it into Bishop's hands, the better.

Bishop's bar, Suerte, was up in the hills, on a winding road that held only a few widely spaced houses and the occasional gas station. I wasn't too surprised to see a few vehicles in the parking lot as I pulled in. It was a little before noon, but I got the feeling they had a few regulars who popped in for lunch, as well as a few who made it a habit to hang out in the bar all day, or night, long. Parking my bike beside Bishop's old truck, I checked to make sure my bandage hadn't slipped and I wasn't bleeding all down my side before heading in. Blood-soaked wasn't a good look for me. It wasn't a good look for anyone. Normally I wouldn't care, but I had a bit of a thing for Bishop and found myself oddly concerned about my appearance whenever I expected to see him.

I'd learned early on that Suerte wasn't always a welcoming place, so I hesitated once I was over the threshold to survey the patrons. A guy wearing a cowboy hat and looking to be a leathery eighty sat at the corner of the bar watching the news and drinking a beer. Four middle-aged women chatted at a table covered with coffee cups and half-eaten sandwiches. HB was behind the bar. I took a few steps toward her then hesitated as I saw there was another patron off to the side. He seemed to be mid-forties with his long, wiry dark beard shot through with streaks of iron gray.

Fuck. Our eyes met and for a few long seconds he held my gaze. With an exaggerated yawn, Dale turned his back on me and focused his attention on one of the TV screens.

Dale had been at Suerte the first night I'd come here looking to ask for Bishop's help to find my kidnapped sister. He and his buddy had attacked me. It didn't look like he was aiming to repeat the events of that night, but a person couldn't be too careful.

Keeping a careful side-eye on Dale, I finished my walk to the bar. HB was her usual platinum blonde perfection except for a faint scar running from her jaw down her neck and across her chest. It hadn't been there when I'd last seen her at the bar, but given the way the scar was indented and puckered, it looked like it had been a very serious wound—one that shouldn't have healed to this extent in a couple of weeks.

It was one more thing that gave me reason to put HB in the not-a-human category.

The woman looked up at me, smiled, then took a few careful steps over to fill a glass with ice and tea. She moved like she was still recovering from a bad accident.

"Are you okay?" I asked as she set the tea down in front of me.

"I will be in a few more weeks." She shrugged. "At least I'm up and walking. Broke six ribs and fractured my pelvis as well as two vertebrae. That shit takes a while to heal."

If you were human, that shit took a good sight more than three or four weeks to heal. HB, obviously, wasn't human.

Demons walked among us. Dragons occasionally flew overhead. Weird creatures were now the norm in Los Angeles, and that included shifters—although from what the news reports said, there had always been shifters, living right beside us for eons, pretending to be human. I was convinced Bob was a shifter—a weredog or werewolf or something. Bishop either wasn't human, or he was a human like me with magical abilities. Clearly HB was *something* as well if she was up and walking around two weeks after being crushed like an aluminum can and sliced from jaw to sternum.

I thought back on that night in the customs warehouse, when a mountain lion had saved my life, when Bishop had spoken to that mountain lion as if she were an old, valued friend. Desiree had nearly killed the mountain lion, but Bishop had picked the animal up and taken it to safety—*her* to safety. Bishop had known the mountain lion, known it was a she. He and HB were close. All this supernatural shit might be new to me, but I wasn't an idiot. Even I could tell that two plus two equaled HB being a cougar shifter.

"I never had a chance to say thank you. For everything. For that night," I finished awkwardly, not positive about my identification of HB as the mountain lion, or her willingness to admit to being "other."

She shrugged. "Bishop's not the only one who's got a soft spot when it comes to kids. I'm just glad you got your sister back. Is she doing okay?"

"She's fine."

Hopefully she *would* be fine, eventually. Nevarra was the queen of bottling it all up and refusing to show any pain—physical or emotional. I couldn't exactly cast stones on that front, so I let her deal with it however she wanted. It bothered me that she hadn't burned that lacy, frilly white dress the moment she'd changed out of it, though. It was still balled up in a corner of the girls' room, in plain view, where she had to see it every time she was in there. Why would she want that constant reminder? Was she harboring some guilt, some silly belief that what she'd gone through was her fault? Or did she need that dress to keep her anger stoked up, because if the anger faded, that's when the fear and sorrow crept in?

Knowing Nevarra, it was probably some combination of the two.

"Eden?" HB's nose twitched. "You're bleeding."

Damn it. I hiked up my tattered, bloody tank top and saw that she was right. Blood had soaked through the second bandana and was dripping down my hip, leaving a dark wet stain along the side of my olive-colored cargo pants. I grabbed a fistful of bar napkins and undid the belt. Letting the blood-soaked bandanas drop to the floor, I pressed the napkins to the wound. None of the patrons in the bar seemed bothered about my bleeding all over the establishment, but I wasn't sure how Bishop, or HB, would feel about it.

"Sorry about the mess." I held the napkins in place and bent down to pick up the bandanas, swiping the floor with them. Instead of wiping up the blood, I ended up just smearing more across the shiny oak planks.

I stood, and my eyes met Bishop's. He'd moved with unnatural silence, somehow managing to appear before me from wherever he'd previously been in mere seconds. I didn't know if the guy was just superfast or teleported, but I added either option to my growing list of things that made Bishop scary.

"How in the hell did you get shot?" he demanded. "Or did you manage to do that yourself?"

I bristled at the thought that I was such a noob that I'd managed to put a bullet through my own side. "Some competing Vultures thought I was poaching. One of them got lucky and hit me."

I didn't bother telling him that the two mercenaries who'd attacked me directly afterward hadn't helped the situation any.

Bishop's hand shot forward to grab my wrist. He pulled my hand with the wad of bloody napkins away and knelt down to inspect the wound.

"It's not that bad," I protested. It wouldn't be that bad if I stopped fighting, running, and driving long enough for the thing to clot.

He grunted. The noise carried a lot of disbelief with it. Whether that disbelief was over my being idiot enough to get shot, being idiot enough to try to staunch the wound with a handful of napkins, or being idiot enough to claim the wound wasn't that bad, I didn't know.

"Want me to bandage it up?" HB offered, as if she were volunteering to run the trash out to the dumpster and not perform serious first aid on a gunshot wound.

"I'll do it." Bishop jerked a thumb toward a door behind the bar. "Office. Now."

I wasn't going to decline an offer for medical attention,

especially when the alternative was probably losing another pint of blood before the wound clotted up, so I grabbed my backpack and followed Bishop into the office.

He shut the door, and I quickly looked around. The room was small, or rather, it looked small with everything that was crammed into it. An L-shaped oak desk took up most of the space, and a couch took up the rest. The desk was stacked with papers and three-ring binders, an office chair barely visible behind them. The couch was a dark leather, worn to a shiny gold in spots. Someone had put a tasseled teal silk pillow at one end. Wood paneling covered every wall, and the ceiling was done in a white popcorn finish. Outside of the decorative pillow, I felt as if I'd stepped back into a gritty 1970s cop movie. Yep. I was pretty sure I'd seen this exact same office on a *Starsky and Hutch* rerun a few years ago.

I set my backpack down on the couch and pulled up my shirt, turning to Bishop so he could get another good view of the carnage.

He stared at my side. I stared at him. I got the strange feeling he was waiting for something to happen.

"Well, go ahead." He waved a hand at my waist.

"Go ahead and what?" I gaped at him.

"Fix it. No one can see in here." He waved at my waist again. I kept staring, so he made an exasperated noise and turned around so his back faced me. "There. Is that better?"

Was I supposed to get naked? Dance the Cha Cha? What the fuck did he want me to do? "I thought you were going to bandage me up?" I tentatively asked. "Or maybe heal me."

Someone had healed me when I'd had my knee shot out a few weeks ago. The Fixers who'd grabbed me had been dead, so the only living beings in the room were me, Bishop, and Fluffy the Durft. I'd been out cold, and even if I'd been conscious, I had no ability to speed-heal injuries. I doubted the rabid groundhog from hell was able to magically heal, even if he'd wanted to. That left Bishop.

He muttered something that sounded like "fucking masochists" and spun around.

I'm not sure what I expected, but it wasn't him taking a stapler off his desk and coming at me with intent.

"Whoa, whoa!" I backed up. "Bandages. Or stitches. Needle and thread, buddy, not a stapler."

"Do I look like I have a sewing kit handy?" He clicked the stapler at me, and I held up both hands, prepared to defend myself.

I took another step back. "HB offered to help. I'd rather she bandage the wound then you puncture the crap out of me with a desk stapler."

"HB doesn't have a sewing kit or bandages either." He put the stapler back. "It's not like we ever need to doctor up wounds around here."

Probably not. I imagined shifters healed quickly, especially if HB was any indication. She'd been a mangled mess on that warehouse floor, and here she was walking around two weeks later. Limping and scarred, yes, but still, she'd healed far faster than any human I'd ever seen.

"How about this?"

I looked up to see Bishop holding a roll of duct tape and shuddered, thinking how painful that was going to be to remove after the wound started to heal.

"How about just some more napkins? I'll clean it up with water and use my belt again to hold them in place."

"Suit yourself." Bishop tossed the duct tape on the couch and went out of the office. While he was gone, I had a chance to look around and basically snoop. The three-ring binders were filled with papers that held a solid wall of text in a language I'd never seen before—single-spaced, double-sided. Not a chart or graph to be seen. The other papers were bills, a survey for some property up in the mountains, a flyer with special sale items from a liquor distributor. I saw a name on one bunch of papers that caught my eye and pulled it out from the stack.

Something about a formal request to dissolve a pack and re-establish under new leadership. Off in the margins in blue ink was "Need to take some action on this one!" The comment was signed "HB."

I stuffed it back in the pile as Bishop came through the door. He kindly didn't mention my snooping. I took the bowl of water and clean rag from his hand and cleared a space for it on his desk. Then I took my shirt off.

It sounded sexier than it was. I was filthy, covered in both dried and fresh blood, and I didn't even have on a pretty bra. Sports bras covered more than most bathing suit tops and didn't really do the whole lift-and-separate thing. Basically, I was a mashed uni-boob with a smudge of dirt across the front of my chest.

Ignoring the dirt, I got to work on carefully cleaning the wound while Bishop opened a little first-aid box and rooted around in it.

"Thought you didn't have one of those." I winced as I pressed the wet cloth to the still-oozing wound.

"I didn't think we had one either. HB said she picked it up on a Costco run a few months back." He grumbled something under his breath. "I hate sending her to Costco for anything. She always comes back with eight hundred dollars' worth of jumbo-sized crap."

"You don't know you need eight hundred dollars' worth of jumbo-sized crap until you see it there on the shelf," I countered.

Costco was still open and in business. The only real difference between the mega store now versus two years ago was that the guards at the door eyeing your membership card were armed. I was pretty sure you wouldn't get shot trying to steal a ten-pound pork loin and a six-gallon jug of barbeque sauce anywhere outside of L.A.

I missed Costco. Bea had let our membership lapse two years ago when the demons came. We'd tightened back on a lot of things since then. It seemed silly to pay for a membership to a place when you couldn't afford to buy stuff in mega-sized containers.

"I get that we need the crate of paper towels and two crates of toilet paper, but an entire case of pumpkin spice coffee pods? And a four pack of sonic toothbrushes? And this thing?" He waved at the first-aid kit.

I was glad she'd bought the first-aid kit, especially when my only other alternatives were duct tape or a desk stapler.

"You've got pumpkin spice coffee pods?" I said with a grin. "Sold. I'll be here every morning from September first until spring."

He pulled out a box of Band-Aids from the first-aid kit. "Good. Because if we don't get rid of that shit, I'm going to sit HB in a chair and make her drink it all herself in one go."

I took the box, selected a few items, and started to open them.

"Here." Bishop knelt down beside me, taking the edge of the rag and blotting around the wound. With one hand he held the ragged edges together. I handed him the Band-Aid, and he secured it on the lower edge, snugging it tight on the top so the wound remained closed. Then he continued with a second and a third bandage.

I suppressed a shiver at his touch. Looking down at the top of his head, I wondered how soft that wavy sun-streaked blond hair was. Having him kneeling down beside me made my mind detour to all sorts of fantasies. I could strip off my pants, sweep all those papers and binders off his desk, sit up on the edge and lean back while he drove himself into me.

Or better yet, he could kneel down and get busy with that sexy mouth.

"There." Bishop had finished with the Band-Aids and put a thick square of gauze over them. He looked up at me, and I saw the golden sparks in his ocean-blue eyes. For a second we were frozen in time, our gazes locked.

Then I sucked in a breath, turned my head, and picked up a roll of gauze. As I wrapped it around my waist, I wondered at this attraction I had for him. He was strong. Confident. Dangerous. When I'd said he wasn't my type, I'd meant his looks. His personality most definitely was my type—in spades. Which meant *I* probably wasn't his type at all.

He and HB were close. I could feel a bond between them that came with a long, affectionate relationship. Were they partners? Lovers? Just really good friends? I couldn't believe that two such gorgeous people *wouldn't* have fallen into bed at one point or another. It was really going to suck if I continued to be desperately in lust for Bishop only to find out he was committed to a woman I admired, respected, and might even consider a friend.

What had he said when I'd offered sex in trade for his help in finding Nevarra? Had it been *if* I were ever in his bed, it wouldn't be because I owed him? Or was it *when*? Either one hinted at a future possibility.

Yeah. I was totally grasping at the slightest bit of hope here.

I held the gauze while Bishop cut the end and taped it in place. The wound still hurt, but it was down to a dull ache now, muffled by layers of gauze and bandages. He'd done a good job. This should keep it from bleeding again unless I had to sprint a few blocks, jump over a fence, or fight off a pair of bounty hunters.

Not bad for a gunshot wound. I'd been lucky it was so

minor, even if I'd been unlucky enough to catch one of Karen's poorly aimed bullets.

He stood, his hand lingering for a moment on my waist. "Hope you've got another shirt. That one's trashed."

My laundry basket at home was filled with trashed clothes. When I got a few seconds in my day, I washed the blood out of them, hung them up to dry, then turned them over to Bea for repair. Some were usually beyond repair, but most were wearable again if I didn't mind having big Frankenstein-looking patches on my clothes.

"I've been carrying a spare in my backpack." I turned away from Bishop, feeling a sudden chill. He radiated heat, like someone who was in the throes of a high fever, or like someone who'd just come out of working at a kiln. He wasn't sweaty, just warm. It was the end of summer, which in L.A. meant it was still upward of one hundred degrees on the regular. You wouldn't think standing next to a Bishop furnace would be comfortable, but it was.

The spare shirt I'd packed was a little snug, and the layers of gauze wrapped around my waist plus the bandages didn't do my silhouette any favors. It's not like I was going on a date, though. I doubted Detective Juke would care if I looked a little thick around the middle.

"I've got something for you," I told Bishop as I pulled a wad of blood-stained cash out of my backpack. I counted my stash for the last few days. Nine hundred in total—seven just from the salvage this morning. I hated to hand the majority of it over to Bishop, but Bea had told me that we were good with food at home. She was back to work now that Sadie was healing, while Nevarra took care of her sister with some unusually eager help from Javier down the street.

If I paid the debts off, then we could start to save again. I hated being in debt to anyone, and I especially loathed owing Bishop money. Not because he was any sort of hard-ass when it came to me paying him. It was the fact that my pulse raced like a thoroughbred at the track every time he touched me that made me not want to be in debt to him.

I wanted to fuck him, and he'd made it clear that wouldn't happen while this obligation stood between us. It might not happen even after I'd paid up, but I was still going to give it my best shot.

And if he and HB were involved…well, I'd need to take an icy shower, dig that vibrator out of the dresser drawer, and never see this man again.

Actually, I should probably find that vibrator sooner rather than later.

I peeled a hundred in twenties off the stack, shoved it in my pants pocket, then handed the rest over. Bishop took the money, recounted it, then pulled a receipt book out of the mess on his desk. I took the receipt with some reluctance, not comfortable with this business-like formality. I wanted trust, and a receipt for what I'd paid—a declining balance on the ledger books—wasn't trust in my mind.

"Thanks for the doctoring," I told him as I stuffed the receipt and my ruined shirt into the backpack. "I almost brought you a necklace, but got chased off before I could take it off the dead guy."

"A necklace?" Bishop shot me an incredulous look. "You were going to give me a necklace?"

"Not to wear or anything. It was insanely ugly." I shrugged. "Could have been worth something at one of those places that buys crap jewelry and melts it down. Although with my luck it was probably electroplated and not even real gold."

Bishop grunted. "Do me a favor and don't bring me ugly necklaces."

"Got it. I'll only bring you the pretty ones, not gaudy chains with big-ass dragon pendants." With a name like

Bishop, he was probably into rugged-looking crosses. Or maybe those leather and bead surfer necklaces.

If I'd been able to grab the necklace, I might have taken it to the Gray Dogs first. They were good about paying a finder's fee for salvage that was gang-related. Although I doubted ruby-eyed dragon pendants were a symbol a gang named the Gray Dogs would choose. Still, maybe one of them was a friend of the deceased and would want his hideous necklace to remember him by. A finder's fee would have been more than I'd have gotten anywhere else.

But all that was moot anyway, since the ugly necklace was probably gracing the stocky neck of either Karen or Chad right now. I'd gotten what was important—the cash. And I'd managed to get away from both the salvage and the following attack with only a minor gunshot wound and some bruises.

Once more I thought about the two guys who'd tried to grab me under the bridge. Yes, I'd gotten away, but next time I might not.

And with five thousand dollars in bounty on my head, there would definitely be a next time.

CHAPTER 2

I left Suerte behind and rode into Glendale, parking in a pothole-strewn lot behind an abandoned building that used to be an art gallery. Finding a spot to park was sometimes a crapshoot, but the joy of having a motorcycle meant I could park places where those with cars would hesitate to venture.

Not wanting to risk my helmet in pretty much the exact location my previous one had been stolen, I tucked it under my arm and took it with me. It was big, awkward, and if I needed to grab my pistol and start shooting, I'd lose a fraction of a second dropping it to the ground. Normally I wouldn't expect to be involved in a shootout on what was actually a pretty decent retail area of Glendale, but I was alert and prepared for the worst. Those two guys this morning wouldn't be the only ones after me now that the bounty on my head had been raised.

I was meeting the detective in a place called Grits. It was a narrow building sandwiched between an antique shop and a jewelry store. Inside was a long counter with the kitchen on one side and a line of two-person tables on the other. A stout woman cooked, her frizzy dark hair making a valiant attempt to escape from her net cap. A younger and thinner version of the cook sat on a stool behind the cash register, her gaze firmly fixed on her phone.

I'd arrived first. Which meant I needed to order something or risk getting thrown out for loitering. Looking up at the menu board, I realized that the place's name wasn't all that creative. They sold grits. Just grits.

Good thing I liked grits.

The young woman looked up as I approached the register. I ordered a small shrimp grits with bacon and extra cheddar, then dug some money out of my pocket. The woman didn't even bat an eyelid at the bloodstains on the twenty. In fact, a few of the bills she gave me back were just as stained.

I pocketed the cash, took the plastic card she gave me with a number "eight" on it, and went to sit in the rear of the dining area. Back to the wall. Eyes on the door.

Detective Juke arrived the same time as my grits. She placed a quick order, then sat down opposite me with a grimace.

"Wanna switch seats?" she asked.

"I'm not having *my* back to the door," I told her as I shoveled a spoonful of grits into my mouth. Mmmm. Not as good as Bea's, but definitely worth the eight bucks I'd paid for them.

"This is killing me." The detective turned her chair sideways, twisting her body around so she at least had a peripheral view of the entrance.

"Cops," I scoffed.

"Vultures," she scoffed back.

I liked her. Bags had been right. Sarah Juke was a good cop. She had integrity but was smart enough to know that in this new world, cops that allowed themselves to do some creative deviating from the rules were the ones who delivered justice.

After I'd brought Nevarra home, I'd splurged on a pay-by-the-minute phone at a convenience store, and one of my first calls had been to the Detective. It seemed she'd been trying to reach me on my old stolen phone number and was eager to meet. When Bishop had taken the trafficked kids from the customs warehouse, he'd dropped them off at the Crenshaw station. While they were contacting the kids' parents, the cops had handed the case off to a detective who was smart enough to call Juke. Juke had worked in the Human Trafficking division before the demons came, and although homicide was every detective's first priority now, she was the go-to cop in the city for this sort of thing.

Juke had hauled herself down to Crenshaw, interviewed eight kids and their parents, and gone to visit the customs warehouse where the police had already set up barricades and called in the techs.

I'd told her a roundabout and incredibly vague tale about tracking the operation to the warehouse where I'd found the kids as well as a bunch of dead guards seemingly mauled by a mountain lion. I claimed that one of the guards confessed who Nevarra had been sold to and where the guy lived as some sort of dying penance. In the story I'd told the detective, I'd arrived at that house to find the buyer already dead and Nevarra locked in the basement.

She hadn't believed a word. And that was okay with me.

"I wanted to let you know there's been progress on the human trafficking case." Juke set her plastic card with a number "nine" on the table between us. "We arrested Jimmie Pollis. He's given us some information on a few other of the Disciples that were involved, but a good number of the key players died in the warehouse that night. He claims that

Desiree blamed the Disciples who were guarding the customs warehouse for losing the kids, and that she said she killed the lot of them as punishment."

I wasn't sure how to take that. On the one hand, I was glad she hadn't blamed the whole thing on me because then I'd have the Disciples after me in addition to all the other shit I was facing. On the other hand, her taking credit for the massacre gave me cause for concern. As a demon, Desiree probably didn't give two craps about any vengeance the Disciples might decide to pursue, but why potentially burn that bridge? Why not blame the whole thing on me, or Bishop, or the cops?

"That doesn't exactly jive with your story." Juke didn't appear at all surprised by that fact. "You said you arrived to find the guards all dead or dying, and the kids locked in the back. The demon's story, admittedly told through a third party, is that the kids were gone when she got there, and she killed the guards in retaliation."

"Demons lie," I informed her, taking another bite of my grits.

"So do humans." Her eyes narrowed. "Where does this Bishop guy fit into any of this? I get that you couldn't transport eight kids on a motorcycle, but why not call the police? Why call a guy who lives all the way up in the Valley and have him drive over an hour to the airport just to take the kids into a nearby police station?"

"I trust him." I suddenly realized that I'd implied I didn't trust the police. Oh well. Not like *that* was a lie anyway. "I knew he was in the area, and that he'd help me out. Plus, I wanted to go rescue Nevarra. Any minute she was with that asshole who bought her was one minute too long."

Juke nodded at that. "Agreed, but you could have called us to help you with that as well."

You could have called me was the unsaid rest of that statement. Juke was hurt that I hadn't brought her in on the operation she'd been working on for years. She was hurt I didn't trust her enough to, at the very least, ask her to be my backup.

She shouldn't be hurt. I didn't trust many people. That number used to be all of three, but in the last few weeks it had expanded to more like six. Maybe seven. And only a few of those were people I *completely* trusted. Bea. The girls.

Bishop.

Including Bishop in my trust list made me very uneasy. I hadn't known him that long. He'd earned *some* trust, but I couldn't figure out why he'd become someone in whose hands I'd put my life or the lives of my family. It couldn't just be hormones. There were a lot of guys I'd be happy to screw, but I wouldn't trust most of them with a used Kleenex. No, there was something more between Bishop and me.

"I couldn't call you because my phone crapped out." I had gone over this with Juke before, but she was clearly bothered about the whole thing.

"It crapped out because you'd stolen it, and the owner canceled service," she muttered.

I sighed, pulled my new, cheap-ass phone out of my pocket, and set it on the table. "Well, I *bought* this one." Although that didn't mean I'd call her if I was about to do something like break into a pedophile's house, kill him, and rescue my sister.

"Right. So back to the topic at hand, our intel says Desiree has put the whole human trafficking business on hold, saying she can't run the enterprise with subpar help."

I snorted. "Meaning the Disciples aren't willing to hand over half a dozen of their best only to have them slaughtered in one of her temper tantrums."

It made me wonder once more why she'd taken the cred-it/blame for killing the guards. Maybe she figured it was fitting that the guards had died if they couldn't fight off one woman and a mountain lion. She probably would have killed them if I'd managed to sneak the kids out under their noses. Maybe she wanted the extra street cred, although demons didn't exactly need to prove they were top of the badass food chain around here.

Maybe she didn't want me to take the blame, to have an additional bullseye on my back. It would probably suck if the Disciples killed me before she got to claim her own pound of flesh from me.

I poked at my grits, thoughts of the demon killing my appetite. I owed Desiree a favor, and since she was a demon, I was pretty sure she'd want me to do something horrible. I had no confidence that one favor would be it either. I'd traded myself for Nevarra. It was a trade I'd make again in a hot second, but thinking about it still sent a wave of fear rolling through me.

Fear and anger. I was glad to hear Desiree had taken Bishop's advice and stopped her human trafficking operation, but I knew it was only a matter of time before she started it up again, maybe with a different gang for muscle.

I couldn't let her do that. I couldn't let her gear up a business that preyed on stolen children. I'd done a lot of bad shit in my fairly short life. There were times where I put far more than a toe over the line between right and wrong. But selling children was a mile into the evil territory.

Juke looked up and smiled her thanks as the cashier brought over her grits, then waited for the woman to leave before turning back to me. "Sure you don't have anything else you'd like to tell me about that night in the warehouse? Or at William Cumberland's house in Santa Monica?"

I shoveled in another spoonful of grits, eyes on my bowl. "It was shocking to find all those dead bodies. And the dead man in Santa Monica."

"Right." Juke stirred a few pats of butter into her cheesy grits. "I get the feeling you didn't lose any sleep over Cumberland."

"Nope. I'm guessing you didn't either."

"Nope. Your prints were all over that house and basement."

"I'm sure they were. I heard someone shouting for help and went in."

"There was no mountain lion in the customs warehouse. Nothing on any of the manifests that showed a live animal shipment passing through the warehouse. There was no crate that might have been used for an animal."

I looked up and met her gaze, because this time I was telling the truth. "There was a mountain lion there. I saw it myself. I got the kids out and had my friend take them to the police station while I went to find my sister."

"Lots of dead in your wake, Alvaro." Juke took a bite of her grits. "Lots of dead. Most of them Disciples gang members."

I nodded. "It's a strange coincidence. And I doubt you're losing any sleep over their deaths, either."

She snorted a laugh. "Can I interview your sister at least?"

"No."

Absolutely not. Over my fucking dead body not. There was no way this woman was going to make Nevarra live through that nightmare again. The detective would just need to make her case without my sister's help.

And honestly, most of the work was done as far as the ring went. She had Jimmie. She was probably breathing down Thumbs's neck as well as any other Disciple involved in the enterprise. I'm sure once she had Thumbs, she could get into the website data and track down the buyers. Juke might look like a cross between Orphan Annie and Zorro with her freckles, her poof of red-orange hair, and her black leather, but I got the feeling she was a pit bull when it came to catching these guys. I'd given her a lead, and she'd follow it until she caught them all.

"I wanted to fill you in on how the trafficking case was going, but I also wanted to see if you could help me out with something," Juke said.

I ate another spoonful of grits and eyed her, wondering if she wanted me to kill someone or provide information. "Like what?"

"There was this dead guy in the morgue that we picked up about three weeks ago. One of the Gray Dogs. Guy went by the name Dragon, although legally he was Herbert Adams."

I laughed, thinking I'd go by a nickname too if I'd been saddled with Herbert at birth.

"It's weird," Juke added.

"Weird how?" Everything was weird nowadays. Demons. Kittens with laser eyes. Shifters. Elves. I wouldn't be surprised to see a unicorn walking down the street. Well, I'd be surprised, but not shocked out of my mind.

"All his bones were gone."

I paused the spoon halfway to my mouth and put it back in the bowl. "Deboned? Like a chicken tender? Was he cut up into pieces? How the hell does that happen?"

Juke shrugged. "The man didn't have a mark on him. We get the call and find him like a deflated balloon sprawled across his sofa. The guy's girlfriend was hysterical—she'd have to have been to call us for a gang member's death. She said she came home from work and found him like that."

That *was* weird. Gross and weird.

"We bag and tag the guy," Juke went on. "And less than a week later, we've got another death. One of the women from the M.E.'s office."

"Some kind of bone-dissolving plague?" I speculate, thinking Juke should probably call in the CDC—except we're no longer part of the U.S., and I doubt New Hell has their own CDC. Maybe there was a state-level equivalent who could suit up and rush in before half the state was boneless.

"That was my thought, although 'plague' in my mind now includes magical curses or the weird way demons sometimes kill people."

Hmm. The demon thing made sense. I'd heard all sorts of twisted things they did to torture and kill people. Deboning wasn't that much of a stretch to imagine.

"The woman at the M.E.'s office didn't handle the body. She worked in admin, so I haven't been able to figure how she'd get a bone-dissolving plague and not any of the people doing the autopsy. If it *is* a plague, that is." The detective took a few bites of her grits before she continued. "So, I started thinking maybe there was some connection between her and the dead gang member outside of the morgue. Then around a week later, I get *another* call for a boneless dead woman—the sister of the woman from the M.E.'s office yesterday, and another one the *exact same day*. A local pawnbroker."

I nearly choked on my grits. "What? Who? Which pawnbroker?"

Bags. I hadn't seen him in over a week. Was he okay?

"Slinky Moore." Juke eyed me curiously. "From ABC Pawn on Vanowen Street. Did you know him?"

I exhaled, weak with relief. "Not well." Slinky was an asshole who had been known to collect taxes on a fence, then change the documentation and pocket what he wanted. I never did business with him unless I had to. A guy like that was bound to get caught sooner or later. Looked like his luck had finally run out.

"So, what do you want me to do about all this?" I asked the detective.

It's not like I knew anything about sucking the bones out

of someone without leaving a mark. I had a few magical tricks, but *that* certainly wasn't one of them.

"You run across the Gray Dogs a lot in your business dealings, right?"

I nodded. They were a gang in the Valley even before the demons came. I'd gone to school with a few of them. I'd dated one of them.

"Can you ask around and see if the dead guy pissed any demons off? I'm digging into the county employee and her sister, as well as the pawnbroker, but the Gray Dogs won't talk to me."

A demon executioner. It made sense. It's not like people's bones vaporized on the regular. I didn't mind asking around, but I was going to stay as far away from this thing as possible. Having already attracted the attention of one demon, I really didn't want to cross paths with another.

"I know a few Gray Dogs," I offered cautiously, wondering what the hell Juke was going to do about it if she found the horned murderer. It's not like the police could arrest a demon or hold them accountable to our human justice system. Maybe she just wanted to close the case, to write *Demon-killed* in big red letters and file the four deaths in the solved cabinet.

She slid me over a manila envelope. "I'd appreciate anything you could find out on this—from the Gray Dogs or even word-on-the-street. You've got your ear to the ground in places I don't."

I opened the envelope, then abruptly shut it. It was too early in the day to look at crime scene photos of boneless dead people. I'd check these out later, when I wasn't in danger of puking grits all over the table.

In reality, I was too busy trying to stay alive to bother about this case, but there *was* something I needed from

Detective Juke, and this would be the perfect opportunity to make my request in the spirit of some quid pro quo.

"I'll get your information, but I need your help on something." I leaned in a bit, even though I was reasonably sure neither the cook nor the cashier was moonlighting for the Fixers. "I was in North Hills on the third working a job. A hit went down, and everyone died, leaving behind a Buick loaded down with seventeen cases of bullets in the backseat and trunk. It was a huge haul. I was salvaging when an officer stopped me and asked for my license number."

Juke nodded. "Standard procedure. Is this the haul you didn't pay taxes on? You're still in the system as delinquent and your license suspended."

"I didn't pay taxes on it because I didn't make the haul." I paused to let that sink in. "The cop ran me off. She even made me leave my backpack behind. I left with a few guns and whatever boxes of bullets I'd managed to shove in my pants pockets. That was it. That's all I took."

Juke leaned back in her chair. "Shit. That's a serious accusation, Alvaro. Do you have any proof?"

"Proof that I don't have what I never took?" I resisted the urge to punch something. "She ran me off, put me in the system for the take, then made off with the whole lot. She set me up, Juke. I'm in serious trouble over this. There's a bounty out on me, and they just upped it. My family got hurt by the mercs sent to pick me up. The Fixers are after me. They're the ones who took Nevarra and sold her to the Disciples."

Juke put her head in her hands, then stared at the wall for a few moments. I knew what was going through her head. They had a dirty cop somewhere in the city.

And I might end up paying for her greed with my life.

"She could work for any of the precincts," Juke finally said. "I can ask around, but I doubt she'd be stupid enough to unload that stash and show up the next week driving a Ferrari."

"I'm in big trouble here, Juke. Two guys tried to grab me this morning. The bounty's at five grand. Five grand. I'm going to get hauled in, the crap beaten out of me, possibly killed over something I didn't do."

Juke pushed her grits aside. "I'll talk to my lieutenant. I'll tell him about your allegations. We'll look into it. I promise you I'll personally make sure we look into this."

I trusted her. She was a good cop, and I knew she'd do what she said. My only worry was that whatever she did might come too late.

"Is there some way you can flag the report in the system? Tell the tax office that the report was a mistake? That one of your cops screwed up, and IA, or whatever the fuck you have now, is investigating?"

Juke shook her head. "We can't just cancel the report or do any of that prior to the investigation. I'll talk to some people and see what I can do to move this along as quickly as I can. I know you're in a jam here, but I need to at least find something to back up your claims before I go flagging or changing reports."

I'd hit dead ends for weeks trying to straighten this out on my own. I needed her help. I needed *someone's* help, and I wasn't sure where to turn at this point. By the time she found her evidence and changed the report, I could be in a holding cell with some demon who was dissolving my bones or something equally horrible. But who else could I turn to?

Bishop. Except I already owed him money and who knew how much it would cost me to have him track down a cop whose name I didn't even know?

"Thanks." I met her eyes. "Thank you for believing me. Anything you could do to help me…well, I'd really appreciate it."

Juke pushed her grits away. "I don't want you dead, Alvaro. Just hang in there. Lay low. I'll work as quick as I can."

Lay low. I couldn't lay low. And I couldn't just wait around and hope I didn't get caught. I trusted Juke to work things at her end, but I needed to work things at mine, just in case.

CHAPTER 3

*A*rtemis Books was one of four shops that still remained open in a dilapidated strip mall on the corner of Oxnard and Willow Crest. I wrestled open the heavy metal door and entered, wincing as the static shock of the magical security system washed over me.

There were three customers in the bookstore, which made me feel a bit better about being here to ask a favor. Unlike the last time, I actually had more than eight bucks to my name, so I resolved myself to actually purchase something. It was typical to pay for information, and besides, I liked books. Surely I could find something here I'd enjoy for twenty bucks.

The owner, Alfie, had helped me out when I'd been looking for Nevarra a few weeks ago. I was hoping he could help me out once more.

Alfie shot me a distracted smile, then went back to helping a woman who was handling a large leather tome, literally with white gloves. The other two customers were browsing in the history section. Heading down an aisle close to the counter so I could grab Alfie's attention once he was done helping the woman, I found myself eyeing rows of what looked to be books on religion and mythology.

"I'm not sure I trust Salvor's translation," the woman told the bookseller. "The man had a solid grasp of Aramaic and Greek, but he had an agenda. I wouldn't put it past him to substitute a word here and there."

"The original spells are in this book," Alfie informed her. "You don't have to trust his translation."

The woman sniffed, tucking a strand of auburn hair behind her ear. "I don't have *time* to check his translation. Can't you get the DeMeo version?"

Alfie turned to the computer, calm and friendly in the face of this woman's snotty attitude. She was thin in an A-line olive-colored dress. Not thin like a model or actress, but like someone who often forgot to eat and didn't bother with exercise. Her hair was thick, wavy, and I absolutely envied her the color. I hadn't gotten a look at her face when I'd come in, but from her voice, I'd peg her to be in her forties. I eyed the auburn locks. Or fifties if dye was covering up her grays.

Forcing my gaze away from the woman's back, I scanned the books in front of me. Demonology. I pulled the text from the shelf and glanced through it. Desiree wasn't the demon's real name according to that back-and-forth between her and Bishop in the warehouse, so I doubted I could just look her up like I would a celebrity's Wiki page. Still, I might find something helpful in here while I waited. Any information was good information.

Principalities. Legions. Households. Huh. According to this book, demons had a real hard-on for rigid social structure, at least among the really old ones. The younger demons formed a hierarchy based on the skill level they were born with as well as scrappy attitude. I wondered where Desiree fell into all this. She was definitely scrappy. I didn't get an aristocracy vibe from her, but I didn't know if the really old ones would act like a stuffy Earl in *Downton Abbey* or not.

I flipped through a few charts showing a list of who's who in hell, then onto the specifics of known demons. The author had included a nineteenth century woodcut illustration of the Morningstar, Samael, the original Satan. I pursed my lips and turned the book sideways, wishing the artist had done away with the drapey cloth over Satan's junk. Damn. If the devil was this hot, then no wonder we humans were constantly falling into sin.

But this sexy dude was no longer Satan. He'd retired or resigned, and the new leader was some batshit crazy woman I'd seen on TV a few times. I got the impression she'd assumed the office fairly recently since every Christian religion was still pointing out Sexy Dude as the leader of the damned.

I heard the ding of the old-fashioned cash register and looked up to note that the customer had decided Salvor's translation was good enough. She paid cash and carefully wrapped her purchase in cloth before putting it into a leather tote. Only then did she remove the white gloves.

Alfie stuck his head around the corner. "Let me go take care of these other two customers, and I'll be right back." He did a double take when he saw my reading material and came forward to pull it from my hands and replace it on the shelf. "Here. Bathalzar's *Households and Minions* is more accurate. If you're going to do research, it's always best to go to the source."

He vanished, and I pulled *Households and Minions* from the shelf, curious that Alfie had implied the author was a demon, or, at the very least, had spent time in hell.

Hel. Not "hell." The page that I'd flipped to mid-book informed me that the actual place was called Hel. Hell with two "L's" was a religious concept of punishment in the afterlife and should not be confused with the realm the demons now occupied. According to Bathalzar, the fallen had gone to live there after losing The War and being tossed on their asses out of Aaru.

Aaru was the home of the angels. Not heaven. I'd need to remember that if I ever encountered an angel, which I prayed was *not* going to happen. It was far more likely I'd come across demons since pretty much the entire west coast of the continent belonged to them. According to Bathalzar, demons and angels didn't get along.

No shit, Sherlock.

I glanced at the price of the book, just about had a heart attack, then sat on the floor to binge-read as much as I could until Alfie came back, and I'd reluctantly have to return it to the shelves.

A half hour later, Alfie appeared once more, his smile apologetic. "So, was I right about the book?"

I sighed, putting it back on the shelf. "You were right about the book, but not the price. I'm sorry, Alfie. It's amazing, and I want it, but I need to save up a bit to afford something that expensive."

"I understand. What exactly are you looking for? And what's your budget? I'm sure I have something that's in your price range."

"Twenty bucks." I winced, thinking that wouldn't go far in this store. Although the last book that he'd given me had been damaged and was only fifteen. Maybe there was a copy of *Households and Minions* in a back room that was missing a cover? I'd totally spring for that.

"Oof. That's a little light if you're looking for anything comprehensive. I've got some fairy tale compilations in the bargain section up front at that price. And by fairy tale, I mean human folklore, not stories by actual fae." He looked wistful. "People who try to write those down usually wind up dead. The fae don't freely give up their knowledge or stories."

Yikes. Maybe I should be glad it was the demons who had taken over L.A. and not the elves.

"You could put the twenty down on the Bathalzar book, and I'll hold it for you until you pay it off," he offered. "It's one of four copies in existence. You might want to grab it now if you really want it."

Four in existence? I glanced longingly at the book on the shelf. Alfie was like a damned drug dealer. He'd given me my first hit for free, and now I was hooked. I could put the Bathalzar book on layaway and make payments, but I wanted it now.

No. I couldn't spend that much money on books when I knew I'd need it for things like bribes, or bullets, or maybe even additional cell phone minutes. I had a price on my head. My license had been suspended. Although researching demons might help me in confronting the ones at the tax office or Desiree, I had more pressing problems to deal with first.

"I'm actually hoping you can help me with some research." I squirmed a bit, hating to ask a favor of anyone, even if I intended on paying for their efforts. "Do you have an hourly rate? Or charge per job? I can buy one of those fairy tale books from the bargain bin?"

He smiled and rubbed his hands together. The gesture gave me a bad feeling that the price was going to be more than I could afford to spend.

"Why don't you explain what you're looking for, and I'll let you know what I'd charge for that information."

Here goes nothing. Alfie was my last chance. Detective Juke probably wouldn't be able to help me until it was too late, and no one else had been able to identify who the cop barely visible under her riot gear had been.

"I'm trying to find a cop that set me up a few weeks ago. She ran me off a salvage, kept the goods herself, and reported me as having taken it." I paused to let that sink in. "The tax office thinks I took it all and kept it or sold it off the books. They've got a bounty out on me. That fucking cop is the reason my house got raided, and one of my sisters got shot and the other one kidnapped and sold. I need to find out who she is and either make her clear my name or get the money from her to pay the tax office."

Alfie let out a low whistle and shook his head. "Girl, you are in some serious shit."

Tell me about it. "I know. Can you help? Is that the sort of information you can find out?" I suddenly had an alternate idea. "If you can't find out who the cop is, then maybe you could somehow get into the online reporting system and delete the report? Or change it so I'm no longer on the hook for the salvage? They've got a huge bounty on me. I'm gonna get nailed for something I didn't even do. Maybe if the report gets deleted or changed, then the tax office'll revoke the warrant and pull the bounty."

Alfie headed toward the cash register and the laptop sitting next to it, talking over his shoulder as he walked. "You definitely don't want to go hacking into the computers at the tax office. That's a bad idea. They'll know someone's been in there changing records, and they've got ways of tagging and tracing anyone trying to sneak into their systems. It's not like hacking into the IRS."

I followed him. "I figured demons wouldn't be all that good at technology."

Alfie sniffed. "First off, demons are smart, and they have thousands of years or more to learn whatever they want to learn. If some aren't savvy about technology, it's either because they haven't been out of Hel in the last century, or they haven't felt the need to learn about it. Secondly, there is a particular class of demons who excel when it comes to knowledge—whether that's how to fertilize a field for optimal wheat production or how to steal encrypted data from a global finance company. Don't underestimate demons, even if they occasionally appear to be rock-headed warmongers."

I nodded. Every time I was here, I learned new things. My biggest fear was I wouldn't remember it all.

"It *is* possible to hack into their computers," Alfie admitted. "But they'll have systems in place that would detect a change. Plus, if you have a big bounty out on you, those mercenaries are going to question why it's suddenly revoked, and that's going to cause questions about who made the change and why."

I sighed. "Okay. So, hacking the tax office isn't going to work. I'll have to clear my name the old-fashioned way—by finding the cop who set me up and beating the crap out of her until she either changes her report or gives me enough money to pay the taxes I allegedly owe."

Alfie pointed a finger at me as he typed with the other hand. "There's a better option. Let's see if I can get into the police system and change or delete the record at their end. If I get caught, they'll be a whole lot easier to deal with than the demons at the tax office would be."

Huh. I hadn't thought about that. Pulling a stool over, I sat across from Alfie and watched him work, noting that he had a tendency to stick his tongue out of the side of his mouth as he concentrated. There were little display cases of items for sale on the counter. Brass bookmarks. White gloves like those the one customer had worn to handle old books. Embossing kits. Wax seal kits. Document preservation kits. I eyed the different wax seals, thinking the girls would have fun with that. Maybe I'd buy one if I had any money left after paying Alfie.

I abruptly straightened, realizing that Alfie hadn't quoted me a price. Hopefully, his fee wouldn't take most of my hundred dollars. Hopefully, it wouldn't be *more* than one hundred dollars.

"Their system is a mess," he muttered. "A damned mess. They don't need additional security measures because it would take a hacker two years to find anything in here."

"Um, Alfie?"

"What was the date of that alleged haul?" he asked. "There are thousands of reports for the last month, and they're not indexed properly. How the hell do these people find anything? Every search term I put in comes up a big fat zero."

I hesitated, really wanting to know how much this was costing me, but really wanting the information either way. Better to ask for forgiveness than permission. If Alfie's fee was too much, then I'd just have to work out some sort of payment plan like I had with Bishop.

I gave him the date and waited, looking around the store as he mumbled, stuck his tongue out, and typed like a fiend. Ninety percent of the store was books and more books, but there were a few shelves along the back wall with little packets of herbs beside hanging racks of keychains, bookmarks, and rolls of Washi tape.

Wandering over, I picked up a packet of herbs and eyed the label. It looked like the sort of thing printed off a home computer. Even the company name, Herb-a-licious, sounded like a home-business. The packet I'd picked up was called "Strong and Calm". Lavender. Chamomile. Peppermint. A bunch of other stuff I'd never heard of before.

Three bucks. Three bucks was definitely worth some "Strong and Calm" if the herbs lived up to their name. I carried the packet up to the counter, think that no matter what Alfie was charging me for this research, I probably should buy something. Although what I was buying, I had no idea. Was this some sort of spell component? Magical incense? Seasoning for roast chicken? Maybe I should ask Alfie before I tossed the herbs into a bonfire and inadvertently blew up the neighborhood.

"This report is in here like glue. I can't delete it and can't alter it without hacking into the admin side and setting up a fake profile. Which I could do if you've got a few days...?"

I didn't have a few days. And more to the point, I didn't have the money to pay Alfie for that much work. I wasn't sure I had enough money to pay Alfie for *this* much work.

"Can you get into the report? See the name of the officer that filed it?"

The man continued to type. "I don't have a username, but I do have some initials from the report. And cross referencing the initials with their database, I've come up with three possibilities."

Hot damn. A lead. An actual lead. I yanked my phone out of my pocket, ready to take notes. "Go on."

"Officer Cristin Balefort with the twelfth precinct. Officer Carly Bliss with the eighteenth precinct. Officer Ches Bingham with the fourteenth."

I frowned. "Are Cristin and Ches male or female? Because this was a woman."

Alfie shrugged. "Their system hasn't tracked gender in the last three years. Not since the *Peabody v. San Diego* ruling."

I didn't know anything about that ruling and really didn't care enough to bother asking about it. Three names, and because I didn't know whether these three officers were male or female, I was going to need to check all three of them out.

"Can you print out a map of the precincts?" I asked Alfie. Officers weren't assigned patrol areas based on the geography of their precincts like they had been before the demons came, but I doubted a cop who normally worked in Koreatown would be checking out crime in North Hills.

Although if the cop had gotten word of the hit and had somehow known about the stash of ammo that would be in the Buick, maybe she *would* have come up to the Valley.

Just happen to see a murder. Just happen to run off any Vultures. Just happen to drive off with the loot. Perhaps this hadn't been a random-chance windfall for the cop after all.

Alfie handed me a copy of a precinct map and also sent one to my phone. I grimaced and asked the question I'd been dreading.

"Thanks. How much do I owe you?"

He smiled. "Eight thousand."

I gasped.

He laughed. "Okay, how about two hundred?"

I didn't have eight thousand, and I didn't have two hundred, either.

"How about a twenty?" I pulled a bill out of my pocket and set it on the counter.

"A *twenty*?" Alfie lifted an eyebrow. "That's a whole lot less than two hundred."

I scooted the twenty toward him. "I don't have two hundred. How about I give you twenty and come back to buy that book once I can get some money together?"

He rolled his eyes. "You do realize you should have asked what my fee was before I provided the service?"

"Or maybe you should have told me your fee before you went ahead and provided the service," I countered. "Come on, Alfie. You spent all of thirty minutes hacking into the police system and looking the data up." Two hundred for a half-hour's work was Bishop-rates, and he was no Bishop. "A twenty is fair. And I'm going to buy this as well." I held up the bag of herbs.

"That's three bucks," he protested. "Two hundred. And I'll toss the tea in for free."

Tea? Not magical herbs? Although for three bucks, I should have known.

"Sixty. Take the twenty, and I'll pay off the remaining forty in two monthly installments," I offered.

He barked out a laugh. "This isn't Rent-a-Center."

I sighed and glanced down at the little packet, knowing I'd been backed into a corner. I could always refuse to pay and leave. I had the information. But I also didn't want to burn this bridge. I'd needed Alfie in the past, and I knew I was going to need him in the future. I'd just have to start holding back extra money for these sorts of things and get used to bargaining before I was over a barrel.

Alfie sighed. "Okay, sixty. Twenty now, and the rest when you get it. But you're buying that tea. I'm not throwing that in."

I grinned. "How about you throw in that demonology book? The Bathalzar one you recommended, not the other one."

Alfie smirked. "You've got a set of balls. You know that, right?"

"Is that a yes?"

He sighed. "Pay me in the next two months—for the book and the other forty. Go get your book, and I'll wrap it for you. And give me three more bucks."

I dug some ones out of my pocket for him, then practically danced down the aisle, because I really did want that book. Tea. Book. The first lead I'd been able to get on the cop who'd set me up. It was definitely worth two hundred and sixty bucks. Or actually two hundred and sixty-three bucks.

CHAPTER 4

I parked my bike five blocks away and took a circuitous route home through backyards and across parking lots. Mercenaries still occasionally lurked around the neighborhood, and after what had happened this morning, I was worried. As it was, I hadn't been home more than five times in the last two weeks. I couldn't be here all the time to protect Bea and the girls, and I'd begun to worry that my presence endangered them as well as the others in the neighborhood. I'd figured that if the Fixers thought I no longer lived here, they'd leave my family alone, so I'd found other places to crash at night, shacking up in abandoned buildings and even once in Telaney's spare bedroom.

Nevarra was sitting out on the front porch, a pistol within reach. Sadie was beside her, relaxing back on a bedspread and pillows, her leg propped up. Both girls were scarfing down handfuls of M&Ms from a gallon-sized plastic bag.

"Hey, Peanut!" I greeted Sadie first, planting a gentle kiss on the top of her head. "How are you feeling?"

"Great." Her face was pale. The lines of strain bracketing

her mouth belied the statement. "It's good to be outside in the fresh air, even though it's hot as an oven today."

Doctor Mwangi had insisted Sadie start getting up and around, even though moving was painful, and her leg wound still wasn't fully closed. The girl was tough. She gritted her teeth and used a combination of crutches and ropes to help her get up and down and around. The crutches hurt her still-healing shoulder, but I knew she was determined to follow the doctor's orders to the letter.

"And you, my mini-me?" I teased Nevarra, reaching in to grab a handful of the candy for myself.

She shrugged. "It's been quiet today. I thought we might have trouble after Linda shot that Fixer sneaking through the backyards last night, but so far, so good."

My stomach clenched. Maybe it hadn't been a good idea to visit tonight. Now that the bounty was up to five grand, there was a chance the Fixers showing up here wouldn't be so easy for the Neighborhood Watch to handle. I was torn between staying and helping them fight off any intruders and leaving to lure the mercenaries elsewhere. Stay? Or go?

"Last night was the first one we've seen in almost four days," Nevarra reassured me. "Stay here for the night, Eden. Please? Or at least stay for dinner?"

If I left, I'd fret all night that my presence had led to them being attacked again. I might as well stay so I could defend them if needed. In the morning, I'd be completely obvious about leaving and act as if I wouldn't be back soon. Haul a duffle bag of clothes away or something. Anything to draw the heat off my family.

"I'll stay."

Sadie squealed at my announcement, but Nevarra just smiled and reached down to touch the pistol on her lap.

Nevarra worried me more than Sadie. Sadie's wounds were physical. Nevarra's were deep under the surface. She'd been tough and brittle since I'd brought her back home after she'd been kidnapped. Everything she said and did was about protecting the family, the neighborhood. I wasn't kidding when I'd called her mini-me. I didn't want a life of bitter toughness for her. I wanted her to enjoy the last few years of her childhood, not become a hardened, distrustful woman at the young age of fourteen. It hurt me to see her like this.

"Where'd the candy come from?" I asked, grabbing more. I still hadn't made good on my promise of chocolate from three weeks ago. Candy was hard to find and pricey, and my priorities had been on paying Bishop, making sure we had money for utilities and food, and paying for the cell phone I'd come to realize was a necessity in my line of business.

"Javier." She munched another handful. "I told him if he was going to be coming by every day to annoy me, then he needed to bring a tribute."

I hid a grin, because I'd been here once when Javier had come by, and I knew exactly what was going on between Nevarra and the good-looking boy down the street.

"Hell of a tribute. I think he's sweet on you," I teased. "I've got some condom packs in the top drawer of my dresser if you need them."

"Ewww." Sadie laughed.

Nevarra scrunched up her nose. "That's not gonna happen. I don't care if he brings me a Gucci handbag and a Tiffany necklace. I saw that boy lift a car once. That's a hard no for me."

I flinched. "There are a lot of people who cross the line of what's legal and what's not. Doesn't mean they're not good in their hearts. Maybe they had reason for what they did. I've boosted a few cars in my day. Not that I had a good reason for doing it, but I hope someone won't rule me out as a romantic partner just because I have a checkered past."

And a checkered present. Probably a checkered future. In

reality, someone probably *should* rule me out as a romantic partner.

Sadie giggled, covering her mouth. Nevarra stared at me as if I were a total idiot.

"*Lift* a car, not *steal* one. He picked up the front end of his dad's F350. From the side. He was changing the tire, and the jack was slipping. He looked around and didn't see me, then picked the thing up with one hand and changed the tire with the other. That's not something normal people do."

"Maybe he's one of those shifters," Sadie chimed in. "I saw a documentary on them last year when we were borrowing internet from the Patels. They're supposed to be super strong."

"Or maybe he's a demon." Nevarra sent a narrow-eyed glance across the line of front yards toward Javier's house. "Demons steal souls then assume their victim's physical appearance. I wonder if his parents know?"

I had a second of instinctual panic. But having been up close with one of the infernal host, I was pretty certain Javier wasn't counted among their ranks.

"Are you sure?" As soon as the words left my mouth, I realized I'd said the wrong thing. Doubting Nevarra, questioning her experience, only added a layer of distance to what she'd been building between us all for the last few weeks.

"Yes, I'm sure," she snapped.

I backtracked. "I have magic. Telekinesis." Plus, the electrical thing I hadn't let either of my sisters know about. "That doesn't make me a demon or a shifter. Maybe he just has magic."

I watched her consider that, watched her posture relax. She trusted me. She loved me. And if she could accept that I had magic, I could see she was considering maybe she could accept the same about Javier.

"He replaced our front door and most of the kitchen cabinets," I reminded her. "And windows. And repaired our furniture."

"Didn't his parents make him do that?" Sadie asked.

I glared at her. *Not helping.*

"He came by and helped me fix my bike that night before I found you," I told Nevarra. "He asked how Sadie was doing. He asked about you. That wasn't just simple politeness, Nevarra, because I don't believe Javier is all that skilled in everyday social graces. He cares about you. And he cares about the people that matter to you. That's something worth considering."

She stilled, a flash of panicked terror flickering across her face before her expression settled back into typical teenage scorn. "Yeah. Whatever."

I hid a grin and took another handful of the candy. "Yeah. Whatever. I'm going inside. Are you girls on neighborhood watch duty for much longer?"

"Another hour." Nevarra looked over at Sadie. "I can manage alone."

Sadie straightened, but the determined glint in her eyes quickly faded. "I *am* a little tired."

"Then let me help you inside." I put the bag down that held my book and my tea, slid my backpack off, and linked my hands together into a fist that Sadie could use to pull herself into a standing position.

Once she was upright, I held her upper arm to give her stability and felt her weight on me. "Crutches, or should I carry you?"

She considered that for a second. "Crutches. But when I'm inside, I might need you to help me back to my bed."

Nevarra handed Sadie's crutches up while I balanced her and waited for her to get situated. Following her closely, I held my breath as she wobbled her way to the porch and in through the door. Once inside, I scooped her up and carried her gently back to her room, every strained whimper like a knife to my chest. Settling her in bed, I noted her eyes glazed with pain and the sheen of sweat on her forehead.

"You're pushing yourself too hard, Peanut." I slid a pillow under her leg and checked the bandage. "When the doctor said you should start getting up and moving around, I don't think she meant taking on a neighborhood watch shift."

"Sittin' out front with a pistol in my lap isn't much more than lying in my bed," she argued. "Aunt Bea's working all day. You're working. There aren't a lot of people in the neighborhood that are home to take the day shifts. I'm old enough to help. Even with my leg, I can still shoot straight."

"You're a good shot, Sadie." I smoothed a hand over her forehead, thankful that she didn't seem to be running a fever. "But you need to take time to heal. There'll be plenty of opportunities to shoot bad guys and defend the neighborhood once you're better."

"It's been forever," she grumbled.

"It's been two weeks," I reminded her gently. I'm sure that felt like forever to an eleven-year-old girl, but when I thought back to how I'd found her huddled in the cupboard under the sink, how hot and swollen her leg had been when she'd tossed and turned in the throes of feverish dreams, I was still shocked at how far she'd come in such a short time.

It helped that an actual doctor was coming by the house with medicine, checking her wounds and guiding her care. Once more, I sent up a quick prayer to whoever might be listening, thanking the person who had sent Doctor Mwangi to our house and ensured there was one less debt we'd be struggling to pay off.

Her lower lip quivered, and her lashes lowered. "I just want to walk again. I want to run. And…I'm scared. What if my leg isn't ever right? What if I'm always limping? What if it always hurts this bad?"

"Hush." I bent down and kissed her forehead, smoothing my fingers through her silky golden-brown locks. "It hasn't even been a month yet. It's too soon to be scared about that sort of thing."

I wanted to soothe her, but I couldn't make promises when I myself had the same fears. It was funny how easily I lied to everyone else but found myself struggling to do the same with those I loved.

She sighed, but still didn't lift her gaze.

"Rest. I'll get dinner started, and we'll eat once Bea is home. Oh, and I bought some tea at the bookshop this afternoon." That got her attention. Big dark eyes met mine. "Let's have a fancy tea after dinner. We'll use those china cups I won at the dime toss three years ago. Pinkies out and everything."

She giggled. "Tea is supposed to be before dinner. At four, I think."

I snorted. "Well, we do things different here in the Valley. Tea is when the sun goes down, and it's not a hundred degrees out."

Her lips quivered upward. "It's still going to be ninety. If we're lucky."

"Practically winter," I teased. "Rest. If you're up to it, I'll do your hair into a bun for tea." I had a sock I could sacrifice to make her bun ballerina-worthy.

"Nevarra too?" She turned her head, her voice softening as she edged toward sleep.

"Nevarra too." I wasn't sure how the heck I'd get Nevarra's crazy corkscrew curls into a bun, but if the girl agreed to it, I'd make the effort.

I stayed until Sadie's eyes fell shut and her breathing deepened. Tucking the blanket around her leg, I tiptoed out of the room, down the hall, and back outside. Nevarra was still on the front lawn, guarding the neighborhood and my backpack. The bag from the bookstore gaped open.

"You spoiled the surprise." I grinned at her. "I got some tea at the bookshop. We're going to do it up all fancy-like after dinner. Dime-toss china cups. Buns in our hair. Pinkies out."

Her gaze continued scanning the street. "Good luck getting my hair in a bun."

I sat beside her. "I'm game if you are."

Nevarra sighed, her shoulders relaxing a tiny fraction with me by her side. "Sure. Go for it. I'll need a whole tub of Shea butter to smooth it back, though."

She was clearly in a mood, so I kept quiet, pulling my Glock 43 from its holster and placing it on my thigh. The air over the road was wavy with heat. The faint smell of cumin tickled my nose, the neighbor's cooking overlaying the usual smell of hot tar, pine sap, and garbage from the giant expanse of landfill transfer station across the street. Lightning shot across the horizon, ending in a burst of sparks. I wasn't sure if it was from the heat, some demon, or that kitten with the laser eyes that seemed to have taken up residence among the piles of junk and sometimes-fragrant garbage awaiting transport.

"That's a big book in the bag." Nevarra's voice was flat as she broke the silence. "Thing weighs a ton."

"Demonology." I was pretty sure she'd peeked at the cover, and maybe the inside, but I was going to pretend she hadn't. "They're clearly here to stay, so I figured I should learn as much as I could about them. This book was recommended by someone I trust."

She glanced over at the bag. "I like the Gilgamesh and Enkido stories you brought home, but maybe we should be reading this at night instead."

No. Absolutely not. "It's kind of dry. If you want to look at it during the day, in between your school lessons, then that's fine."

Nevarra rolled her eyes at my mention of school lessons. The girls were supposed to be following a homeschool curriculum since there hadn't been actual public-school classes for the last two years. Bea had been insistent about checking their schoolwork for the first year, but while she still tried to keep the girls on track with their studies, it had become less of a priority lately.

I stood and stuck my pistol back in the holster. With my backpack in one hand and the bookstore bag in the other, I turned toward the house. "I'm going to start dinner. Come in and help me when your watch shift is over."

She didn't respond. Not that I expected her to. My heart ached at how Nevarra had changed. She'd always been guarded and tough, but what she'd endured after the Fixers had taken her had caused a wound I wasn't sure would ever heal. Bea's love had eventually won me over, but I'd never gone through what Nevarra had. If only I could help somehow. I'd do anything to change what had happened. I'd do anything to make it all better.

I just wasn't sure what that "anything" was.

The food our neighbors had dropped off following the raid by the Fixers was long gone. Now that Bea was back to work, we felt free to splurge a bit on things like meat and fresh vegetables, but it was important to stretch those valuable commodities as long as we could. I plopped my backpack on the living room sofa, set the bag with the book and the tea carefully on the kitchen table, then went to survey our available food.

Little chicks peeped from the corner of the kitchen; the lights that would keep them warm at night off during the heat of the day. Taking a quick detour, I refilled their water and added to the little cup of feed they'd been pecking at throughout the day. Last week they'd been tiny downy birds, fragile in my hand as I'd placed them in the box that would be their home until they grew large enough to jump out. After six days, I was thinking we needed to get a larger box. Chickens grew fast, and already their fuzz had been replaced here and there by thin reddish-brown feathers. Bea's friend down the street had given us four, and I sincerely hoped all four were hens. Or maybe one rooster. More than one would mean a young rooster would be destined for the pot.

The girls had already named the chicks and grown attached to them. If it needed to be done, I'd be the one who butchered the bird. None of us were vegetarians. We all enjoyed meat when we could. It would be difficult, though, to end the life of a creature you'd raised and named, let alone consume his flesh.

Chicks taken care of, I turned my attention back to the contents of the fridge and the cabinets. The electricity was on—a miracle—so I took my time eyeballing the choice of leftover bits of pork, cabbage and carrots, eggs, and an assortment of cheeses. Closing the fridge, I checked the dry goods and decided we were going to have ramen à la Eden tonight.

Noodles in a miso soup. The leftover pork. Some shredded cabbage and carrots. It probably wasn't the best choice in one-hundred-degree weather, but it would leave the eggs, cheese, and a little bit of pork and veggies for another evening. After that, we'd need to go shopping.

Reaching down a hand, I patted the pocket with my money in it. At least I had cash if Bea didn't get paid today. Sometimes her employers stretched payday out an extra week. It sucked, but they always made good on what they owed her, and a job that paid late was still better than no job at all.

Miracle of all miracles, the water was on as well. I put on a stock pot to boil and went ahead and washed the dishes, refilling the various buckets and jugs we had around the kitchen to hold water in case we went days without. Adding the meat, veggies, and broth packet, I went back down the hall with my backpack and washed my bloody clothing in the tub, cleaning the battered porcelain with Ajax after I was done. Before I headed back to the kitchen, I filled the tub with clean water so Bea and the girls could get a bath later, even if the water had been shut off by that point.

I put the noodles in once I heard Bea walk through the door, then called everyone for dinner as I was ladling the Ramen into bowls. Going to check on Sadie, I saw she was still sleeping and decided to just let her rest. I could always sit with her and let her eat dinner in bed later.

We all sat down. Bea talked about work. I gave a sanitized version of the events of my day, surprised to realize I had completely forgotten about my gunshot wound. It didn't hurt. Not even a twinge.

"I'm glad you're working with the police to get your name cleared and your license back in order," Bea said.

"Yeah." I pushed the noodles around in the bowl. I knew Juke would do her best to help, but the detective was limited in what she could do and how fast she could make things happen. I didn't have such constraints, but I also didn't have her resources. And I wasn't sure how to resolve this problem if one of the three names Alfie had given me turned out to be the cop who'd set me up.

Killing her wouldn't do anything besides make me feel a bit better emotionally. I'd still have my license suspended and have the tax office thinking I owed them a shit ton of money. Plus, if I killed her and it got traced back to me, I'd have every cop in L.A. gunning for me. Those guys stuck together, and unlike the mercenaries I'd dealt with to date, the police were a whole lot more skilled at bringing in someone and locking them behind bars.

If I didn't kill her…well, there still weren't a lot of options there, either. Ideally, I'd find her laughing maniacally while sitting on a pile of money. She'd leave, and I could steal the money while she was out and pay off the tax office. That scenario wouldn't do anything about that need for revenge burning a hole in my chest, but at least I'd be able to make a decent living again and not constantly be dodging mercenaries trying to collect a bounty.

Hopefully, Juke would handle the situation. She'd fix things with the tax office. They'd fire that bitch's ass and lock her up. Then maybe I'd stumble across the pile of money and just keep it for myself.

After dinner, Nevarra did the dishes while Bea went to give Sadie her dinner and check on her. I cleaned my guns, made sure the magazines were full, then pulled the thick demonology tome out of the bag and set it on the coffee table.

At the bookstore, I'd just read a few random pages, but now that the book was mine, I started digging in from the beginning. Unfortunately, chapter one started with an agonizingly long drawn-out history of angels and some war that took place millions of years ago. My eyes glazed over and ten pages later, I still wasn't sure what the fuck these angels were fighting over. Some shit about humans and their worthiness or potential, and whether they should be getting gifts from the angels or not.

I'll admit the gift thing perked me up a bit. Sadly, these "gifts" were never really spelled out. I got the impression that it had something to do with sentience, self-awareness, and evolution, and not Gucci purses and Tiffany jewelry. I started skimming, losing interest in the hundreds of unpronounceable names and thousands of battles. Flipping a few chapters forward, I found myself still in the midst of a history lesson, this one about some angelic choir who went off the rails and started boinking human women, producing Nephilim and bringing down the wrath of the other angels after they were discovered.

You'd think illicit sexy-times would be interesting, but it wasn't.

Bathalzar was probably celibate, given the lack of any titillating details in the story. Basically, the angels were tempted by sensory pleasures (not just sexual ones, according to the author), got caught, then got hauled back to Aaru for punishment, leaving responsibility for the humans in the hands of a surly archangel and a rotating group of angels.

At least this chapter had illustrations. I turned the book sideways, thinking that the surly archangel wasn't as hot as the drawing of the male Satan in the other book. I'd do him but…

I'd rather do Bishop.

I stuffed that thought back where it belonged, thinking I'd bring it out later when I was alone in my bed tonight. I was looking through the book, hoping there'd be *some* sort of kinky porno pics of angels doing it with humans, when Nevarra came into the living room and plopped down beside me.

"What do you think?" I asked as I showed her the drawing of the surly archangel. The guy stood on top of a pile of rocks, a flaming sword in his hand, a legion of blurry-faced, golden-haired angels behind him.

Nevarra looked at the illustration. "They're a lot scarier in real life."

None of us had actually seen an angel in person, thankfully. There had been lots of television coverage, though, and I agreed with Nevarra. The guy in the drawing looked powerful, determined…and as if he were a judgmental asshole. But the artist hadn't conveyed that terrifying sense of otherness, or the power to take a life with one glance from their impersonal, burning gaze.

"Yeah, but I'd still fuck him." I was half-teasing. Okay, not even half, but it still got a laugh from Nevarra.

"Eww. I'll stick with humans, thanks."

"Or teenage shifters who can pick up a truck with one hand?" I jostled her with my elbow.

Her smile faded. "Maybe. I don't know. I just…I just don't want to think about that right now."

I watched as she fisted her hands together and shoved them in her lap. "A good person will be happy just spending time with you," I told her. "They'll be okay waiting, even if it takes years. Anyone who isn't okay with that deserves your boot in their ass."

Her white-knuckled grip eased a bit. "I know."

"If you ever want to talk, I'm always ready to listen. So is Bea."

She sighed. "I know."

We sat together in silence. I watched her breathe, slowly beginning to relax. With another sigh, she leaned against me. "That dress he made me wear…"

I gave her a few seconds, then spoke when she didn't continue. "Why haven't you gotten rid of it yet, Nevarra?"

Her hands twisted in her lap again, but her head still rested on my shoulder. "I want to, then I think maybe I shouldn't. Maybe I need to see it there every day, to remind me. Sometimes I want it all to fade away, like a bad dream. Sometimes I want to keep the memory fresh in my mind, to burn it into my soul. That way I'll stay strong and hard. That way it won't ever happen again."

I put my arm around her shoulder, worried that she *wanted* to stay hard. Strong, yes. Hard, no. "That dress, those memories…that's not what will keep you going. You survived. You killed that bastard. You walked out of there, and he'll never take another breath again. You survived, and you destroyed the man who hurt you. *Those* are the memories that can stay in your mind. Let the rest fade into the ground where they belong."

She nodded, and I saw the splash of a tear on my shirt. "Will you help me? Burn it?"

I squeezed her shoulder. "I thought you'd never ask. We're gonna burn that fucking dress and celebrate as it goes up in flames."

"Then we'll drink tea?" I barely heard her watery laugh.

"Then we'll drink tea."

CHAPTER 5

*N*evarra shook the last few drops of lighter fluid onto the lacy white dress currently balled up in our old Webber grill.

"You need to stand back a bit more," I warned. The girl had enough flammable liquid on that dress to blow up the yard.

"Ready?" Nevarra glanced over at the kitchen window where Bea stood filming with my cell phone. Sadie had wanted to be here, too. She'd insisted she was well enough to get up, but after an exhausting struggle to shift to the edge of the bed, she'd confessed tearfully that she couldn't do it. We'd show her the video. And afterward, we'd all squeeze into the bedroom and take tea together with our pinkies out and our hair in buns.

"Ready." I tensed, prepared to grab Nevarra and shield her from the flames, or roll her in the dirt if need be.

Nevarra pulled a match from the box, struck it along the side, then tossed it into the grill. The whole thing went up with a *whoosh* of flame. I winced at the heat.

"Stupid ugly dress," Nevarra muttered, her mouth trembling as she said the words. "It's a baby dress. I'm not a baby."

"No, you're not."

Fourteen was that weird dawning stage of a woman's life. I remembered wanting to be sexy, wanting boys to look at me with interest, but being absolutely repulsed if anyone over the age of eighteen eyed me with so much as the faintest hint of desire in their eyes.

Nevarra was looking anything but childlike this evening. She'd changed clothes for the occasion and the jeans from Ms. Carlson's donation bag fit her perfectly, showing off her long legs and slim hips. She'd paired them with an old Black Eyed Peas concert T-shirt of mine that was so soft and worn I'd been reluctant to let it go.

She should have been going to high school this fall. But there was no high school, and honestly, she was probably better off studying that demonology book I'd brought home than geology and algebra anyway.

"I'm okay," she whispered. "He didn't touch me. He didn't hurt me." She continued to repeat the phrase, like a mantra.

Her words didn't convince me. They probably didn't convince her, either. I'd gotten there as fast as I could. If only I had been faster.

"It was just stupid clothes and baby talk," she said as she turned to me. "He fed me on those dumb plastic plates with the sections in them. I had to eat mac and cheese—the kind from a box. Not even the stuff with the squeeze packet of cheese, either. There were lumps of orange powder on the noodles. Guy was a shit cook."

"I hate that powdered stuff," I agreed.

"He cut the grapes in half for me."

"Disgusting," I said.

"He gave me a lollypop and wanted...he had me..." She

clenched her jaw tight for a second. "That mac and cheese was the worst."

"You killed him," I reminded her. "It was a hell of a good shot, Nevarra."

"I did." Her whisper was fierce. "It was a good shot. I killed him. I burned the dress. I'm never eating powdered mac and cheese again. Ever."

"Never again," I pronounced, knowing she meant something very different than just powdered mac and cheese.

We watched the dress burn. It didn't take long. It felt like seconds from flame to a smoldering pile of ash and melted polyester. If only the other memories would burn that fast.

"I wish I had something else to burn." Nevarra's laugh held a bitter edge. "That was cathartic. Maybe I should take an extra watch shift or go across the street to the junkyard and shoot at old cars."

"It's getting dark," I reminded her. "Maybe save the target practice for tomorrow?"

She smiled. "Deal. Let's ditch this burned dress and go drink tea."

I eyed the grill, thinking there was one more thing I wanted to do first. "You go on in and show Sadie your video. Get your hair in buns and start boiling some water. I'll be in soon."

She headed inside. I waited until she and Bea had left the kitchen before hauling the Webber around the side of the house and down the street. I wanted to dump the smelly ashes somewhere Nevarra wouldn't be likely to see them. Normally that would be right across the street in the three-block lot used to store trash before it was sent off to the landfill, but we'd mentioned her doing target practice over there, and I wanted to make sure I discarded this shit far enough away from our house that she'd be unlikely to stumble upon it.

When I'd first moved here, any wind from the north would send the acrid smell of garbage across our lawn and in through any open window. The transfer station was still operational, but they either seemed to be moving less garbage than they had years ago, or perhaps they were hauling it away with greater frequency. That, or I'd just gotten used to the smell.

Our little street was at the far end of the operation, so we thankfully didn't have to deal with the noise and sight of trucks and heavy equipment shifting piles of waste around. Normally that was a good thing, but tonight I was wishing that I didn't have to drag a rusty grill on two wheels through blocks of rock-strewn dirt and weeds. The sun was rapidly vanishing beyond the horizon, lengthening shadows and giving the landscape that grayish tinge of twilight. The grill rattled behind me. I hugged past a pile of scrap aluminum and another pile of rotted wood, deciding to dump the ashes next to a heap of black trash bags that smelled like urine and rotted produce. I contemplated just leaving the grill here, but an old rusty grill was better than none at all. We might need this one day if the electricity stayed off, and we were forced to use it to cook everything we ate. So, with an annoyed growl, I started to drag the thing back to the house.

I'd just passed the pile of aluminum when someone zapped me. I yelped, dropped the grill, and dove to the side, more out of surprise than anything else. The electrical jolt that should have knocked me to the ground had about the same effect on me as getting hit with a particularly soft bean bag. I'd discovered when I was a child that my stun gun magic worked both ways. Electricity was a weapon I could wield, and I was oddly immune to it myself. At four years old, a knife jammed into an electrical socket had nearly set the house on fire, but hadn't so much as singed my fingers or frizzed my hair.

Another jolt hit me, this one with a bit more punch than the first. I abandoned the grill and rolled, managing to get behind the pile of rotted wood before the third strike carved a smoking path through a patch of sedge.

There were no electrodes with wires attached to me. No one had been close enough to shove a stun gun or a cattle prod against my skin. That meant whoever was trying to electrocute me into submission had the same magical ability that I did.

Huddled behind a rotted hunk of chip board, I peered around the edge to see if I could lay eyes on my attacker. I'd never met anyone who could do what I did. It sucked that the first time I encountered someone with this ability, they were directing their magic against me. I was excited and curious, but I drew my weapon because I wasn't stupid. I'd prefer to sit down and have a nice long chat with this person about our weird magic, but if they were going to continue to zap me, I was going to put a bullet through them.

Another burst sent splinters of chip board flying, and another lit some plywood scraps next to me on fire. I cursed, backing away from the flames, and heard a laugh from the pile of scrap metal.

"Throw your gun on the ground and walk out with your hands up, and I won't zap you," a male voice called out.

Fuck that. "I don't have any money on me. I've got nothing of value aside from my gun. And maybe that grill," I replied. "Take the grill and leave, and I won't shoot you."

This time something that felt an awful lot like a bolt of lightning hit a stack of two-by-fours, charring them and knocking them to the dirt. I ducked and scrambled out of the way of the falling lumber.

"Come out, and I won't hurt you."

Right. Like I believed that. Random attacks did happen, but I got the feeling this wasn't a plain old robbery or some guy wanting to get some nonconsensual action on top of the trash bags. The mercenaries who wanted to bring me in for the bounty had begun to realize venturing onto our street and neighborhood would get them shot. I'd dealt with a few who had been lying in wait for me to leave, but this guy was taking things a step further. Out here, there would be no one to help me. I had my gun, but my magic would probably be just as useless on him as his was on me. Should I stay behind the lumber and hope he'd show himself enough for a quick shot? As I pondered my options, a burning piece of plywood slid off the pile, nearly landing on my head. The fire was spreading, and I needed to make a decision soon.

Hoping to keep a few cards close to my chest, I holstered the pistol and came around the pile with my hands up. A man cautiously appeared from behind the aluminum, one hand extended outward and the other at his waist on a set of handcuffs. He had a military haircut along with desert camo attire, but no gun that I could see. Reddish stubble shaded his square jaw and firm chin. He was young and good looking in a rugged, lean muscle kind of way.

He was also a liar, because he zapped me before he was less than five feet from the aluminum pile. The jolt of electricity didn't do shit to me, but I hammed it up, screaming and falling to the ground. I even twitched a little, just to enhance my award-winning performance. The guy clearly wasn't an L.A. native, or he would have realized everyone, including me, was an actor here. Thinking his magic had done the job, he pulled the handcuffs from his belt and walked toward me. The asshole even whistled a little, swinging the handcuffs around one finger as he approached.

I did my best to look helpless. When the merc knelt down to cuff me, I grabbed his ankle and let loose a stream of electricity that should have fried him to a crisp. As expected, he didn't die, but he did yelp with surprise and fall onto his ass, dropping the handcuffs as he scrambled backward. I jumped on him and decked him in the face, straddling him as he fell back. I'd never taken any martial arts classes, but I'd been in enough street fights to know to take the advantage when I had it and to use my thighs to keep his arms pinned to his sides. I got in one more punch before he bucked me off and flipped us over.

"Bitch. How the fuck…?" He swore again, trying to hold me still with his weight while he searched me. My gun got flung out to the side, my pockets patted down. He even pried my hands open. I twisted and turned, trying to get him off me, but the guy weighed close to two hundred pounds, and I couldn't budge him. I could hardly breathe.

"How did you do that?" His eyes narrowed. "What are you?"

Same as him, I supposed—a human who had a few magical tricks up their sleeves. I zapped him again, hoping to dislodge him enough to get out from under him.

He grunted at the shock, then leaned over and tried to reach his handcuffs. Looking around for anything within reach to grab, I saw something stir over near the wood pile. A small, fluffy gray kitten walked out of the burning pile of wood and fixed us with a stare from big yellow-green eyes.

Fuck. Oh, fuck.

I kicked and managed to wiggle one arm free. With another curse, he abandoned the cuffs and grabbed at my arm.

"Kitten," I hissed at him, far more worried about the little ball of fluff than the Navy SEAL with superpowers sitting on my chest. "Kitten. Run."

He glanced over, then gave me an incredulous look, still sitting firmly on my torso.

"Kitten." I tried to keep my voice at a whisper, hoping it didn't notice us even though it was already staring a hole right through me. "No sudden moves. Ease off me, then slowly get the fuck out of here."

He laughed. The booming sound made me wince, but it did shift the kitten's attention from me to my attacker, so that was a plus.

"You're joking. Ooh, I'm so scared! It might purr at me, kill me with cuteness, scratch me with its widdle tiny paws."

The kitten's eyes widened, the fur on its arched back rising. The air around us grew thick and wavy, then half a dozen aluminum rods shot toward us, slamming into Navy SEAL Guy and sending him ten feet through the air. He landed in the dirt with a groan, and I took that opportunity to slither away on my back as fast as I could. The kitten hissed at me, and I froze, knowing I could never outrun any magic attack this adorably fluffy thing might launch at me.

Navy SEAL Guy groaned again and rolled to a seated position, pushing bent aluminum rods away from him. The man must have been wearing some sort of protective vest because the only thing that seemed to be injured was his shirt.

"Stay down," I whispered. The only way we were going to get out of here alive was if we held still long enough for the kitten to get bored and go elsewhere. I wished I had a laser pointer or catnip, but honestly, I had no idea if either would work to distract this cat from hell.

The man ignored my directive, glaring at me as if he thought I was the one who tried to magically impale him with scrap metal. "Do that again and I'll break your arms. And your legs. I'm trying to use minimal force to take you in, but you're pissing me off."

Oh, for fuck's sake. "That cat did it, you moron. If I could shoot metal rods at you from ten feet away, do you think I'd still be lying here? No, I wouldn't. I would have gotten up and ran. Or I would have gotten up, grabbed my gun, and unloaded it into your chest. Or I would have picked up one of the two-by-fours not yet on fire and bashed your head in with it. But no. I'm lying here in the dirt, hoping the kitten doesn't kill me, because *I'm* not the scariest thing in this dump. And newsflash, neither are you, buddy."

I sucked in a breath because my rant had gotten the attention of the kitten, but instead of laser-eyeing me or burying me in a shower of burning wood, it simply cocked its head and began licking its paw.

The man turned his frown on the kitten, then picked up a piece of aluminum and threw it at the animal.

"No!" With a burst of speed, I launched myself in front of the cat, knocking the metal aside. Pain shot through my arm, but I ignored it and rolled away. I'd heal from a bruise or a hairline fracture far easier than I'd heal from whatever was coming next.

The kitten yowled, its yellow-green eyes glowing red. The air sizzled as light shot from its gaze, barely missing me. Whatever flak jacket Navy SEAL Guy had on, it wasn't kitten-laser proof. The light carved a round hole right through the middle of the man's stomach, exiting the other side and burning a black line through the dirt. As the cat sprang forward, I took advantage of the shift in its attention and dove behind the pile of scrap metal. There I huddled, hearing a series of yells, curses, and explosions. The air pressure changed, causing my ears to pop, then all I heard was an angry hiss followed by a tomcat yowl that was surely designed to send any other felines in the neighborhood running for cover.

I waited until the only sound left was the pop of burning wood, then counted to two hundred before carefully looking out from my hiding place. When I didn't see anything move, I eased around the pile of metal, picking up my pistol and looking around. No kitten. No Navy SEAL Guy, either. The wood pile burned. There were some smoking black skid marks radiating out from where I stood. There were some trampled and blistered sedge patches. That was it.

I had no idea if Hellkitty had killed Navy SEAL Guy and taken him back to its lair to eat, or if the man had somehow managed to survive and crawled off to die behind a pile of rubbish. Didn't know. Didn't care. Yeah, the guy had claimed he'd been trying to use minimal force, but he'd still zapped me with enough electricity to power a large appliance. If he'd managed to get those cuffs on me, I had no doubt that he would have proceeded to haul me off to the tax office and collect on the bounty. I'd warned him about the kitten. In fact, I'd warned him about the kitten *twice*. In my opinion, that was all I owed a mercenary who was too stupid to realize dangerous shit sometimes came in cute fluffy packages. Dead. Dying. Not dead and trying to wrap gauze around a truly horrific gut wound. Not my problem.

Dusting off my pants and holstering my pistol, I left the now twisted and broken grill where I'd dropped it and headed for home.

CHAPTER 6

"What in the world happened?" Bea exclaimed as I walked into the girls' bedroom.

It wasn't the *worst* I'd ever looked. My clothes were dirty with some smudges from the fire and a few burn marks from where Navy SEAL Guy had zapped me. Other than that, I was peachy, which was something my attacker certainly couldn't say.

"Had a run-in with a Fixer." I pointed at Nevarra. "Don't do target practice in the dump after all. In fact, neither of you girls should go in there. That kitten is still there, closer to our end than I'd thought. I don't want any of you to run into him."

Bea sucked in a breath. "The kitten? With the laser eyes?"

I nodded. As much as that kitten freaked me out, it had saved me from being hauled off to the tax office where the demons would have probably killed me when I couldn't come up with the money they thought I owed plus whatever penalty and interest they'd tacked on. Not that I thought the kitten had saved me on purpose. I'd lucked out.

"It's a cute kitten," Sadie said. Her hair was in a bun, and she was wearing Bea's pearls with her T-shirt.

"It's a scary, deadly kitten," Nevarra reminded her. "There are plenty of cute kittens that won't try to kill you." She also had her hair in a bun but was without pearls.

"Can you bring the tea in?" I asked Bea, thinking that I was a bit unprepared for our party.

"Of course. You go get ready and meet us back here."

Bea went to the kitchen, and I headed into the bathroom to strip out of my clothes and wash the worst of the dirt and blood off me using a cloth at the sink. As I yanked my shirt off, I realize that I'd completely forgotten about my earlier injury.

The gauze was still wrapped around my waist. The padded part covering the Band-Aids was as clean as it had been when Bishop had doctored me up this afternoon. I lifted my arm and began to unwind the gauze, expecting a twinge of pain, or, at the very least, the pull of a newly formed scab. I felt neither. The gauze fell to the floor. Grimacing, I gently eased off the Band-Aids that Bishop had used to hold the edges of the wound together, then I turned to look in the mirror.

I saw unbroken skin, a smooth expanse of warm gold without even a hint of a scar. This morning I'd had a gaping wound. Now there wasn't any sign at all that I'd been shot.

Weeks ago, when I'd awoken to find my knee uninjured after that mercenary had shot it, I'd assumed Bishop had healed me. He refused to admit to his mind-whammy and head-twisting abilities, so it wasn't a shock to think he'd deny having the skill to make an injury just disappear. But this…?

I'd still been wounded when I'd left Suerte—not bleeding all over the place but bearing an injury that should have taken weeks at the very least to heal. Yet here I stood, good as new. Did Bishop have some sort of ability to heal from a distance? To delay the timing of his magic? Or did I unconsciously do this myself?

Was this his magic or mine?

But there was no time to contemplate that—not with tea awaiting my arrival. I quickly put on clean clothes, threw my hair into a messy bun, and headed into the girls' bedroom for our little party.

As I poured the fragrant brew into the little flowered cups, my thoughts kept straying back to my healed waist. We drank our tea, the girls adding a bit of sugar to theirs. Bea surprised us with some shortbread cookies she'd bought. The girls giggled as I faked a horrible British accent, and we did indeed put our pinkies out as we drank from the dime-toss cups. All too soon it was over with Sadie and Nevarra tucked in for the night and me washing up. It seemed that loose leaf tea went a long way because even with us having several cups each, there was still half a bag left of the mix. Best three dollars I'd ever spent.

"So, fess up and tell me what's gotten you so distracted this evening." Bea's voice was soft behind me. "Is it that monster kitten, or the bounty hunter that came after you?"

The bounty hunter was dead, and as terrifying as the cat was, it wasn't what was preying on my mind tonight. I desperately needed to get the situation resolved with the tax office, like yesterday, but instead of those three names, I kept thinking about the gunshot wound that should have decorated my waist.

"When I was a kid, did I seem to heal faster than normal?" I put away the last cup and turned to face Bea. "Like scraped knees where the scabs were gone in days instead of weeks? Cuts that closed up quicker than normal? That kind of thing?"

Bea eyed me solemnly. "You were never sick. Someone

could cough right in your face, and you never even got a sniffle. And you did heal fast. Not so fast that it was noticeable, unless you really thought about it, though. Once I knew about your special talent, about how you could move things without touching them, that's when I started to notice how quickly you healed."

"You never said anything." That came out more accusatory than I wanted, but I was really feeling on edge tonight.

"Why would I say anything? At first, I wasn't even sure it was out of the ordinary. Some people have real good immune systems, and some people just heal fast."

"But you suspected something? That maybe I was…different?"

"We're all different one way or another." Bea took a step toward me. "Eden, you are my *daughter*. I wasn't going to say anything that might get you taken away from me. Besides, it wasn't my secret to share. And now we live in a world with demons and elves, and kittens that shoot lasers out of their eyes. Moving things with your mind and healing fast ain't exactly different compared to all that."

I laughed. Maybe she was right. Who the fuck cared if I could bat balls out of midair and heal a gunshot wound in a matter of hours with the shitshow we were living in.

"Fair warning, the fast-healing thing seems to have speeded up." I bit my lip, then went on because of all the people in the world I could trust, Bea was top of the list. "And I can create electricity. Like out of my fingers. Sometimes it's no more than a static shock. Sometimes it's like a lightning bolt."

She shrugged. "That's a good thing. Next time the power goes out, I know who to call. Think you could run the stove long enough to cook a meatloaf if we need it?"

I laughed again, relief flooding through me. "I'm not good

at controlling the output. There's a good chance I'd blow up the stove. And the meatloaf. And probably the house, too."

Bea smiled and stepped forward to plant a kiss on my cheek. "Then you should probably practice more, honey. We're counting on you, Eden. You might be the only thing standing between us and raw meatloaf one day. Goodnight. Sleep well. I hope to see you in the morning before I head to work."

Just being here in my home with my family around me made me relax. Just that short conversation with Bea made me feel accepted, loved, and not as freakishly weird as I'd thought I was. I was a walking stun gun. I could sorta move shit with my mind. I healed super quick. It didn't matter. I was still human. I was still Bea's daughter, Nevarra and Sadie's sister. I was loved, no matter what.

It had been insanely hot this week, and with spotty electricity, the air conditioner had been unable to keep pace with the outside temperature. Outside the temps had dropped to the upper eighties, and it wasn't much cooler inside. Just as Bea and I were headed to bed, we heard the all-too-familiar click that plunged us into darkness and silence.

Bea pulled a small flashlight out of her pocket and switched it on. "Let's open the windows. Hopefully there will be enough of a breeze tonight."

Even with a breeze, we were going to be hot and sticky all through the night. "I'll get up and close the windows if the power comes back on," I told her as I headed to my room.

The tiny window at the bottom of my bed wasn't going to provide much relief from the heat, but it was the only option I had. Stripping naked, I climbed into bed and kicked the sheets to the bottom. Already, I could feel sweat pooling under my breasts. I lay there thinking of the mercenaries after me, of the cop I needed to find, of my magically healing wounds, and of boneless corpses. I had enough on my plate that the boneless corpses were a low priority, but with Juke helping me out, I felt like I should do her this favor in return.

I needed to warn Bags, since one of the dead was a pawnbroker. I wanted to see him tomorrow anyway to ask him about the names Alfie had pulled up for me. Bags knew stuff. He knew about cops, and he knew where they liked to hang out. If anyone could point me in the direction of these three officers, it was him.

Thinking of everything I needed to do, of all the issues I needed to resolve, I fitfully drifted off.

What felt like seconds later, I was awakened by a noise. Normally I would have jumped out of bed, gun off the nightstand and in my hand ready to shoot, but some instinct kept me still in bed.

A small shadow moved along the windowsill. With a quiet slice, the screen mesh fell as if it had been tissue paper, and something slid through the window. It leapt with agile grace to the foot of the bed and stared at me with yellow-green eyes.

The kitten. I nearly wet myself with fear. Had it tracked me here? Was it not just more murderous than most cats, but more intelligent as well? After devouring Navy SEAL Guy, had it decided to hunt me down and eat me too?

I didn't want to move. I didn't want to endanger Bea or the girls, who would come running to help if I screamed. I didn't want to try to fight this thing off right down the hall from where they were sleeping. Hopefully, it would just kill me quietly without setting the place on fire or realizing there were other tasty morsels in the house for it to devour.

But instead of attacking me with razor-sharp claws and laser eyes, the cat blinked, kneaded the sheets I'd kicked to the end of the bed, then curled up in a little fluffy ball at my feet. The yellow-green eyes winked out, and the only sounds I heard were the faint noise from the freeway, and purring.

I lay there absolutely still for hours, too terrified to move. Eventually I must have dozed off, because suddenly there were thin streaks of golden light coming through my window. The cat was no longer on my bed, but I remained where I was, only my eyes moving as I made sure it wasn't clinging to the ceiling or poised on my nightstand, ready to pounce on me.

It was gone.

I let out a breath, moving muscles that had tightened with hours of rigid inactivity. Getting up, I searched the room, the anti-magic gun in hand just in case the kitten was under a pile of laundry or hiding under the bed. I wasn't sure it would work on the thing, but I figured the spelled blue pellets would be my best chance of disabling the kitten long enough to attempt to kill it.

It was truly gone—which was a good thing because I might be pretty emotionless when it came to shooting people who were trying to attack me, but killing a kitten wasn't something I could easily do, even one like Hellkitty. Shutting the window, I put the gun down and sat on my bed to think. Was this a one-time visit? If I kept the window closed, would that keep the kitten away, or would it just burn the damned house down to get to me? And why me? It didn't seem the sort of animal that would get attached to anyone, let alone a woman who'd disrupted its home in the dump and who'd been in the company of a man who'd attacked it. Maybe the kitten knew I'd also been attacked? Maybe that made us kindred spirits in its mind?

Maybe I was going crazy. Still, if this kitten was after me, it was one more reason for me to stay away from home.

Getting dressed, I headed down the hallway and saw Nevarra already awake. She was sitting on the sofa, reading the demonology book.

"Learn anything?" I teased her.

She nodded. "Demons are pretty much like young angels. Except there's some inbreeding weirdness, and they don't seem to have much in the way of powers for their first thousand years. And some are just born more powerful than others."

"Lows." I headed for the kitchen, remembering something HB had said a few weeks back. "Lows are really limited in what they can do demon-wise."

"Yeah. But the really old demons, the Ancients, are basically angels. They're fallen angels from that stupid war a gazillion years ago. So, angels and demons? They're the same thing outside of some philosophy crap."

I grabbed an apple and poured the somewhat cold coffee from the fridge into a mug. "So, angels steal souls and take on the human form of their victim as well?"

Ugh, I hoped not. It was one thing for the denizens of hell to do that sort of thing, but it weirded me out to think that the supposed good guys were capable of the same horrible acts. I could accept angels being impersonal, cold, and lacking in empathy, but soul stealing just didn't jive with my rather secular Catholic upbringing.

"No, that's just a demon thing. Or a fallen angel thing. The fallen ones are ruled by chaos, and the non-fallen ones are ruled by order. Philosophy stuff. It sounds like that's what really caused the boring war that took up the first hundred-some pages of this book."

"Huh. How about that." Relieved that angels didn't steal souls, I had turned my attention to the cold coffee in my mug. Could I use my electrical power to heat it up? Did zapped liquid get hot, or would it just explode the cup and splash ionized coffee all over the kitchen? I went to stick my finger into the cup, then decided against it. As hot as it was this morning, iced coffee was a more appealing option.

Besides, I really didn't have time to clean up the mess if things went wrong.

I went back in to see Nevarra loading the book into my backpack.

"When do you think you'll be back?" Her question was casual, but I caught the worry in her voice.

"I'll swing by in a few days to visit, but it might be another week or two until I spend the night again. You guys are safer if these bounty hunters don't think I actually live here." Hopefully by then my situation would be resolved, and I could be home every evening.

She nodded, then held out the backpack. "Better grab some spare clothes if you're not coming back for a few days."

I took it from her, then went back to my room to grab a few things. Spare clothes. Spare ammo. Travel-sized toiletries in case I found myself needing to clean up in a fast-food restroom. A multi-tool and a few knives went into the pockets of my cargo pants, and the rest went into the backpack with the book. I debated taking the anti-magic gun. There were only four of the spelled paint-ball bullets left, and I kinda wanted to hold them back for an emergency. Plus, I liked the idea that the gun was here in case Bea or the girls needed it. Most of what I encountered on a day-to-day basis was human violence, but the gun would have come in handy last night against Navy SEAL Guy.

Or not. His magic hadn't done shit to me, and I wasn't sure if neutralizing his abilities would mean he'd suddenly be susceptible to mine or not. Was our innate immunity magical or just part of who we were?

I knew little about this new world we'd all been thrust into two years ago, and I needed to remedy that. Keeping my head down and just shrugging off things like Hellkitty, lizard people on the beltway, magic spells, shifters, Durfts, and everything else had been my way of coping, but that way of coping was going to eventually get me killed.

There was so much shit I didn't know. Figuring out what demons could and couldn't do, how to avoid them and how to wiggle out of their grasp when I couldn't avoid them was high on my priority list. And after last night, I realized that I needed to know more about my magic and how it worked. I didn't use spells or magical ingredients. I didn't invoke any sort of deity or infernal creature. My magic came naturally, and I wasn't sure if that made me more like the mages or more like the elves.

Or more like the demons. But I wasn't going to even think about that one.

Walking over to the mirror on my dresser, I examined my ears. Could I be part elf? I was a foundling child, and the police had never been able to locate my parents or any of my family. Folklore of changeling babies swirled through my mind. It fit. A fussy difficult baby, abandoned in the parking lot of a church, naked and without even a blanket to cover her. But weren't the babies left behind in a changeling swap dead or dying? Otherwise, why would the elves leave one of their own behind for a bunch of humans to raise? Unless I was some illicit bastard-child of a human and elf, unwanted by both.

Did elves even have sex with humans?

Hell if I knew. I'd never met a mage or an elf—at least I thought I hadn't. Demon, yes. Hellkitty, yes. Shifters, I was sure, yes. I'd probably know if I saw an elf, but a mage would look just like any old human.

My ears didn't have the slightest bit of point to them, though. And I'd never managed to keep even a pot of basil alive. Wasn't elven magic supposed to be all about nature and the elements? The only thing I could do was electrocute stuff and some minor telekinesis. And heal myself, evidently.

But figuring out what I was had to go on the back burner. First, I needed to get the tax office and the mercenaries off my back, and my license reinstated. Then I'd deal with demons, magic, shifters, and the rest.

I packed the anti-magic gun, stopped to say goodbye to Bea, Sadie, and Nevarra, then headed out, swinging by the dump just to see it all in the daylight. Keeping a careful watch out for Hellkitty, I nosed around the burned pile of scrap wood, the stack of aluminum, and the rods scattered off to the side where the kitten had launched them at Navy SEAL Guy. The grill lay dented and twisted off to the side of the stack of metal. Flecks of dried blood were splattered on the packed dirt and a few bunches of sedge, but not nearly the amount I'd expected to see given the injuries the man had sustained. Maybe kitten eye-lasers cauterized wounds, but I still would have thought there would be more blood.

Kneeling down, I picked a dried red blob off the dirt and held it between my finger and thumb. It looked like any other blood I'd seen, but it felt…weird. Touching it sent off a cascade of vibration and static that ran from my fingertips through to my toes. Pulling a Kleenex from my pocket, I wrapped the dried blood in it and stashed it safely away. With a shudder, I wiped my fingers on the dirt to rid them of the sensation.

"Sorry you're dead, Navy SEAL Guy," I said as I got to my feet. Not that I was really sorry he was dead, but it would have been nice if he'd lived long enough to answer a few questions.

But him dead with my questions unanswered was better than him alive and me having my guts pulled out my ass by a bunch of angry demons.

I had come out of this fight alive and unhurt, and in the last two years, I'd learned that was what was truly important. Questions might be answered later, but dead was dead.

CHAPTER 7

Two blocks from my neighborhood, a gray sedan and a white SUV pulled in a few cars behind me. Five miles and six turns later, they were still tailing me at a careful distance. Then the sedan changed lanes, slowly easing closer while the SUV pulled in behind me. The sedan was going to flank me and squeeze me over into the parked cars or pull ahead and block me, sandwiching me between him and the SUV.

I rolled the throttle and accelerated. They realized they'd been made and quit pretending to be casual drivers. The sedan sped up, abruptly jerking to the right. I hit the brakes, ducked behind him, then cut across oncoming traffic, darting back into my lane and narrowly avoiding a head-on collision. Swerving in front of a minivan, I leaned in to make a sharp right at the next intersection, then immediately swung onto the on ramp for the 5 South.

By some miracle, traffic wasn't a complete gridlock. I swerved into the fast lane, cursing when a quick glance in the rear view revealed the SUV and the sedan on the freeway behind me and moving up fast.

My Yahama Fazer was old, but she could still get up and go when I needed her to. Top speed on this bike had been around one hundred forty way back in the eighties. I didn't think I could top one hundred ten in it now without parts vibrating off it. The vehicles chasing me could go faster than that. I couldn't outrun them, but I sure as hell could outmaneuver them.

I started evasive maneuvers, weaving in and out of traffic, but they were doing the same, growing closer by the second.

Shots rang out, and I instinctively ducked down. The cars around me swerved. A pickup in front of me sideswiped a Toyota, then spun around, skidding to a stop on the shoulder. The Toyota careened into my lane, and I swung right to veer around it, hitting the loose grit on the shoulder for a few seconds. The bike skidded, but I held her straight, keeping a little brake on for control as I accelerated hard.

I could hear the sounds of twisting metal behind me, the crash of vehicles colliding. Pushing the bike as fast as I could, I wove in and out of the traffic, relaxing when the only sounds I could hear were the typical L.A. traffic noises.

I was worth far more alive than dead, and even more if they brought me in with the loot, but I still worried. They'd shot at me. They would have tried to force my bike off the road if they could. Just as the guys who'd grabbed me a few weeks ago had said, alive didn't mean I wouldn't be delivered to the tax office with broken bones and a few bullet holes in me.

The wreck I'd narrowly avoided allowed me to put some space between me and the bounty hunters, but I had no doubt they'd be after me again. Soon. I'd need to be careful when I went to visit Bags later this morning. I'd need to make sure I wasn't followed. And I needed to get off this damned freeway before those goons got free of the wreck and caught up with me.

Exiting at Los Feliz, I doubled back north, heading up a winding road that led to a cliff-side neighborhood nestled up against Griffith Park.

When I was a kid, I'd made the usual obligatory trips to the observatory as well as the zoo. A friend during high school had convinced me to hike a few of the trails with her. L.A. and the Valley were full of beautiful places, but for some reason I'd always been drawn to this iconic park. I loved it here. There was something about the area that spoke to me. High above the L.A. basin, I could look down at the city like a goddess from on high.

There was one way into this neighborhood and one way out. It was defensible. It had an amazing view. And the houses here weren't pocked with bullet holes or scorched with dragon fire. These people didn't live across from a dump or where laser-eyed kittens snuck into bedrooms at night. Here it felt…safe.

Ever since I'd seen Telaney's house, I'd dreamed of finding a place of my own to claim squatters' rights on. Home would always be home, but it would be good to have an alternate place to crash that wasn't an abandoned store or a bridge abutment. And after what had happened last night with Navy SEAL Guy and that kitten, I was starting to think about a safer place for Bea and the girls as well.

I'd hoped that by now we would have saved enough money to get out of New Hell, to start a new life in Dallas or Denver or somewhere. The Fixers had smashed those dreams when they'd invaded our home, stolen all of our money, hurt my family, and taken Nevarra. We might never get out of New Hell, but maybe we could carve out a decent life here, in a new home, in a new place.

I'd kept my eyes open for a house in a decent neighborhood that seemed vacant but didn't seem so vacant that it had probably been trashed a dozen times over. And four days ago, here, on Canyon Drive, I'd found what I was looking for.

It was a white stucco contemporary that looked to be one story from the front, but actually had a lower level where a wall of glass looked out over the L.A. basin. On a clear day, downtown would be visible. Heck, on a clear day, I might even be able to see the ocean.

I hadn't been inside yet but judging from my drive-bys and stealthy reconnaissance, I knew no one was living there. The lights came on and off at programmed intervals whenever the electricity was on, and the mail was either being forwarded or picked up by a neighbor. I was positive the residents had left town. Maybe not permanently, but these days if you were fool enough to go away on vacation without leaving armed guards at your house, then you could expect to find someone else living there when you got home. Maybe you could pay them to leave. Maybe you could oust them at the business end of a gun. Either way, it would cost you.

I wasn't sure if this house would be a permanent thing for me or not. I might decide I hated the décor or the neighbors. I might just stay here until I got things resolved with the tax demons. Or maybe I'd keep this place, have Bea and the kids over to visit, pretend as if I'd actually bought it and were a successful young woman, not a scavenger who hadn't had a real bath in almost a week. Or maybe I'd move them all in. No easily accessible backyard for Fixers to try to sneak through. No dump across the street for monster-kittens to hide in. No shot-up walls and broken cabinets and windows patched up by a teenage neighbor.

For the last two years, all I'd thought about was getting us out of here. Now all I could think about was surviving. We may never get out of here. I might as well dig in and create the best life for myself and my family with whatever we had left.

Standing astride my bike in front of the house, I wondered that I'd ever thought we'd be able to leave. It seemed like a fantasy to believe that. My whole life was here —in the Valley and in the city. I still wanted a better life for Bea and the girls, but me? I was beginning to think I belonged here. I was beginning to think there wasn't a life for me outside of New Hell, and that I'd been a fool to ever believe there would be.

I was different. I was weird. And it had become harder and harder for me to ignore that. Maybe I belonged in New Hell with all the other weirdos.

If so, I might as well make the best of it.

Making a decision, I pulled my bike into the driveway, then walked up to the front door. It was locked, but after a few minutes with my picks, I had the door swinging open. This was still a nice neighborhood, and I was a little shocked to find there were no magical alarms or defensive spells on the door. Just a basic handle lock and an equally basic dead bolt. Bracing myself, I walked inside and was relieved not to be shot, or incinerated, or tranq'ed, or turned into a frog.

The house was small, simple, and breathtaking. The open floor plan had a dining area to my right, a kitchen to my left, and a living area directly in front of me that looked out across the city. There was a door off the kitchen that probably led out to the small garage, and a spiral staircase to the left of the living area that headed down to the lower level. Shelves were empty aside from a few random knickknacks, but the residents had left their furniture behind. I was too dirty to even think about sitting on the creamy white sectional sofa, so I closed the door behind me and went in search of the bedrooms. The door off the kitchen did indeed lead to an empty garage. Another door revealed an equally empty small pantry; another opened up to a half-bath, and yet another was a closet with a pair of navy-blue Crocs abandoned in the corner. I headed downstairs and found that the bedrooms included one larger room that ran along the cliff-side of the house, one smaller windowless room against the street-side wall, and one giant bathroom complete with a double-headed walk-in shower and a jacuzzi tub big enough for an elephant.

Weird, but I wasn't going to turn up my nose at the layout of a house I was squatting at. Two bedrooms wasn't optimal if I moved Bea and the girls in here, but I could make it work. The girls and I could share the big bedroom, or I could divide it off into two rooms. Javier had proven himself handy with a hammer. I'd bet he'd happily help put up some framing and drywall if I asked. Or rather, if Nevarra asked.

Heading back into the bathroom, I admired the luxurious layout. With a quick prayer, I turned on the shower, squealing when water sprayed out. In seconds, I was naked and wasting hot water with abandon, using up every bit of the little travel shampoo and body wash I'd packed with me. The girls totally had to see this shower. And the tub. We were totally going to have a party in the jacuzzi tub. We'd slap some face goop on, make a few fruity drinks, turn on the jacuzzi jets, and live it up. If I timed it right, I bet I could even make sure the water was hot.

The water slowed to a trickle, and I got out, wishing I'd thought to run some in the tub and in the sinks while it was available. There were a few threadbare towels in the cabinet that I used to dry myself off, then I stood naked in the giant bedroom and unpacked my backpack. When I went to toss my tank tops and T-shirts in the dresser, I found that the pair of Crocs weren't the only things left behind. Making room for my own belongings, I dressed in clean clothes and hauled my backpack and the demonology book upstairs.

There were some canned goods in the kitchen cabinets and a random assortment of what I assumed were everyday dishes that had been left behind. I took a quick inventory. I'd need to do a little shopping before I came back tonight. Maybe I'd eat carryout by the huge window overlooking the city. Maybe I'd just walk around the house naked all night long. My own house. Until I'd walked through the front door, I hadn't realized how much that meant to me, how much I longed for a place just like this. Tonight, I'd sleep here, and hopefully by next week I'd have Bea and the girls moved in.

I loaded the book into my backpack, strapped on my shoulder harness, walked out the front door, and abruptly came to a stop.

There were people standing on their lawns and driveways, and in the street. They were all staring at me. I froze, trying to figure out what was about to happen here. Was this a Neighborhood Watch about to shoot me full of holes or throw me out? Only a handful of the people were armed, but something about them sent my awareness into overdrive.

An Asian man in a light gray business suit took a step toward me. "You're not one of us. You don't belong here."

I tensed but resisted the urge to reach for my gun. "I claim squatters' rights on this house. It's empty. Abandoned."

"We have rules on this street. Protocol for who's allowed to move in and who isn't. There's a reason that house is still empty. We don't allow squatters to come into our territory."

Great. And here all I'd been worried about was some pesky HOA restrictions or the neighbors complaining about how noisy my bike was.

"I won't cause any trouble." It wasn't exactly a lie. *I* wouldn't cause trouble, but the demons and mercenaries after me might. "I'll be in and out a few times a day at most, maybe sleeping here most nights. I want to move my family in here—my mother and two sisters. They're good people."

They were good people. I wasn't too sure I could say that about myself.

"If you're going to lay claim to a part of our territory, then you'll need to fight for it," the man announced.

"Fight…how?" I eyed him, not wanting to be overconfident here. He was slim and not much taller than I was, but I'd seen short wiry guys fight before. Drew had regularly beat the shit out of guys twice his size. Hopefully, the man didn't mean fight as in a brawl. Maybe he meant pistols at twenty paces.

Or rock paper scissors. Yeah, rock paper scissors would be good.

"One on one." He swept his hand outward. "You can pick who among us you wish to challenge."

"Just one? Or the whole lot of you, but one at a time?" I hoped the former.

"Just one. If you win, you can stay. I can't guarantee you won't need to assert your status among individual members, but as a group we will accept your presence."

This was…weird. Strangest HOA I'd ever encountered. Not that I'd encountered too many HOAs in my lifetime. Were they all like this? I couldn't imagine new homeowners in Brentwood needed to brawl with their pissy neighbors, but what did I know?

"And if I lose?" I began eyeing the people, trying to figure out who I might be able to beat in this fight.

"If you lose, then you leave and don't return. We will allow you to go peacefully with any belongings you brought with you."

Okay, that didn't sound too bad. "What sort of fight? Are knives allowed?"

"No weapons." Someone in the crowd to the right made a disgruntled noise at that proclamation. "No knives or guns. No teeth or claws."

Damn. My nails were kept short, but I wasn't above biting if it got me an advantage.

"How is the winner determined?" Was this a first blood sort of thing? Since they would allow me to leave if I lost, then it clearly wasn't a to-the-death fight, thank God.

"Loser yields."

Huh. The whole thing was weird, but I was game. If I won, cool. If I lost…well, I was no worse off than I had been this morning.

Looking through the crowd, I spotted my target, and no, it wasn't a woman. Women fought like crazed badgers. In spite of the no-teeth and no-nails mandate, somehow a female opponent would manage to skirt around those rules, and I'd end up chewed and clawed. Plus, women gave every fight one hundred and ten percent, as if they were in a fight for their lives even if they were just scrapping it up over a cute pair of boots at TJ Maxx. No, I was challenging a man. Men held back on fights unless they truly *were* in a life-or-death situation. And men were generally reluctant to go all out when it came to fighting a woman. Plus, they tended to fight fair. Women didn't fight fair.

I definitely didn't fight fair.

"Him." I pointed at a balding middle-aged dude. He was dressed like an accountant and holding a coffee mug. The man was taller than me, so that put me at a disadvantage as far as reach went. And he outweighed me. But I was willing to bet he wasn't as skilled at fighting or as in shape as I was.

"Dennis, you're up," their leader announced.

The balding guy cursed, then looked around for someone to hand his coffee mug to. Yeah, this was going to be easy. I unstrapped my shoulder holster and set it aside, then pulled my shirt off as well.

"You don't need to fight naked." The leader glared at me. "This isn't mud wrestling."

A few people in the crowd laughed at that.

"I just took a shower and changed. I'm not getting my clean clothes dirty." I was always dirty and covered in blood by the end of the day, but I liked to at least start out reasonably clean.

Dennis finally found someone to take his mug and handed it off. He stripped off his shirt as well, revealing some unexpected muscle. I debated taking off my cargo pants and just fighting in my underwear. Less clothing meant less my opponent could grab onto and use for leverage as we grappled and having a mostly naked woman wresting around on him might provide a distraction. But these were not manicured Beverly Hills lawns here. We'd be rolling around on rocks, thorny decorative plants, and probably the driveway asphalt. Even if my new super healing cooperated, the scrapes and road rash were gonna hurt. Deciding that the added pain would outweigh any half-naked distraction advantage, I just emptied my pockets instead.

The leader motioned us forward, and we squared off on either side of him. I was happy we were doing this on a neighbor's lawn and not mine since the previous residents had gone with the whole-lotta-rocks landscaping and this neighbor had at least made an attempt at grass.

"No weapons," the leader reminded us. "Don't kill her, Dennis. I need to be at work in an hour and don't have time to dispose of a body."

"Got it." Dennis shifted his weight, his gaze laser-focused on me.

I did the same. Then I rushed him. I went low, aiming my shoulder for his gut and hoping to knock him off balance. Hitting his stomach was more like plowing my shoulder into a wall. Pain radiated down my arm. Before I could spin away and try to recover from my mistake, Dennis grabbed me around the waist, flipped me upside down, then threw me to the ground. I landed hard on my back, gasping for air.

Without a second of hesitation, Dennis lashed out with a foot, kicking my side, then landed another kick on my hip. Still struggling to get a breath, I rolled. I managed to grab his leg before he could land another kick and tucked it under my arm, using his momentum and my roll to finally knock him off balance. Dennis landed hard on his ass and yanked his foot free. We both scrambled to our feet at the same time.

Damn, this was not the easy fight I'd hoped it would be. We circled around each other, feinting and trying to gain the advantage. This guy was good. He was really good. Where was Hellkitty when I needed him?

"Hurry up, Dennis," someone shouted. "Your coffee's getting cold."

This was stupid. Why was I risking a beating over a damned house? I had enough to deal with. I should just tap out now, get my stuff, and leave. But then I glanced at the house, at my bike in the driveway, and felt a pang of regret.

Dennis acted in that split second of my inattention, and his shoulder in my stomach was a hell of a lot more effective than when I'd tried the same move. I went down hard but got in a punch to his kidneys and a knee to his face on the way.

"Damn it!" Dennis stepped back, wiping blood from his nose and shaking his head.

The kidney shot hadn't seemed to work, but clearly the guy's nose was a weak point. I scrambled up barely in time to side-step another rush and spun around, mule-kicking Dennis in the back of his knees. The guy finally went down, and I jumped on his back, grabbing his thinning hair and slamming his face down into the gravel.

I hoped hair pulling was allowed. They'd said no weapons, no claws or biting, but hadn't said anything about hair pulling.

Dennis bellowed, bucking with far more strength than a middle-aged office worker should have. I flew off his back, skidding across the driveway. He was on me with a preternatural speed, his nose still bleeding, his face a mess of scrapes and embedded bits of rock. I squirmed, kicked, and punched, but he ignored all that and wrapped his hands around my neck.

I couldn't breathe. Things were starting to get fuzzy. I smacked a hand onto the asphalt, indicating my surrender, but the fingers around my throat just tightened. I patted the ground again, patted the guy's leg, tried unsuccessfully to say something, to plead mercy with my eyes.

His fingers tightened further, so I made the only move I had left—I sent a surge of electricity through him.

Dennis jerked upright. His hands were still around my neck, and I was starting to panic, so I let loose with everything I had and blew the guy off me in a shower of sparks.

I'd tapped out. I'd fucking tapped out, and Dennis had tried to break my neck. My only fear now as I scrambled to all fours, coughing and desperately trying to draw in a full breath, was that my unreliable magic had sent far more electricity into the guy than I'd planned. If I killed him…well, I was pretty sure I was going to be dead as well. There was no way I could escape or defend myself against this mob, magic or no magic.

The crowd was eerily silent as I crawled over to Dennis and tried to check his pulse. He jerked an arm up and knocked my hand away, answering the most pressing question on my mind.

"You're not human." The leader took a step toward me and the air crackled with tension.

"I *am* human," I croaked out. "I just…I just have some magical abilities."

His mouth thinned. "You're a mage?"

I had no idea what I was, and I wasn't about to get into a question-and-answer session with this guy. "Look, I lost. I lost, and I tried to tap out, but your boy here wasn't having any of that. I defended myself the only way I could, to keep him from killing me."

"That's cheating," he snarled. "No weapons. That includes magic."

"It wasn't supposed to be a fight to the death. I lost. I tapped out. I'll get my things and go." I managed to struggle to my feet, swaying a bit as I stood.

Dennis moaned and stirred. I was tempted to kick him, but I got the feeling I was in enough trouble as it was.

The leader snarled, and for a second, I thought I was going to have to zap him and try to make a run for it, but a woman who'd been trying to get his attention reached out and grabbed his arm. She whispered something I couldn't hear, and the tension I was feeling from the crowd changed. It didn't lessen, but somehow, I got the impression they were less angry and more…anxious?

"Get out of here." The leader pointed down the road. "You've got ten minutes to get your stuff and get out."

I didn't ask "or what." I didn't even pause to take a breath. Grabbing my clothes, my gun and gear, and my backpack, I ran for the house. Tearing down the stairs, I dressed, then shoved whatever clothes I could grab into my backpack, strapped on my shoulder harness, and ran outside to my bike. I was on the road with plenty of time to spare, and I didn't look back.

CHAPTER 8

*B*ags didn't know *everyone* in the Valley, but he knew a lot of people, and those people knew a lot of people. So, I headed to the pawnshop, thinking that there was a chance he could get me the information on these three cops. It was a long shot but spending an hour or two to see what Bags knew wouldn't make much of a difference, especially with how my day was going so far. Besides, I hadn't seen him in a few weeks, and I missed the guy. He was more than just my preferred pawnbroker; he was a friend. He was family.

Cristin Balefort at the twelfth. Carly Bliss at the eighteenth. Ches Bingham at the fourteenth.

Two years ago, L.A. was divided into four police commands—or bureaus—with a total of twenty-one precincts or divisions. The dividing lines and budget allocations had shifted quite a bit since then, but the Valley still had its own bureau. That bureau had sucked in all the independent city police departments when the demons came, and those cities found themselves unable to pay for their own law enforcement agencies. That was true outside the Valley as well. Burbank, Pasadena, Santa Monica, Glendale, and even Beverly Hills residents were pissed to lose their police force, but no one had been willing to pitch in the considerable funds to keep the independent offices going. Not that the LAPD had the funds to pick up the slack. For the first year, everyone complained about poor response times, unsolved crimes, and reports that seemed to go straight to the circular file, but we'd all gotten used to it. People still bitched and moaned about the police, but now they also grumbled about paying protection to the gangs or the exorbitant cost of private security or militias.

The Valley Bureau had encompassed divisions nine, ten, fifteen, sixteen, seventeen, nineteen, and twenty-one back in the day, but with the restructuring, we now had precincts that numbered from ten to twenty. My three potential suspects worked at Van Nuys, West Valley, and Burbank according to the map Alfie had printed for me. Bags might know some of the officers who were with the Burbank and West Valley precincts, but for Van Nuys, I was probably going to have to go elsewhere.

I drove by the pawnshop a few times, circling the block and cruising down the side streets. There were no unusually clean vagrants propping up lamp posts, no men with sunglasses just sitting in their cars, no loiterers milling about neighboring buildings, no sketchy vehicles following me. The Fixer mercenaries who'd been staking out Bags's pawn-shop for a few days must have decided their time would be better spent trying to catch me elsewhere, and the guys from this morning clearly hadn't followed me from Los Feliz.

Parking my bike a few blocks away, I called the store, then asked Bags if it was clear for me to come in. Just because I hadn't seen anyone hanging around didn't mean the mercenaries weren't checking here and there throughout the day. Bags let me know he was currently dealing with a customer, but that he was always in the market for a post-hole digger, and I should come by.

"Post-hole digger" was code for "come around the basement entrance." It made me hesitate, wondering about his customer and who else might be in the store. But Bags wouldn't have told me to come on by if it wasn't safe, so I left my bike and cut through the back parking area of an abandoned home improvement store, making my way over fences and between buildings to the back of the pawnshop. After carefully scoping out the area, I snuck through the rear lot and down the stairs to the cellar door. Navigating the locks and security system, I went through the basement and up the stairs. I could hear Bags talking with a customer, so I hung out in the little break room and grabbed a soda while I waited for him to finish up.

I'd just tossed the empty soda can in the recycle bin when Bags poked his head around the corner and motioned for me to come up front. He'd locked the door and slid the security gate closed, but I still eyed the windows nervously.

"So, you've got names?" he asked me.

I pulled out the map Alfie had printed and showed him the precincts I'd circled. "Cristin Balefort, Carly Bliss, and Ches Bingham. Do you know any of these cops?"

Bags scratched his chin. "Don't know any Balefort or Bliss. I've never met any of them personally, but Bingham's got a reputation as a good cop. The others I don't know anything about."

This was so frustrating. How was I supposed to check these cops out? Should I walk into the police stations, ask for the cops to personally see if they were the woman from the hit that day? I'd recognize her, but I was sure she'd recognize me as well, and confronting her in the middle of her station wouldn't go well for me. She'd accuse me of something and get me thrown in holding until the tax collectors came to get me. No, I needed some other way of verifying which of these officers was the cop who'd set me up.

"Please tell me you at least know if Bingham is a man or a woman." I desperately wanted to cross at least one of these names off my list.

"He's a guy."

"The cop that set me up is a woman, so that rules out Ches Bingham." I looked around the store, my gaze settling on a case of phones. "You have anything cheap with a few minutes left on the plan?"

I didn't want to use my own phone for this. I doubted the police would have the time to trace the call even if they thought it was worth the bother, but there was no sense in taking chances.

"Sure." Bags walked over and pulled one of the phones out. "Have at it."

I quickly made two calls, one to the twelfth precinct and one to the eighteenth. I had to leave a message for Cristin Balefort, but Carly Bliss was in. As I waited for her to pick up the line, I suddenly realized I had no idea how to get her to come out to meet me. Telling her I had knowledge of a murder wouldn't work if she was a traffic cop. There was a good chance whatever ruse I used would end up with her transferring me to another department. But the cop who'd set me up was wearing SWAT gear and was clearly a patrol officer. That gave me an idea.

"Officer Bliss."

The cheerful female voice on the other end of the line didn't sound at all like the woman who'd ordered me to leave my backpack and all my salvage behind, but I wasn't going to trust my memory.

"I know what you did." I kept my voice low and raspy. "Meet me at the old Capital One building on Empire Avenue at one o'clock. Alone. If you're not there, I'm going to the tax office and filing a report."

"What the hell are you talking about?"

She sounded honestly perplexed, but I wasn't taking any chances.

"Be there. Or you'll find a demon waiting at your house tonight." I disconnected the call and looked over to see Bags regarding me, an approving smile curling up one corner of his mouth.

"Damn, girl. I nearly soiled my drawers just now. Don't wanna ever be on your bad side."

"You could never be on my bad side, Bags." I held up the phone. "Do you mind if I borrow this for the day? Once that other cop calls me back, I can return it."

He nodded. "No problem. Just bring it back when you can."

I stuffed it in my backpack, and my hand brushed against an envelope. Shit, I'd completely forgotten about the assignment Juke had given me—and about the warning I'd meant to give to Bags.

"There's something else I wanted to talk to you about." I pulled the envelope out of my backpack. "Slinky Moore over at ABC died a few days ago."

"I heard." Bags shook his head and made a *tsk* sound. "I'm not surprised. The man lived on bacon and potato chips. The blood in his arteries was probably thicker than molasses. Slinky was a heart attack waiting to happen."

I sat the envelope of photos on the counter. "That's not how he died. They found him boneless. *Boneless*, Bags. As in, he was a sack of flesh without any bones."

Bags recoiled. "Someone broke all his bones? Pulverized them? Or deboned him like a chicken?"

I shook my head. "Nope. Not a mark on him. Or on the three other people who died the same way. Your buddy

Detective Juke said it was like their bones just vanished, and they slumped into a puddle in a skin wrapper."

I pulled the photos out. Bags's eyes widened, and he slapped a hand over the top picture, shoving them back into the envelope.

"Don't be showing me that stuff. Slinky was no friend of mine, but I still don't wanna see his dead, boneless body."

Yeah. I didn't, either. I put the envelope back in my bag.

"Juke asked me to look into it because one of the victims was a Gray Dog, and they won't talk to her. She thinks they're all connected—and she's probably right. I mean, it would be kinda weird to have four deaths all within three weeks or so, where the victims all died boneless."

"You said there were four victims? Were the others Gray Dogs? ABC Pawn employees? Collateral damage?" Bags shuddered. "And did Sarah have any idea what the hell could have dissolved four people's bones?"

"She's thinking a demon, but nobody really knows at this point." I thought of Hellkitty with its laser eyes and ability to fling shit around. "All sorts of weird stuff came from Hel with the demons. Maybe it's a bone-dissolving monster or something."

Bags pursed his lips. "A monster just would have cut a swath through town, killing a bunch of people before going to ground. I can't see one of them killing only four people over the course of three weeks."

I thought once more of Hellkitty. "Unless they stumbled upon its lair or something. Maybe it tracked down the tres-passers and killed them."

That idea was a bit of a stretch. A gang member, a morgue employee, her sister, and a pawnbroker all trespassing through the lair of a monster? The more likely scenario was that they'd all pissed off a demon somehow who got his kicks out of magically deboning people.

"Just be careful about dealing with demons," I warned Bags. "I don't want to see your boneless corpse on one of these crime scene photos."

He laughed. "Well, you don't have to worry there. I stay as far away from demons as I can. And just in case, I'll be careful not to trespass in any monster's territory, either."

I slung the backpack over my shoulder. "You do that. Front door or basement? Which is safer for me to make my exit?"

"Better do the basement. There's been some kook hanging around front, and I don't trust that he's not after you."

Bags headed toward the back, and I followed him down the stairs and up into the weed-filled patch of yard behind the shop. Walking past him, I turned to tell him goodbye. Something whizzed past my head, splatting a blob of blue paint on the brick of the building.

"Down!" Bags leapt forward and tackled me, but not before a bullet grazed across the top of my shoulder, this one not a magically spelled paintball, but an actual flesh-ripping bullet.

I rolled to get Bags off the top of me and out of danger, pulling my pistol from the holster. Two more shots spat up dirt next to me, and then I felt the sizzle of electricity along my skin.

"Get inside!" I fired in the general direction of the gunshots, trying to lay down enough cover that Bags and I could get out of the open and behind some shelter.

"There's two of them." Bags used the metal cellar door to shield himself, propping it open as he vanished down the stairs into the basement. I jumped to my feet and fired as I ran to hide behind a stack of rotting pallets. A few bullets pinged off the wood, but I didn't feel any further electricity attacks.

The glint of a pistol barrel reflecting in the sunshine confirmed my suspicions that one of the attackers was behind the dumpster. Bags had said there were two. Not needing to look, I recalled the layout from memory and thought through the ambush strategically. Behind the dumpster provided an eleven o'clock angle of us coming out of the basement, but the cellar door would block the shot until we were clear. Not that anyone with half a brain would open fire while we could quickly duck back down underground. But that placement would most likely put the second shooter either on top of the neighboring building, or in the ditch off to the right.

If they were on top of the building, I'd be exposed and probably dead right now, so I was putting my money on the ditch. It wouldn't afford much opportunity to get a clear shot, but if we got free of the first guy, we'd probably run right toward the ditch. Plus, it gave good cover.

Another two bullets splintered one of the pallets.

I ducked down to check my magazine. Two with one in the chamber. Not wanting to have to change magazines in the middle of a firefight, I pocketed the one from the gun and slid a fresh magazine in from one of the pockets of my cargo pants. This had better do it because I'd have no time to reload a magazine with spare bullets from my backpack.

Dumpster Guy was the only one shooting bullets, as far as I could tell. Was he also the one who'd sent that surge of electricity toward me? Or was that Ditch Guy? And who had the anti-magic gun? That was a real concern. If that bullet hadn't missed me, I wouldn't be able to attack with electricity.

And I probably wouldn't be able to super heal any gunshot wound, either.

Three bullets slammed into the pallets right near my head, and I jumped back. Electricity tingled through the air, and the dry wood burst into flame. I'd been hoping to wait for Bags to reappear with an arsenal from the pawnshop, but I was running out of time.

Jumping out from behind the pallets, I sent a burst of my own electricity toward the metal dumpster, not holding anything back. It shot from my hand like a bolt of lightning, and sparks flew as I hit my target. Crouching as I ran, I shot toward the ditch for cover. Rounding the side of the dumpster, I swung my pistol around and found…no one.

Fuck, he was on the move. Which meant I needed to be as well. With one hand on the dumpster, ready to send another blast of electricity into it, I edged forward. No gunshots alerted me to the shooter's location, so I paused at the corner of the dumpster and waited, not wanting to get my head shot off by walking blindly around the side.

The boom of a shotgun rang out, followed by the ping of bullets off the cellar door.

"Oil barrel," Bags yelled. "And ditch."

The cavalry had arrived. Bags might be in his seventies and walk with a limp, but he was definitely someone I wanted on my side in a fight. The man could shoot a pea off a fence at twenty feet.

I heard the boom of another shotgun round.

Running low, I rounded the dumpster, shooting toward the oil barrel and saw a rifle barrel propped up on the edge of the ditch, pointing right at me. Time seemed to slow as the muzzle flared. With that odd sensation of tachypsychia that only seemed to happen in movies, I *saw* the tranq dart make its way toward me. I froze, then with the muscle memory from a thousand games played with the girls, I waved my hand and batted the dart aside from four feet away—just like I'd always done with the balls in the backyard. I did the same with the second dart before I moved with a weird Matrix-like blur to the oil can.

There crouched a man unloading a pistol in Bags's direction. In slow motion, he turned to me, eyes widening as he began to pivot to the new target.

Knocking his pistol to the side, I plowed into the guy. His head cracked against the pavement, and I kicked the gun from his limp hand, not bothering to check him for other weapons as I ran around the side of the oil drum, intent on doing the same thing to the guy in the ditch.

I don't know what the fuck was going through my head. All tactical strategy had fled my mind, leaving me with a weird sense of invincibility partnered with outrage that these fuckers would try to kill me—would try to kill *Bags*. He was my friend. I considered him family. He was *mine*, and no one would be allowed to harm him.

No one hurt those I loved. No one hurt what was mine. No one.

The man behind the ditch stood, and I froze.

Navy SEAL Guy?

How the...? How could...? He should be dead. He should either be dead and kitten chow or just plain old dead. Yeah, he had electrical magic just like I did, so there was a good chance he might also share my newly discovered super healing. But fully recovering from a minor gunshot wound in a day wasn't the same as miraculously healing a laser blast that blew a hole through one's abdomen less than twenty-four hours ago.

While I was in shock and thinking, Navy SEAL Guy dropped the rifle, yanked a pistol from a hip holster, and shot —not at me, but at Bags.

I heard Bags yell, and I fired, hearing the dry click of my empty magazine. Panicked, I dropped my pistol and grabbed a metal pole from the ground. With a wild scream, I threw the pole javelin-style toward the man. It knocked him backward into the ditch. Not sure how long he'd be down, I ran toward him. The fucker might bounce back from a baseball-sized hole through his stomach, but I was willing to bet he'd stay dead if I smashed his head to a pulp with that pole.

I jumped into the ditch, grabbing the pole on my way, but found nothing. He was gone. Vanished. The only thing that remained behind was the rifle he'd shot the tranq darts from.

All the adrenaline drained from me, and I dropped the pole, swaying with sudden exhaustion. *Bags.* Concerned for my friend, I staggered out of the ditch and toward the cellar entrance. Bags sat on the ground, gasping for air and clutching his chest. With a second burst of adrenaline, I ran to him, kneeling down and moving his hand from his chest.

He was wearing a vest. While I was grateful that he'd taken the time to put one on before coming back to help me, I was still panicked.

I wasn't gentle as I yanked the vest off, ripping at Bags's torn shirt to see how badly he was hurt. I'd expected to see a bloody hole and let out a relieved breath when I saw the bullet had done no more than break the skin. He already had a bump forming and some serious color blooming on his brown skin, but no gaping wound.

"Ribs? You need to see a doctor." I gently felt around the impact area. There could still be internal injuries, and I didn't want to take any chances.

"No hospital." He took a few deep breaths. "I've got a friend I'll call to check me out later. I think it's just bruises and a big-ass bump. Glad I bought that vest a few years back. Weighs a ton, but these assholes around here got serious weaponry."

I rocked back on my heels and picked up the vest. It *was* heavy. The smashed bullet had to be laying around somewhere, but I didn't care enough to look for it.

Exhaustion swept over me once more, but I needed to check on the guy behind the dumpster. I was pretty sure he was dead. Certainly, he would have at least tried to shoot at us or crawl away if not but given the fact that Navy SEAL Guy had vanished into thin air, I wasn't convinced the man behind the dumpster hadn't done the same.

The man was still there, sprawled out just as I'd left him. A quick check confirmed that he was indeed dead, so I did what I'd been doing for two years and searched him, salvaging what I could from his corpse.

I piled the goods over to the side, numb and robotic as I went through the motions I'd done thousands of times. Bullets. Knives. The pistol I'd kicked away. The guy had a nice pair of RayBans that hadn't been broken in all the action, so I added them to the pile. His wallet yielded a twenty and an expired driver's license from three years ago. I didn't even bother looking at the name, not wanting to personalize someone who'd come to kidnap me for money.

What the hell am I? And what the hell was Navy SEAL Guy? *I* couldn't teleport out of somewhere like he had, but would that skill eventually appear? I fucking batted tranquilizer darts out of the air. I'd moved with supernatural speed. I'd picked up and thrown a metal pole with a chunk of concrete stuck to the end of it. Reaching up, I touched the graze on my shoulder, feeling sticky, thickened blood, but no wound under the torn shirt. It wasn't even taking hours for me to heal anymore.

It scared me. Growing up with my stun gun skills and minor telekinesis had been weird enough, but I'd gotten used to it. I just figured I was a human who had magic and never questioned it. I never questioned a lot of things. When your life was full of questions there were no answers to, you stopped bothering to ask. You just took each day as it came and shrugged off the rest.

What was I? I'd always pushed aside that question as well as those about my parents, but I couldn't continue to ignore it.

Giving the dead guy a little kick, I gathered up the pile, walked over to get the rifle from the edge of the ditch, then went back to the cellar entrance. Bags was still sitting but had maneuvered himself so he could lean back against the wall of the building. I dropped my salvaged goods to help him inside and up the stairs into the shop. I checked the locks on the door and looked around to make sure no bad guys had broken in and were lurking behind the rack of Weed eaters or the jewelry cabinet, then I returned to the basement. Gathering up the pile of goods, I locked the cellar door and set the alarms, then went back upstairs to check on Bags.

The elderly man was on his feet, applying some white cream to his bruises. I helped him wrap the wound in gauze, then hovered as he limped his way to the store counter.

"I'm fine." He threw a scowl over his shoulder at me. "Stop fussing."

I held back an extra step, which was my idea of "not fussing." Bags opened the register, took out a wad of money, counted it, then handed me a stack.

"What's this for?"

"That stuff you lifted off those guys."

I stared down at the money in my hand. "I was just going to leave it here. It's yours. The whole thing went down right behind your shop."

"Doesn't make it any less of a salvage." He shut the cash drawer on the register.

"But you fought too," I argued. "It's as much your salvage as mine."

"I've had more robberies than you can count. I've faced pissed-off customers who've tried to ambush me coming and going. One point I had four different gangs trying to hit me up for protection money. I wouldn't have survived those two guys out there without you." He shook his head. "Dumpster

Guy maybe. The dude in the ditch with the rifle, the pistol, and that electrical magic? Shiiiit. No military-issue vest is gonna help me against getting hit with the magical equivalent of a live wire."

"But the reason they were here was because of me," I countered.

I noticed he didn't mention anything about my having the same skill. Or about my batting tranq darts out of thin air. Bags was purposefully ignoring my weirdness, and for that I was grateful.

"The reason they were here is because someone set you up. Ain't your fault, Eden. Ain't none of this your fault." He pointed at the money in my hands. "Take it. And grab some bullets to load up your magazines before you go. You let me know if there's something I can do to help you, because I'm gonna be mighty pissed off if these guys kill you."

Yeah. Me, too. I'm not good at accepting gifts, but I realized Bags wasn't going to give in on this.

"Thank you." On impulse, I leaned forward and kissed him on the cheek.

"Stop that." He waved away the gesture of affection, a tiny smile twitching at one corner of his mouth. "And get out of here before that guy comes back with some friends."

I didn't bother to hide my smile as I pocketed the money, loaded my magazines, and slapped a full one into the Glock. With Bags covering my exit, I carefully made my way out the back door and to my bike. Then I hopped onto the freeway and headed north.

CHAPTER 9

The Capital One on Empire Avenue used to be a small branch inside a Target, but when the demons came, the bank ended up lasting longer than the retail store. Two years later, Capital One had abandoned all their locations in the Valley. Most of the branches had been taken over by payday and title loan companies, but this one stood empty—the old Target store as well.

Cristin Balefort called as soon as I'd pulled off the freeway. I knew right away that this wasn't my woman, because Cristin clearly was a guy. I claimed wrong number and hung up, then parked my bike a few blocks from my destination. It hadn't escaped me that the cop who'd set me up might not have been working alone. I'd suspected she had a partner with her that day, and her partner might have been the one who'd signed off on the report to the tax office. If that were the case, one of these three names could be the accomplice, and I'd have no way of knowing it.

It was all so fucking frustrating, but I had to go with what I had. I'd see if this Carly Bliss was the officer who'd confronted me that day, and if not, then I was going to have to throw the whole thing back into Juke's lap and try to find some other way to get myself out of this mess.

Too bad the bank was closed, because robbing a bank to pay off the tax demons was sounding like a pretty good idea right now. I was running out of options. Navy SEAL Guy was better than the other Fixers who'd tried to bring me in, and I had no doubt he'd be back. If Hellkitty shooting a laser-eyed hole through his abdomen hadn't deterred him, nothing would.

The officer pulled up in a black and white that looked like she'd taken it off a movie set. Bold as can be, she parked it diagonally fifty feet from the entrance and got out. As she eyed her surroundings with her hand hovering near her weapon, I was busy eyeing her.

Officer Bliss was short and solid with light brown hair yanked back into a low bun. She rounded the car, her hand easing away from her holster while she took in the empty parking lot. With a sigh, she leaned against the passenger side of her cruiser. Then she lifted her face as she scanned the roofline of the building.

I could tell this wasn't the cop from that salvage weeks ago. This officer was a different build with darker hair and a manner of movement completely dissimilar from the cop who'd set me up. That officer had a smooth, nimble grace. Carly Bliss walked like a seventy-pound pit bull entering a fighting ring.

"Stupid kids," she said, glancing at her watch. "Prank calls are gonna be the death of me."

I suddenly got an idea. It was probably a stupid idea, but I was out of options.

"Hey!" I unstrapped my shoulder holster and held it out with one hand, raising the other hand as I slowly came around the pillar I'd been hiding behind. "Don't shoot me. I just want to talk."

She had her pistol out and pointed at me before I could even blink. "Talk? You call me with some vague accusation and threaten to send a demon to my house? Doesn't sound like talking to me."

"It was stupid, but I needed to get you to come meet with me, and that was the first thing I thought of." I gently set my gun and holster on the ground and stepped away from it, both hands raised.

"Meet with you about what?" She waved her pistol at me. "And stop right there. Don't come any closer."

I complied, keeping my hands up. "A cop ran me off a salvage in North Hills on the third, then wrote me up under my Vulture license as having taken the haul. Seventeen cases of bullets and other stuff. I've now got a price on my head for tax evasion. Mercenaries broke into my family's home, beat them up, then kidnapped my fourteen-year-old sister and sold her."

She frowned. "Wait. Is this related to those kids brought in a few weeks ago that were being trafficked out of the custom's warehouse?"

I nodded. "That's the group who had my sister. She's home now, but the tax demons still think I owe them, and mercenaries are still harassing me and my family. Someone I know looked up the report the police filed on the salvage, and the initials on the report were C. B."

She barked out a laugh. "Well, that's not me. I haven't been in North Hills in three months. And I hate demons. I especially hate the tax demons. I'm the last cop to be filing a report on a salvage."

"I had to know." I gestured toward her. "You're clearly not the cop from that day. She was tall and blonde and dressed in SWAT gear. She moved like a gymnast or something."

"Not a bull in a china shop, like me?" The cop raised an eyebrow. "That description probably fits a hundred cops in the city. And the last two years we all have access to the riot gear."

"My source says there are two cops in the city with the initials of C.B. besides you." I gave her the other names. "I know they're both guys, but maybe they were working with her? A partner? Or just another officer who was in on the deal? She might not even be with one of the Valley precincts. If she's got connections, she might have had the same advanced warning about the hit as I had."

Bliss chewed her lip, eyeing me as if she wasn't quite sure whether to trust me or not.

"I've done some work with Detective Sarah Juke," I continued. "I told her about this, and she said she'd look into it, but I honestly don't have a lot of time to spare here. If the Fixers grab me, or if they get one of my sisters again…"

She nodded. "Detective Juke's solid. If you're one of her CI's…"

"I am. I'm helping her with a case right now." Or I would be if I ever got a chance to go visit the Gray Dogs.

She lowered the gun but didn't holster it. "I'm sorry about your situation, but I don't think I can help you."

"Welcome to the club," I muttered, bitter about how little the police could do. I don't know why I was surprised. I'd grown up surrounded by kids who believed the police were worse than the gangs.

"I can file a civilian complaint; say I'm following up on a tip. But whoever set you up will be monitoring stuff like that and go underground the moment IA starts nosing around. We've got almost two thousand female officers in the L.A. area. With that number and your vague description…"

"I know." Needle in a haystack, I believe the saying was.

"And the initials C.B. on the report don't mean anything. Half the time, we don't even sign the things, not when it's all electronic. We'd need to find out the login credentials of who filed the report, and to get that, IA would need to talk to the techs. Gossip flies faster than a rocket in the department. Your cop would vanish in the wind before IA even questioned her—especially if she's sitting on that much money in ammo. Heck, she probably resigned a week ago and is already halfway to Dallas."

"I know." This was depressing.

"Even if the initials on the report are legit, and are this cop's partner, you're still shit out of luck. It's not me. It's not Bingham. That guy is squeaky clean. And I can't see Balefort doing something like this, either. Dude used to be a school officer. Totally Officer Friendly type."

"I know."

She holstered her pistol. "Look, I know you're in a jam here. I hate a rotten cop. We all hate rotten cops. But you need to realize that finding whoever set you up probably isn't going to solve your problem. She could be long gone and the money with her."

"But the report," I countered. "If it gets deleted or changed or marked as a false report, then the tax office can call the mercenaries off."

"Maybe. Maybe not. The tax office is run by demons. They do their own thing, and it's not always what we'd consider legal or fair. Not to tell you your business or anything, but I think your best chance of getting out of this is to just pay what they say you owe and chalk the whole thing up to this crappy world we're now living in."

Pay for what I hadn't done. Wasn't that pretty much the way things went for people like me? I'd spent my whole fucking life paying for other people's wrong-doings. Why stop now?

"I'm sorry. I know that's not what you want to hear. I'd love to say that we'll catch whoever set you up, that your name will be cleared, that she'll pay for her crimes, and that we'll turn the loot over to the tax office. I'm a police officer. That's the outcome I want for every one of my cases. But I'm also a realist, and I know that bad guys get away, and innocent people get hurt. Sometimes there's no happy ending, and the best you can hope for is to mitigate the damage." She turned and walked around to the driver's side of her car. "Mitigate the damage. Survive. Anything else is icing on the cake."

I watched her pull out of the lot before I went back to get my shoulder harness. Strapping it on, I thought about what she'd said. None of it had been any huge revelation. There'd been a voice in the back of my head telling me those things for weeks now, but I hadn't wanted to listen.

I still didn't want to listen. I was fucking sick and tired of having survival be the best possible outcome. In spite of what I'd told Nevarra, I wanted to do more than just survive a bad situation. I wanted things to be set right. I wanted some damned justice. I wanted that cop to pay. And I wanted an ending where I didn't have to pay for something I didn't do.

There was one more person to go to. If Bishop laughed in my face or couldn't help me, then I'd need to swallow my pride, forget about the cop, and take my lumps.

I was a block from where I'd parked my bike when the sound of a gunshot sent me diving for cover behind a delivery van. The noise echoed off the buildings, making it hard to pinpoint where the shot came from, let alone whether or not it was meant for me. Pulling my pistol from the holster, I waited. When I heard nothing, I eased my way around the side of the van, alert and ready to jump back to safety.

Something hard pressed against the back of my head. "Lower the gun. Finger off the trigger and hold it out to the side."

Navy SEAL Guy. Dude really got around.

I did as he said, knowing I wouldn't be able to wave away this bullet and not wanting to test my newfound super healing against a bullet to the skull. He took my pistol and slid it across the top of the van. I winced as I heard it clatter to the ground on the other side of the car's hood.

"Hands behind your back. Slowly."

There was no Bags or laser-eyed kitten here to help me out. There was no one here to help me. I was going to need to get out of this one all on my own. And that would be difficult with a gun against my skull.

"It wasn't me. I didn't take that salvage. I didn't pay taxes because I didn't take it. A cop ran me off the scene and took everything herself. She filed the report to set me up so she wouldn't get caught."

"Right. It was some other guy. I didn't do it." He said the last two sentences in a mocking falsetto. "Hands. Slowly."

I complied, and somehow, he managed to get handcuffs on me with one hand. There went my plan to fight back once the pistol wasn't pressed into the back of my head.

"I'm not lying. A cop set me up. She's the one with the money and the stash, not me. Help me find her, and I'll split it with you."

Now *that* was a lie. I had no intention of splitting anything with this guy. I'd been hoping to find the cop as well as the money and/or goods. If the police didn't clear me, then I'd pay off whatever the tax demons said I owed and keep the rest.

He grabbed my shoulder and hauled me down to sit on the curb. "The bounty on you has been active for three weeks. If you haven't tracked down that cop in three weeks, then it's not going to happen—probably because there is no cop, and you're lying."

"The bounty on me is what, two or three thousand? Those bullets are worth ten or twenty *grand* at least. Find the cop and find the money—a whole lot of money, not just some shitty bounty. It's a better scenario."

He pulled my backpack off my shoulders with the gun still pressed against my head. I heard the sound of him unzipping my pack.

"No, the better scenario is I turn you in for the bounty after I find where you hid the money. Those tax demons don't need to know I found it. It's not like they'll believe you if you tell them I took it, either."

Fucking dick. "Except I don't have the damned money or bullets. Think, you moron. All I've got is my backpack and a motorcycle. A group of Fixer goons already raided my house and didn't find anything. Where the fuck do you think I stashed it? You think I'm going to stuff twenty grand in a storm drain? Leave it in an abandoned building? And if I had twenty grand, don't you think I would have gotten the fuck out of here already?"

He swore, and it sounded as if he were kicking my backpack away. "You haven't sold the bullets yet. I've been checking pawn reports and asking around. You're either selling it a box at a time—which means it'll take you months to unload it all—or you're waiting for the heat to cool off before you sell."

The pistol muzzle pushed my head forward, and I felt him pat the pockets of my cargo pants.

"Then where the fuck am I hiding *seventeen* cases of ammo? Where?"

He paused then straightened, the pressure of the pistol lessening against my skull. "Where exactly was that hit?"

I didn't dare hope that I might be able to weasel my way out of this, but I was going to try my best.

"North Hills. That little alley off Marilla, near the freeway. It was a cop wearing riot gear, but I don't think that's her normal beat. I asked a few people I know with the Dogs and the Southside Militia, and they didn't recognize my description of her as a local cop. I think she found out about the hit the same way we Vultures do and decided to take advantage of an opportunity."

The pressure against my skull eased a bit more. "So that means she probably knows Vultures and pawnbrokers," he mused. "Maybe works Vice, or worked in Vice before the demons came, so she's got contacts."

"She's got a place to hide the stash where it won't be noticed. Someone who covered for her while she transported it. And she's got to be familiar with the Valley and Encino. That alley isn't on Google Maps."

"She'll fence the goods outside her precinct," he mused. "Hell, probably outside her bureau. I'm betting she'd use one of the downtown pawnshops that deal with the shit the demons steal on the regular."

Huh, I hadn't thought of that. I'd been avoiding down-town like crazy, expressly trying to stay away from demons. I didn't even know any of those pawnbrokers, although I was willing to bet Bags did.

"Thanks." The gun left the back of my head, and I felt myself being hauled upright. "I'll turn you in for the bounty, then find this cop and the loot."

Damn it. "You'll find her quicker if I work with you."

He chuckled. "I don't think so. Besides, I'm not splitting—"

A pop sound cut off the rest of his words. I yanked away from my attacker and spun around, shocked to see a blob of blue paint centered on his forehead, dripping slowly down between his eyebrows. Before either of us could react, there was another pop noise and two electrodes slammed into Navy SEAL Guy's chest. He jerked, then dropped to the ground where he continued to convulse. I followed the wires from the electrodes to a Taser held in Officer Carly Bliss's hand.

"Sorry that took me so long," she called out to me. "I had to wait until he had that pistol away from your head."

Of course, she'd followed me. The surprising thing was that she'd intervened.

"Thanks." I looked down at my assailant, who was no longer convulsing, but definitely wasn't getting up anytime soon. I guess that answered the question of whether the magic-negating paint balls would affect his—and my—imperviousness to electricity.

"How'd you manage to sign out an anti-magic gun?" I knew the police kept those tightly under lock and key. They were only distributed if an officer could prove he or she truly needed to carry one at that particular time.

"Well, let's see. I got a threatening phone call from a woman who implied she was going to sic demon assailants on me. That, and my uncle runs the bureau armory."

"You're interfering with the legal capture of a wanted tax evader," Navy SEAL Guy gasped. "I have the warrant in my pocket. There's a bounty. I'm authorized to detain her and bring her in."

"What? What?" Bliss shook her head. "Damn, the Taser made him slur his words so bad I can't understand a thing he's saying. I might be able to make out what he's trying to tell me in ten or fifteen minutes, unless I need to zap him again because he resisted arrest or something." She grinned over at me. "My report is going to say that I was coming from a meeting with a CI and saw a woman being assaulted at gunpoint from a man who appeared to be robbing her. He was going through your backpack, right?"

I nodded. "Right. Gunpoint. Robbery." I turned around. "He even handcuffed me."

Keeping one hand on the Taser, she dug out a set of keys and motioned for me to come close. "Fucking sexual deviant weirdo. Lucky I came along. He might have dragged you into that van and raped you after he was done stealing your stuff."

The handcuffs fell off. I stuffed them in a pocket, then I picked up my gun. And his gun. And while I was at it, I patted him down and went through his pockets.

"Ah, ah, ah," Bliss warned as Navy SEAL Guy snarled.

I found the warrant from the tax office, the contract he'd accepted that showed he was authorized to bring me in. I also found some knives and fifty bucks in cash, as well as a round blue stone about the size of a quarter.

"He stole these from me," I told the officer. "Took them out of my backpack."

"I did not—" Navy SEAL Guy thrashed as Bliss hit him again with the Taser.

"Bastard." Bliss clucked her tongue. "You're very lucky I was here to help you, Miss. I'm going to read this guy his rights and take him in. Hopefully, by the time I get him to the station, I'll be able to understand him. Probably will take half an hour or so."

So, I had half an hour before Navy SEAL Guy was sprung and after me again. Although the magic negation would last anywhere from an hour to a few days, and I wasn't sure he'd be so brazen about trying to grab me without his supernatural abilities. Plus, I had his gun and his paperwork.

He might decide he'd rather focus on finding the money than going after me. Three times he'd jumped me, and three times I'd beaten him—well, not me. Either way, I'd slipped through his grasp with each attempt. Hopefully, he'd decide a crooked cop would be an easier mark.

I wasn't sure I liked that idea any better. I needed to find that cop and the money, and I really didn't want to keep crossing paths with this guy. I didn't want him to find the stash or money first and vanish into the sunset with me still with the tax demons on my ass.

"Thanks," I told Bliss once more.

Grabbing my backpack, I ran for my bike. Then I went to the one place where I was sure Navy SEAL Guy wouldn't dare attack me—Suerte.

CHAPTER 10

By the time I got to Bishop's bar, I'd worked myself into a mess of frustration. Maybe that cop was right. I'd been trying to find who set me up and clear my name for weeks now and was no further along than when I'd started. Actually, I was worse off. I'd been attacked five times within the last twenty-four hours, and unlike the prior mercenaries who'd come after me, Navy SEAL Guy was a step above the usual idiot-with-a-gun. He had magic. He'd survived a blast from Hellkitty. He'd fucking teleported. If I didn't get things straightened out with the tax office soon, I was going to end up dead or dragged in to face the demons at the tax office, wishing I was dead.

But if I went into the tax office, what would I tell them? They wouldn't believe my story. I didn't have the money to pay them the taxes they thought I owed. I doubted they'd be any more lenient if I gave myself up than if Navy SEAL Guy dragged me in.

What did they do to people who couldn't pay? A shiver rolled through me at the thought.

Bishop…well, Bishop was my last hope, my Hail Mary with two seconds left on the clock—except I wasn't sure how Bishop *could* help.

Yeah, he found people, but from what I'd seen, finding involved Bob tracking someone down with his nose. I didn't have anything for Bob to track. Even if we went to the scene of the hit, I doubted Bob's super nose could detect anything. Three weeks had passed. There had probably been dozens of people through that alley since then.

I was fucked. I was so royally fucked.

I'd parked my bike and was about to get off when a text chimed on my phone. Hoping for a miracle, I glanced down at the screen and saw a message from Telaney.

Got a tip on a big job downtown and could use a hand. You free tomorrow night?

There was so much shit I was leaving in my wake right now, and I didn't want to drag it onto Telaney's doorstep. We'd worked together on occasion, and I knew that Telaney was a straight shooter. More than that, she was a friend. She'd let me crash at her house last week when I was sick of sleeping in flophouses and under bridges. She'd helped me out when I'd been trying to find Nevarra.

License is still suspended. Bounty hunters have been up my ass since last night. You don't need the trouble I'd bring.

She responded immediately. *Fuck the bounty hunters. We can take them if they show up. You're not bringing any more trouble than I see every day of my damned life.*

The text was followed up with a laughing-crying emoji that made me shake my head and smile.

What time? I asked.

Meet me at Sunset and Hammond at ten. Wear a dress. And do something with your hair.

A dress? And do *what* with my hair?

I replied in the affirmative, then shoved the phone back in my pocket, wondering where this job was. Obviously, it was walking distance from our destination if we were going to be wearing dresses. West Hollywood. That close to Downtown meant we might run into demons.

I'd need to get back home sometime tomorrow, not only to find a damned dress to wear, but to check in with Bea and the girls. Last night's run-in with Navy SEAL Guy had unnerved me, but finding out that he'd somehow survived the laser kitty attack and come after me twice today unnerved me even more. A guy like that might not be deterred by the Neighborhood Watch or the sigils Genevieve Planteaux had laid down that may or may not be actual magic.

I needed to have faith in my family's ability to protect themselves. And faith in the neighbors who'd been so upset at the home invasion that they'd sprung into action. But what could a bunch of people with guns and one maybe mage do against Navy SEAL Guy and his magic?

Hopefully fill him with enough holes that he wouldn't be able to heal them all, that's what.

Brooding over the shitshow that my life had become and worrying over my family, I headed into the bar. The door jerked with a slight resistance, then opened. A sharp static bit me as I passed over the threshold, like I'd just walked through an electric fence. The place was empty, which seemed unusual for a late afternoon, even on a weekday. The lights were off—only what was natural spilled through the windows, illuminating the area. HB sat at the bar with her back to me, reading an actual newspaper.

"We're closed," she'd shouted as I'd yanked the door open. "Bishop! You forgot to lock the damned door!"

"I didn't forget."

The low voice right behind me nearly sent me into a

coronary. Bishop *must* have some teleportation skill. I would have thought that improbable, even in this world, if I hadn't already seen one person blink out right in front of my eyes. Compulsion. Super strength. Durft finding abilities. Knows demons, and they treat him with respect. Teleportation. I'd originally thought Bishop might be some kind of shifter, but now my guesses were taking a turn toward the dark side. He didn't *seem* like he was a demon, but the past few weeks had taught me that demons weren't all lizard-eyed psychos like Desiree.

Demon? Or something else?

HB spun around on the bar stool, a grin lighting her face when she saw me. "Eden!"

"Yes, *Eden*," Bishop mocked. "Something wrong with your nose?"

Her eyes narrowed. "She reeks of gunpowder, burned wood, and motor oil. How the hell am I supposed to smell anything over that? Besides, your security system messes with smells. I've told you that a million times."

Motor oil? I guess that leak on my bike was back again.

"She smells like blood too, but that's typical of our clientele." HB snorted. "It's especially typical of Eden. At least you're not bleeding all over the floor like you were yesterday."

Bishop shook his head. "So, you get shot up every day, Trouble? This is a regular thing for you?"

"No, this isn't a regular thing for me," I snapped. It was becoming a regular thing, and that made me cranky. Even if I'd developed the magical ability to speed-heal myself, getting shot still hurt like fuck, and my healing wasn't instantaneous.

"Looks like it is." He cocked an eyebrow at me. "Should I get the first-aid kit again? The stapler?"

"I'm fine." I dug the fifty out of my pocket that I'd stolen from Navy SEAL Guy and slapped it against his chest. "Here. Another payment."

He took the money and stuffed it in his pocket before spinning around and walking into the office. I guessed he was going to record the payment and get me a receipt. The guy was really strict about his financial records. I appreciated that but wasn't used to such bank-like formality when I'd owed people money in the past.

HB set a glass of tea on the bar, so I walked over and sat down, taking a sip. I don't know what it was with her and the iced tea, but it was cold, sweet, and refreshing on a hot day like today. Taking another sip, I felt my anxiety ease a bit.

"Shitty day?" she asked, leaning her elbows on the bar.

"Yeah, but I got some unexpected salvage." Actually, it was stolen and not technically salvage, but I wasn't going to make that distinction when it came to Navy SEAL Guy. "The fifty I gave Bishop. A nice H&K nine mil. This blue rock."

Hopefully, she'd want to buy the pistol off me. It would be one less thing weighing down my backpack. But instead of eyeing the gun, she picked up the blue rock, rubbing it between her thumb and index finger like a worry stone.

"Lapis. That's a weird thing for someone to be carrying around. Was the dead person you scavenged from a mage?"

"Maybe? He can shoot electricity out of his hands. And he teleports." I'd not thought to ask HB about the mercenary dogging my tail, but she did seem to know a lot about these things—more than me anyway, which wasn't saying much.

She didn't seem surprised at either revelation. "Can? As in, the guy isn't dead? Why am I not surprised that your salvage license extends to stealing in your case?"

"Only from assholes who deserve it," I assured her.

She set the rock down. "Sounds like a mage to me. Scrolls, incantations, wands. I haven't run into a lot of them in my life, but I know sorcerers can craft items that allow the user to teleport. Magical weapons as well. One guy in Compton specializes in wands that create chickens."

My mouth dropped open. "As in *live* chickens? Or chicken nuggets?"

HB snorted. "Live chickens. Although a wand that creates chicken nuggets would be cool. Someone needs to get right on that. I'd buy the shit out of that wand."

A wand that created live chickens. I envisioned that for a second, wondering what good would that do? Maybe as a distraction? If I were surrounded by Fixers and could shoot a bunch of chickens out of a wand, it might just be weird enough to be a distraction.

"He didn't have a wand or say anything like a spell or incantation though," I told her. "The electricity just happened. So did the teleportation. And…telekinesis. Batting stuff out of midair like darts and balls and stuff."

Okay, I was kinda talking about myself, except for the teleportation thing. If I could figure out how Navy SEAL Guy got his abilities, maybe that would give me insight into my own.

HB shrugged. "It's not always wands and spoken spells. Maybe he's got a magic ring that does the electricity spell. Was he wearing any rings?"

"Not that I remember. Do mages just *do* magic? On the fly? Without imbuing an object with a spell beforehand or anything?"

"No." Bishop slapped a receipt onto the bar beside the blue stone. "Elves can do magic on the fly, but humans need some prep, even if it's just a handful of herbs and a spoken spell. They need a ritual or something to focus and project their magical energy. In a hundred thousand years or so, they may be able to do magic the way the elves do."

I tucked the receipt away. "So, evolution then? Could

there be outliers born with those abilities that might be commonplace in a hundred thousand years?"

"Sure. Humans received the gifts of Aaru in bulk instead of on the slower timeline the angels had originally planned for. It's made their evolution…unpredictable."

I got the feeling Bishop had read the book I was lugging around in my backpack. "The tenth choir, right? They're the ones who screwed up ten thousand years ago, giving all the gifts at once and boinking human women?"

Bishop tensed. "That's what the stories say. Who knows if they're true or not?" He pointed at the blue stone. "Where'd you get this?"

"I stole it off a guy. I think maybe he's a mage, although he might be one of those outliers I was speculating about."

Bishop picked the stone up and frowned at it. "Lapis. Odd choice for a Kirby's Marble."

"A *what*?" I stepped closer, thinking this rock didn't look remotely like a marble.

"It's the name of a teleportation device. There's a matching set. One item allows you to teleport to the other. If you have three of them, you can teleport back and forth between two locations."

"Holy shit," I muttered.

"Magic, but not holy magic," he drawled. "They have a certain number of charges on them and can be recharged. Very high-level magic stuff. Very expensive."

"How is it activated?" HB and I had both held the thing and neither of us had vanished.

"I'm not sure. I think just by intent." He set the rock down. "Any idea where it leads to?"

"Nope." Probably Navy SEAL Guy's house or something. Which meant he had to live somewhere in the Valley to tele-port from outside Bags's shop then be back to attack me again an hour later.

"Actually, I'm not here just to pay you fifty bucks or to find out about this stone." I turned to face Bishop. "There's a mercenary who's after me, and he's proven hard to kill. I've gotten away from him three times in the last twenty-four hours, but I get the feeling the next time my luck might not hold out."

Bishop leaned against the back of the bar, folding his arms across his chest. "So, what do you want me to do?"

What *did* I want Bishop to do? Kill Navy SEAL Guy for me? Find the cop who set me up? Strongarm the tax demons into forgiving the debt they thought I owed? Just listen to me whine and complain?

To be honest, I didn't know what to do. I wanted ideas. Taking action, doing what I needed to do, wasn't my dilemma. My problem was that I didn't know *which* direction to head in, *where* to act. I needed clarity. Bishop might not be the right source for that, but I trusted him. And surly as he was, the guy cut through bullshit and got right to the heart of the matter.

I started counting things off on my fingers. "Find the cop who set me up and all the money from the salvage she took. Keep Navy SEAL Guy from dragging me downtown to the tax office—"

"*Navy SEAL Guy?*" Bishop scowled.

I waved a hand. "It's what I call him. Everyone gets a nickname."

"What's my nickname?" HB called from the back room, proving to me that she did have supernatural hearing, and that she was unapologetically listening in on our conversation.

"Hot Bitch." I shouted back the first thing I could think of.

"I'll take it," she replied.

"So, you want *me* to solve all of *your* problems?" Bishop

asked as if the brief segue in the conversation had never occurred.

"Yes, please." Hey, it was worth a shot. "Find the cop. Find the loot. Get rid of these mercenaries, especially the one who actually might be capable enough to haul me in. And while you're at it, make those assholes in Los Feliz let me move into the Canyon Drive house. Oh, and install solar panels at Bea's and my new home. Ensure the fucking water doesn't shut off every time I'm in middle of a truly epic hot shower. And throw in a fancy dinner at a place downtown with steaks and drinks and a waiter-guy who pairs wine with every course."

I was on a roll; might as well ask for the moon.

Bishop blinked, then shook his head. "Trouble, you don't have enough money to pay for me to do all those things."

It wasn't like I really expected him to do any of that, but his words still sent me spiraling downward.

"What the fuck am I supposed to do?" I hated the way looming tears thickened my voice but couldn't do anything to prevent it. "Navy SEAL Guy is going to haul me in, and the demons will torture and kill me because I can't pay what they think I owe. Some fucker set me up, and I can't find them. I just keep sliding farther down into this damned hole."

Bishop stared at me for a moment, his expression unreadable.

I turned away from him and put the pistol into my backpack and the blue stone into one of my pockets. I shouldn't have bothered to come here.

"They're demons, not idiots," he finally said. "You're worth more to them alive than dead. If they kill you, they'll never get the money or the goods—well, not unless you're standing over it all when they kill you."

"But I don't have the money or the goods," I argued. "And when they finally believe that, they'll kill me because they don't give a shit whether I'm innocent or not. They're demons. They'll kill me because I won't be of any use to them alive, and setting me free isn't as much fun as slowly carving my organs out."

His lips twitched. I was pissed that he'd think a demon disemboweling me would be even mildly funny.

"Don't give me that shit, Trouble. You can lie with more skill and conviction than anyone in the Valley. I guarantee that within an hour you'd have every demon in the tax office out trying to find this cop that set you up *and* believing you're the only one in the universe that can lead them to the treasure they seek."

I thought of my desperate conversation with Navy SEAL Guy. Yeah, I might have convinced him that it really was a cop and not me who had the money and the bullets, but he still was ready to turn me over for the bounty. Would demons be any different?

"The *Fixers* are trying to kill me even if the demons want me alive," I argued. But were they? The ones who'd grabbed me in the parking lot of the Scientology church were just roughing me up. They'd shot me when I'd attacked them to try to get away, but even then, they'd shot me in the knee and knocked me out. Navy SEAL Guy had repeatedly said he wasn't trying to harm me, but outside of Bags's shop, it had certainly seemed as if his partner was shooting to kill. Or maybe not. Outside of the one bullet that grazed my shoulder, none had hit me. They were either terrible shots, or they actually *were* trying to take me alive.

"Those Fixer mercenaries, this Navy SEAL Guy included, won't get much from the tax office if they bring you in dead." Bishop shrugged. "Of course, there might be someone else with a bounty out on you who does want you dead."

Well, that was reassuring. I shot him an annoyed glance.

"Now, if they thought your family had the money, they

might torture you as an incentive for them to give it up." He counted off the ideas on his fingers. "Or they might grab a member of your family and use them as leverage to bring you—and the money—in."

"They already tried that," I shot back.

"No, the Fixers took your sister and sold her because they're idiots. Anyone else would have used her as leverage, as a hostage for ransom money."

He was right. The Fixers had just seen Nevarra as a quick buck, and the Disciples had no reason to use her in some blackmail scheme. As horrible as Nevarra's experience had been, I shuddered to think it could have been much worse. I didn't even want to contemplate what demons would do to a hostage to force me to come in.

"How much do you owe?" Bishop demanded.

"I don't know." It seemed silly to admit that, but I'd been too afraid to call up the tax office and ask them. Not that it mattered. I didn't have the money to pay them. It seemed like a better idea to try to get the report changed and my record cleared, than to figure out how I was going to make over a year's worth of earnings in a week or two.

"What's the bounty they're offering on you?" Bishop asked.

"Last I heard it was five grand."

Bishop sighed and dug his phone out of his pocket. He made one quick phone call, hung up, then turned to me. "Ten thousand."

I choked a little at the number. "*That's* what they say I owe?"

"No, that's the bounty they'll pay if you, as well as the haul or the money, are brought in. It's still five grand if someone just brings you in. One if you get delivered dead. Originally it was a hundred dead, five for you alive, and a thousand for you and the stash." Bishop looked oddly pleased at that.

"They've upped the bounty three times since they put the original warrant out on you. That means they're having a hard time getting mercenaries to bite at the contract. You're getting a reputation, Trouble."

A very unwanted reputation. "If they set the bounty on me and the salvage at *ten grand*, then the tax debt they think I owed is probably a hell of a lot more."

"Total tax bill of fifty-two thousand."

Bile rose to burn the back of my throat. *"Fifty-two thousand?* How the fuck are the taxes on seventeen cases of ammo, a few guns, and a beat-up old Buick worth that much? I couldn't have gotten half of that in pawn."

A case was a thousand bullets. Two years ago, that would have retailed for around seven hundred bucks. Now wholesale was a thousand per case. A dollar per bullet. Retail was anywhere from twenty-five hundred to three grand. Even if the tax office was calculating one hundred percent tax on the high-end of retail, it wouldn't have been fifty-two thousand.

"They're valuing the goods at three grand a case," Bishop said, echoing my thoughts. "Fifty percent in taxes. Double that for penalties and interest. The extra thousand is for the Buick."

"That's fucking bullshit," I sputtered. "I couldn't have pawned that stuff for full retail. I couldn't even have pawned it for full wholesale. They can't expect me to pay that. Even if I did take that salvage, they can't expect me to pay more than double what I would have gotten above board for the take!"

"Demons." Bishop lifted one shoulder, as if that would explain it all.

I'd spent the last two years avoiding demons, shoving my head in the sand, focusing every bit of effort on earning money and trying to get my family out of here. I knew demons were brutal, violent, greedy, and cruel. But this? This was fucking insane.

"What can I do? I can't find the bitch that set me up so she or the other cops can make things straight. I can't find her to steal everything back to pay the tax office off. I'm trying to work, but with my license suspended I'm getting run off jobs. Plus, I risk getting hauled in for the bounty every time I do a job." I ran a shaky hand through my hair. "I could work for the next five years and not be able to pay that debt. The penalties and interest are going to keep piling up, and I'm guessing the demons won't let me pay installments for the next thirty years like a mortgage."

He leaned one elbow on the bar. "You've got three choices, Trouble, but smartest is to make a deal. No one has been able to bring you in. You've left a trail of dead bodies, and they had to up the bounty to even get this Navy SEAL Guy to bite. In their minds, every day that goes by is one more day for you to sell off a bit more of the stash, skip town, or end up dead. They're likely weighing the odds of getting *anything* and not liking those odds. You can bullshit with the best of them. Walk your fine ass downtown, into their office, and start bullshitting. Cut a deal."

The idea terrified me. "What if they don't believe me? What if they haul me into a back room and torture me? Then kill me once they realize I'm telling the truth and don't have the money?"

Wait. *Fine ass?* Did he just say I had a fine ass?

"Think, Eden. Do you seriously believe the powerful demons sit around an office doing clerical work? It's mostly humans doing that shit—that and a bunch of Lows. Talk your way out of it. And if that doesn't work, shoot your way out of it."

Fine ass. *And* he'd just called me by my real name. I was stunned speechless for a few seconds.

I looked around the bar, calculating how long it would be before Navy SEAL Guy hunted me down again. I was so tired of running. I just wanted a normal night where I could pretend I was a normal girl and not someone on the verge of being dragged off for a bounty and tortured by demons for money I didn't have.

"Is there somewhere here I can crash for the night? Storeroom? Shed? Basement?"

Bishop burst out laughing. "One more thing to add to your wish list, Trouble? You don't need me; you need a genie."

"Oh, let her sleep in the storeroom, Bishop," HB called from the back. "She can waitress. Talina called off for tonight, and we could use the help."

The thought of waitressing tonight was oddly exciting. Normal girl. Normal life.

"Who's coming in tonight?" Bishop called back.

"It's Kevin's night," she replied. "And Sabrina's group down from Bakersfield. They've got some trivia and karaoke tournament going on."

Bishop nodded thoughtfully. "Moderates, then. They're not likely to raise a fuss."

I heard HB's snort all the way from the storeroom.

I bit my tongue, thinking that I may have been right about Suerte being less of a public establishment and more of one that served a very specific clientele. I'd been in biker bars before and knew how the bikers viewed the place as if it were their own private clubhouse. It seemed like Suerte was the same, with Bishop juggling the calendar to accommodate several different groups.

I could handle that. I'd gone to school with gang members, even dated a few. This shouldn't be a problem.

"Okay, you're in." Bishop pointed to the storeroom. "After we close, you can sleep in there. I'll get some blankets together for you. HB's got a spare uniform. Don't worry about collecting money or anything because it's all on a tab.

Just take orders, deliver food, and drink. And, by all that's holy, try to be polite. I don't feel like breaking up any fights tonight."

"Got it." I grinned. "And thank you."

For one night I'd get to be normal. For one night, I'd feel safe.

CHAPTER 11

About three hours in, I decided the normal life wasn't for me. The good news was these people weren't the racist assholes from my first encounter with Suerte. There did seem to be a whole lot of white people in the room, but the scattering of brown faces here and there at least made me feel as if I wasn't completely alone. No one yelled out or even whispered slurs, but their politeness was stiff.

The bad news was that these people ate an enormous amount of food and downed beer and mixed drinks as if they were at a mead hall in Valhalla. My feet were killing me. I couldn't deliver food and drink fast enough. I was literally running back and forth across the bar to make sure the customers didn't have to wait.

But as the food vanished from plates, and pitchers of beer were refilled four and five times over, people stopped glaring at me. Instead, they acted as though I were a robot delivering their orders.

I'd take it over the suspicious glaring.

It was a lot of work for just a place to crash for the night, but there were a few fun moments. The Bakersfield group sucked at trivia, and both groups delivered some of the worst karaoke performances I'd ever heard. I was giggling to myself over a young woman attempting to sing Halsey's "You Should Be Sad," when I nearly crashed into man coming out of the restroom. We both did that little dance people do when they're trying to get around each other in a narrow hallway, then I looked up into his face and recognized him.

Fuck. It was one of the guys from the Canyon Drive neighborhood—one of the guys who'd watched my disastrous fight with Dennis.

He paled. I was pretty sure I did the same.

"It's…you're…why are you here?" he asked.

"Just filling in for Talina," I told him as if I knew Talina, and it was a normal thing for me to take her shift here at Suerte. "She's…not here. So, I'm waitressing tonight."

He caught his breath, his expression a mix of horror and dread that would have been funny if I wasn't worried that what had happened this morning was going to bite me in the ass.

"This morning—"

"I won't say anything if you won't," I cut him off. "Bishop doesn't want any trouble, and I don't want to be the cause of any trouble. As far as I'm concerned, it was a fair fight. I lost, and I'm bummed because I really wanted to claim that house, but whatever. Shit happens. I'm okay with it if you are."

He tilted his head and regarded me for a second. "You're really okay with that? I mean, Dennis *did* take things too far and didn't respect your tapping out. Some of us aren't cool about that. Rules of the fight, you know."

I thought of the amazing house, the luxurious shower I'd taken, the view looking down into the city, and the odd feelings that had stirred in my chest as I stood in a place that I wanted so badly to be mine. But I wasn't going to fight an entire neighborhood of hostile people for the right to live there—especially if these people were customers of Bishop.

"I'm okay with it. Let's just pretend we've never met, and that this morning never happened."

He nodded and went back to his table while I picked up an order from the kitchen. I knew right away that the guy had blabbed everything because the second I walked in with three plates of Prime rib, half the room turned to look at me. Instantly, I wished I could go back to the invisibility of just minutes ago. I wanted to run, but I'd made a commitment, so I put my head down and just worked, not meeting anyone's gaze, every word out of my mouth polite and deferential. Bishop had said no fuss, and I was determined to make sure my presence didn't cause any dustups.

The night felt like it stretched on forever, but finally it was closing time, and both groups were cheerfully making their way out of the bar and home. I bussed tables as they emptied and was surprised to find tips left on a few of them. The guy from the bathroom had left me a twenty, which I gladly pocketed. When the last table left, HB locked the door and got to work cleaning up the bar. I wiped down tables, then went into the kitchen to see if I could help. The sooner everyone left, the sooner I could take these polyester clothes off and curl up in the storeroom with the half dozen blankets Bishop had left for me.

"What can I do?" I asked the cook, who'd been introduced to me as Marita.

"*Saca la basura,*" Marita instructed over her shoulder.

I went over to the pile of black bags and grabbed two, grimacing at the weight. Staggering to the door, I shoved it open with my ass and hauled the bags out. There was nothing out back besides a rocky flat area dimly lit by one flickering bulb over the kitchen door. The dumpster was a giant hulk of metal way out back and to the left, just past the edge of the light. I took three steps, then gave up trying to carry the bags, dragging them across the ground instead and praying they didn't split open and dump potato peelings and grease all over the place. Hopefully, HB splurged on the extra-strength ones when she'd done her Costco run for the bar.

I wrestled the heavy dumpster door open. Then, with quite a lot of cursing, I managed to haul one bag up and inside. Wiping my hands on the polyester pants HB had loaned me for tonight's job, I bent over to grab the second bag and felt a sharp sting in my arm. I slapped at whatever bit me, and my palm knocked against a tranq dart.

The realization of what had happened hit me about the same time as the drugs. I staggered around the side of the dumpster, yanking the dart from my arm. Something thunked against the heavy metal—no doubt a second dart that I'd miraculously avoided. I was woozy, disoriented, but aware enough to realize that a second dart would have knocked me out cold.

Fuckers. They had the nerve to try to grab me here, right outside Bishop's bar, the very place I thought I'd be safe. Apparently, *nowhere* was safe.

I didn't have my pistol, not wanting to waitress armed and thinking I wouldn't need it. I also didn't have my cell phone. I was weaponless, aside from my magic—which I hoped would work with the narcotics coursing through my body.

I slid to my ass, trying to stay awake and think of a plan. I'd never make it to the kitchen door without taking at least another dart. HB's hearing was pretty incredible, but I wasn't sure she'd hear me through the walls, especially with all the noise from the kitchen between me and the bar. Then there was the fact that I wasn't sure I could even shout.

Time to play possum. I'd have one chance to take these

guys down, and I needed to make it count. I slumped against the dumpster, fingers touching the metal side, and waited.

It felt like hours before I heard footsteps and whispered voices. I watched from under mostly closed eyelids as four figures cautiously rounded the dumpster.

"She's out…"

"Dose her again…make sure."

"…don't wanna kill her—least not before we find the loot."

"…cuffs…search her."

Struggling to keep conscious, I felt rough hands on me, and knew I needed to act before it was too late. I sent out what was supposed to be a lethal amount of electricity and heard a squeal.

"What?"

"I don't know. Felt like a static shock."

"Probably some magical alarm triggering. Grab her, and let's go."

I gave up trying to look as if I were knocked out and opened my eyes. I must not have opened them too far because none of them noticed. Instead of jumping back in alarm, they cuffed the hands I was trying to fight with. Then, someone picked me up and tossed me over his shoulder.

"Go, go, go," was the hissed mantra as I felt myself jostled around.

It was dark, and I was pretty sure I still had my eyes open, so we must have left through the back undeveloped land behind Suerte. Made sense. These guys would hardly pull up and park in the well-lit front lot if they wanted to grab me and go. They must have left their vehicles further out, and snuck in through the trees and bushes.

I was in trouble. Big trouble. It was getting harder and harder to focus or to even keep my eyes somewhat open. If only my super healing would kick in and purge this shit out of my body, I might have at least a minimal chance at fighting these guys off. They sure were making a ton of noise though, crashing through the brush like a fucking heard of elephants. Maybe they'd startle a bear, or a mountain lion, and get killed. Or maybe Marita would realize I was taking forever at the dumpster and send HB out to find me. Now *that* was the mountain lion I really needed right now.

Suddenly the world lit up to white, like a nuclear bomb had gone off. There was a second of abrupt, total silence, then I fell, landing hard enough to knock the air from my lungs. I felt the handcuffs fall away, but I was too busy trying to catch my breath and blink my half-blinded eyes back into focus to try to get up and make a run for it.

Strong, gentle hands eased me upright, brushing gritty sand off my face and smoothing my hair back. I looked into Bishop's face and felt a wave of gratitude. When had he come back to the bar? How did he know I was gone? And where the hell were the Fixers who'd abducted me? They must have dropped me and took off like a shot the second Bishop appeared. Must be nice to inspire that sort of fear.

"You okay?" His voice was gruff, and I got the feeling he was barely holding back some serious anger. Hopefully, it wasn't me he was pissed at, but the four men who'd dared trespass on a place under his protection.

"Mwabbble ah," I replied. Saliva bubbled from my mouth, and I felt the spit roll down my chin. Lovely. How sexy. I get rescued by a hot guy, and here I was drooling, rolling my eyes around in my head, covered with this sandy dirt that had cushioned my fall.

"I'll take that as a yes." He scooped me up as he stood, and just like my abductors had done, he tossed me over his shoulder to let me bounce around with no dignity whatsoever as he carried me back to Suerte.

"Oh, thank *God*," I heard HB say once we were back in the

comforting glow of the bar's outdoor lighting. Marita added her praises to Mother Mary in Spanish.

I frowned, because both women sounded…frightened. Well, Marita sounded frightened. HB just sounded worried.

"Blabbmehh bma," I informed them, my spit dampening the back of Bishop's shirt.

He smelled good. I could feel the warmth of him, the firm, solid wall of muscle under the fabric. Maybe he'd tuck me into my little nest of blankets in the storeroom. Maybe he'd lie down next to me, big spoon to my little as we slept. And sleeping would be all we'd do because I was incapable of sex right now, and Bishop didn't strike me as the kind of guy who would enjoy getting it on with a drooling, barely conscious woman.

But Bishop didn't carry me inside. Instead, I found myself being dumped into the passenger seat of his truck, held somewhat upright by the seatbelt. He closed the door, and I leaned against it, listening to the noise of him loading something into the back of the truck and the murmur of conversation. He got into the driver's side, started the truck, then looked over at me. His blue eyes were full of tiny gold sparks, and the light from the bar illuminated his sun-streaked blond hair from the back like a halo. I thought for a second he was going to say something, but then he grunted, faced forward, and put the truck in gear.

I was asleep before we were even out of the parking lot.

CHAPTER 12

I awoke with no clue where I was. My mouth was dry. My skin and hair were gritty with sandy dirt. I was in my underwear and bra, on a king-sized bed, covered with what felt like a million-thread-count sheet and a lightweight blanket.

Cool air trickled from a nearby floor vent. Sweet Jesus, *air conditioning*.

Sitting up, I noted the mahogany head and footboard of the sleigh bed, a set of matching dressers, some watercolor prints of the ocean decorating the walls. The only personal items were my clothes neatly folded on a leather wingback chair with my backpack beside them.

The Fixers. The tranq dart. Bishop. This must be his house. While I could see HB taking me home, it had been Bishop in the truck with me last night. Plus, this room definitely did not have any sort of female vibes to it.

I jumped out of bed, then caught sight of myself in the mirror and winced. Shower. I needed to shower and clean up a bit before I went in search of my host.

Just to check, and because I was nosy, I pulled up a few of

the dresser drawers. They were full of men's shirts, men's socks, and men's underwear, all neatly folded and wrinkle free as if this were a department store display and not a guy's bedroom. One door opened up to a walk-in closet with the clothes organized and color coordinated with near OCD attention. Strange. I hadn't expected this from the guy who looked like a surfer who did CrossFit three times a week and drove an old truck with primer paint on one of the bumpers. But his truck was very clean. I didn't recall ever seeing old chip bags or napkins or even so much as a nose print on the window from Bob. Maybe the guy just liked his belongings orderly and his space neat.

The second door revealed a bathroom, and I darted inside.

After taking care of business, I availed myself of the toothbrush and paste still packaged and left neatly by the sink, then I hopped into the shower. It wasn't as gigantic as the one at the Canyon Drive house, but the water was steaming hot, and the soap and shampoos left me smelling of cloves, sandalwood, and ocean breezes—a scent I'd come to associate with Bishop.

I dried with a fluffy towel, combed my hair, then dressed in spare clothes from my backpack. On impulse, I checked the wicker hamper in the bathroom, hoping to find a shirt to steal. Sleeping in a shirt that smelled like Bishop? I loved the idea, even though I knew I probably wouldn't get all that much sleeping done.

The hamper was empty, so I did the next best thing and grabbed a button-down from the closet and a T-shirt from the dresser. My hand hovered over the underwear, but I decided that would be crossing the line into weirdo territory. Stuffing the shirts into my backpack, I gathered up my belongings and headed out of the bedroom to hopefully find my host.

The house revealed itself to be a sprawling hacienda-style with a mix of southwestern décor, nineteenth-century European furniture, and the occasional nod to the nearby ocean. I ran my fingers through a bowl of pastel sea glass and glanced out the huge picture window that looked out over the hustle and bustle of the Valley below. I hadn't been awake on the drive up here, but from the view I'd guess Bishop's house was somewhere in the mountains above Altadena, just north of Pasadena.

Continuing my search, I realized to my disappointment that Bishop was not home. His truck wasn't in the driveway, but my bike was, the keys sitting on the seat next to my helmet. My cell phone said it was eight in the morning, so I guess I shouldn't have been too surprised that Bishop was up and out the door by now, but I was still bummed that he wasn't here.

I wanted to thank him for saving me last night, for taking care of me, for letting me sleep in his amazingly comfortable bed.

Since my host was gone, I decided to snoop, downing a glass of water and grabbing an apple off the counter to eat as I checked out the rest of the house. There were a total of three bedrooms—one of which had been turned into some sort of office. The other bedroom held two empty dressers, a queen-sized bed, and was connected to the office room by a jack-and-jill bathroom. I ate my apple and eyed the queen-sized bed, wondering why Bishop had put me in what was clearly his room instead of here. I'd been dirty, drooling, covered in sand. Why strip me to my underwear and put me in your own personal bed?

Lurid fantasies ran through my mind. Not that I thought Bishop had tried anything with my passed-out body. It was rather the implication of him tucking me in on his own bed that had me visualizing us sweaty, hot, and

naked—and me fully conscious, as well as eagerly partic-
ipating.

I needed to finish paying this guy what I owed him so we could get down to some bedroom antics. In the meantime, I planned on making use of those shirts of his wherever I managed to be sleeping tonight. Oh, yeah.

Bishop was right. I needed to take care of business because I couldn't keep running away from mercenaries forever. Sooner or later, my luck was going to run out, and I'd rather negotiate on my terms than try to do it after being shot, darted, and hauled in for a bounty. The very idea of walking into the tax office gave me chills, but I was running out of options. None of the CB names had panned out. My last hope was Detective Juke. If she wasn't close to fixing my situation from the administrative end, I was going to need to work up the nerve to beg for some sort of payment plan.

I left Bishop a quick thank-you note, got on my bike, and headed into the Valley. Once I'd gotten down into Pasadena, I pulled over and dialed the detective.

"You've got info on the boneless dead?" Juke demanded without so much as a "hello" first.

The dead, boneless people. I'd been too busy trying to stay alive to worry about the favor she'd asked of me.

"I'm working on it," I lied. "Although it would be a whole lot easier for me to work on it if I hadn't been attacked *five times* since I met with you at Grits. Five. You're lucky I'm not locked away in some demon torture room downtown right now."

"I'm trying to get you out of this mess," she snapped. "I looked into your claims. I saw the initials on the report and checked up on every officer in L.A. with those initials. Then I had a buddy in IT check the login for the report. It's a dead ID. Dead as in that officer, Conner Bah, died last month, and with the backup of work, they hadn't gotten around to deleting his login. I had them trace the login, and it originated from a computer down in Torrance. I'm trying to figure out if Conner Bah actually filed the report or someone just used his login, and that's been kinda hard since he's dead. I've been working this, Alvaro. I'm working as fast as I can here."

I was stunned—stunned that she'd put that much time and effort into my problem, and that she'd actually gotten a heck of a lot done in the last two days.

"How long do you think it'll take? For that report to get deleted or changed, that is. How long?" Maybe I wouldn't have to go make a deal with the tax demons.

"Another week or two at least. I'm trying. Just try to stay alive, okay?"

A week or two. I didn't have a week or two. I couldn't keep dodging these mercenaries for that long. Damn it. I was going to have to cut a deal.

Juke sighed. "Look, I could put more time into this problem of yours if I didn't have the Lieutenant on my back about those four dead people. Can you at least talk to someone in the Gray Dogs about Dragon? I really need to get this case off my desk."

Spend the morning doing a little digging around? Or head downtown to the tax office? As much as I wanted to procrastinate, I knew it would be stupid to delay the inevitable. The report wouldn't get changed for weeks. I wasn't going to figure out who the cop was or get the money from her. And I had a bunch of mercenaries who would probably be hauling me downtown if not today, then tomorrow.

If I came out of the tax office alive, I'd still have time to drive back to the Valley, meet with the Gray Dogs for Juke, then head back downtown to meet Telaney and do that job with her—although I wasn't going to have time to grab a dress from home. Telaney would have to just deal with me in my usual cargo pants and tank top.

"I'm going to talk to the Gray Dogs as soon as I run an errand downtown," I promised Juke.

Then, pocketing my phone, I pulled into traffic, made a U-turn, and headed for the freeway.

CHAPTER 13

By the time I managed to make it downtown, it was close to noon. I wasn't sure if demons took business lunches or not, but hopefully someone would still be there with the authority to cut a deal with me.

Downtown had…changed. I hadn't done more than look at the skyline from the freeway in the last two years. Between the demons and the occasional dragon, this area had truly become a den of sin. The stores had been looted and stood empty. Entire floors of high-rises had gone dark when businesses fled. Occasionally an enterprising human would set up shop in what had once been a high-rent business district, but that human would fail unless there was a powerful demon backing his business.

That's what had happened with the big hotel chains. Some had abandoned their real estate, but a few had bargained with the demons and arrived at a mutually beneficial agreement. The Westin Bonaventure was one such hotel. I didn't know if the original corporation still owned it or not, but the building still bore the signature branding and names, and the human employees still wore the same uniforms. The top-floor suites were all occupied by demons who called this place their home. I'd been told that they received a regular delivery of food, booze, and whatever else they wanted. In return, the resident demons made sure the place didn't get trashed and allowed the hotel's owners to keep a portion of the revenues. If the rumors were true and the occasional guest vanished without a trace, well, that was the risk one took for staying in any hotel in Downtown. Or living anywhere in New Hell, it seemed.

The tax office was a boring block of concrete with evenly spaced small windows that went up ten stories. The thing looked like it had been built in the seventies, and no one had done anything to even attempt to beautify it since then. I pulled into the parking deck below the building and readily found a spot. There weren't a lot of cars—but that wasn't surprising.

Any human who could afford a Bugatti or Lamborghini wouldn't risk their life working in a place like this. I walked past the Hondas and Hyundais, wincing at a Chevy Malibu under enough dust to indicate that it hadn't moved in months. Hopefully, the car had just died, and the owner had abandoned it. That was a much better scenario to think than one where the owner had walked into the tax office and never left.

Would that be me? Would someone months from now come through this garage and see my Yamaha bike covered in dust, still where I parked it just now?

I shook off the morbid thoughts and took the elevator up to the lobby where a woman sat at the receptionist desk painting her long, curved nails a neon lime green. She looked up at me and smiled, revealing a row of jagged, pointed teeth. I'd seen my share of body modification in my life, but I'd be willing to bet this creature manning the phones was not human. No guards. No visible weapons. Teeth like a shark.

Yeah, this was a demon, no matter how pleasant her smile seemed.

"I'm here to see someone about my tax bill," I told her, trying not to stare at her teeth.

The smile broadened to inhuman proportions. "Your name."

"Eden Alvaro." I gave her my Vulture license number and watched her type that into the system.

Her eyes widened. "Holy shit. Where's your briefcase, girl? You know we don't take checks or credit cards here."

I swallowed hard. "I know. Is there someone I can speak with? I need to talk about the situation surrounding my alleged debt and see if there's something that can be done."

She practically bounced in her chair with excitement. "I'm shocked you're still in one piece. There's been a bounty on you for…over three weeks now. They even upped it twice. Damn, you must be like that woman from *The Terminator* or something."

"Or something," I agreed.

I'll admit I was flattered. And I was also more than a little shocked how easy it was to talk with this demon. Unnerving appearance aside, she wasn't particularly scary. Not like Desiree. Not like the lizard-like demons who menaced the freeways. Not like Hellkitty. Not even like that demon with the herbicide sperm who'd come through our neighborhood that one time. I could see myself sitting down for a beer with this demon, and that was probably more terrifying than anything.

She got up from behind the desk. "I'm going to put you in the third-floor conference room and see who's free. Come with me."

"Should I leave my weapons somewhere?" I looked around, perplexed.

"Pfft. Like anyone gives two shits about your little pea

shooter. Now that anti-magic gun our security system says you've got in your backpack is impressive, but those bullets are hard to come by. You've got six max in there, and there are over a dozen demons here right now. Even if you were a good enough shot to disable six of us with that thing, the rest of us would tear you to shreds." She sent me a saucy smile over her shoulder. "You're too smart for that. And I'm too lazy to take care of your shit while you're getting your ass handed to you on the third floor. So, keep your weapons. For now."

Well. *That* didn't exactly reassure me.

We took the elevator up to the third floor. Outside of her teeth, the receptionist had a cute little set of yellowish horns poking out of the top of her head. It made her look like an anime character.

She whirled around to face me, walking backward as we exited the elevator. "So how the fuck did you manage to rack up fifty-two K in tax debt? That's some serious coin."

"A cop set me up. Reported me for a salvage she took herself."

The receptionist rolled her eyes as she continued to walk backward. "Girl, that lame-ass excuse is not gonna fly. If I had a nickel for every human or demon who used the 'it was some other guy' defense, I'd be rich. And I'm not rich."

"Why not?" I was genuinely curious. "You're a demon, aren't you? Why aren't you rich? Take what you want. Kill whoever stands in your way. Isn't that what demons do?"

"Well, yeah, but lots of demons who do that stuff die. There's always a bigger demon and occasionally a smart human. Better to weigh your risks and not do stupid shit that gets you killed."

Amen, sister.

"Besides..." She shrugged. "I'm a Low."

She halted before a door and reached out for the handle.

"A Low?" I remembered they were supposed to be demons without a lot of powers, but beyond that, I didn't know anything about them. And I didn't want to have to look through this giant book in my backpack at the moment, either.

Her smile twisted. "The lowest caste of demons. Lowest in powers. Lowest in abilities. Considered disposable and basically no more than cannon fodder."

I hated bullies, always rooted for the underdog, and now I liked this woman even more. "That's bullshit. Fuck them."

She blinked, then opened the conference room door. "I like you, Eden Alvaro. Hope you walk out of here alive."

Yeah. Me, too. "What's your name?"

"Blister."

I walked into the conference room. "Nice to meet you, Blister."

"Good luck, Alvaro. Hope to see you walking out of here and not being carted out in a body bag." She winked at me and closed the door, leaving me in a long, narrow conference room.

The mahogany table had long gouges down the center as if some creature had dug in with talons and been dragged from one end to the other. One of the chairs had been broken into palm-sized bits of metal and plastic, the upholstery and stuffing strewn across the floor. At the far end was a bookshelf and a coffee maker with no pot. A cracked off-white mug sat next to the coffee maker with the Merrill Lynch logo in red emblazoned on the side.

I walked over to the windows, looking across at another office building, then down to the street below where traffic slalomed around potholes and debris.

I heard the door open behind me.

"Eden Alvaro. You are not who I was expecting when

Blister told me there was a delinquent account in the third-floor conference room."

I turned around instinctively yanking my pistol from its holster, and swallowed a gasp.

Before me stood a minotaur—if minotaurs had scaled bodies, hands like tiger's claws, and a massive set of bat wings folded behind them. The guy was completely nude, and the scales covering his extremities weren't hiding anything. He blew out a snort of steam through his ringed nose, and I noticed his flaring nostrils weren't the only thing pierced. There were hoops through his ears, dangling from his nipples, and decorating his junk.

His junk was more terrifying than the horns or the claws. The thing was a fucking club. If this turned to violence, that's where I was aiming. In preparation of that very thing, I lowered the muzzle of my pistol and pointed it right between his legs.

"I'm unarmed." His voice boomed, and he spread his arms wide.

Right. He flexed his paws, revealing three-inch claws. Unarmed my ass.

"Me, too." I kept my aim steady. There was no such thing as an unarmed demon, and I wasn't letting down my guard around this guy for one second. My bullets might not be able to kill him, but I'd unload the mag, try to do as much excruciating damage as I could, then run like hell.

He chuckled. "I'm impressed. You evade every mercenary sent to collect you for weeks. You kill so many of them that we were forced to up the bounty twice. Then you waltz right on in here and have the guts to point that little thing at me. It won't kill me, you know."

"It won't, but I'm willing to believe a nine mil to the dick would hurt like fuck." I gestured with my free hand. "Sit. I'd like to talk, and I'm hoping to walk out of here with some sort of amicable arrangement between us."

"Then put the gun away, and we'll talk."

There was a mini stand-off between the two of us, but after a moment, I holstered the pistol and sat.

He grinned, the expression weird on a bovine face, then he sat as well. "You haven't fenced the bullets. Or at least you haven't tried to pawn them in bulk, because we would have caught that transaction. And no pawnbroker, even one that's your friend, is going to risk buying that large of a salvage without recording it."

"A cop set me up. I didn't take those cases of bullets. She ran me off the job, took everything herself, including my backpack. Then she filed a report saying I'd taken the salvage." He probably wouldn't believe me, but I felt like I had to at least attempt to assert my innocence.

The demon ignored me. "There are enough pawnshops around that you could have gone through the city, through the Valley, fencing small quantities here and there, maybe even selling some to gangs and militias directly. It would have taken you a week or two maximum. But if you'd have done that, why are you still here? With that money, even if you had gotten fifty cents on the dollar, you would have had enough to bribe your way across the border and set up a life where we would have to exert considerable effort to reach you." He shifted his weight on the chair and adjusted his wings. "It was a big haul, but not *that* big. Not big enough that we would bother wasting resources tracking you down across the states. So why are you still here? And more to the point, why are you *here*?"

"I don't have the bullets. I never did. And I'm here because I don't have the money to leave, and I'm sick of killing the mercenaries trying to collect the bounty on me. I don't owe you all jack shit, but I'm willing to deal. I'm willing to make some sort of arrangement so I can live my life in peace."

He leaned forward, his eyes flashing with red lights. Once more, I reached for my pistol. Should I shoot the guy? Continue to try to talk my way out of this? Make a break for the door and hope I had a slim chance of getting past him?

"You haven't left. Why? You're either sitting on a bunch of cash or seventeen cases of bullets. Why are you still here, trying to salvage without a license? Why are you still here, having to evade and fight off mercenaries who want to collect the bounty on your head?"

Did those furry ears with the hoops in them work, or were they just for decoration?

"A cop set me up," I repeated, very slowly and somewhat loudly this time. "I didn't take the bullets, *she* did. Then she pinned it on me. I'm still here because I don't have any money, and I don't have any of those fucking cases to sell."

"Three weeks, and no one has been able to bring you in." The demon examined the claws on his left paw, scraping a bit of dirt—or was that dried blood—free from one.

I stood, unable to remain seated. The minotaur-demon did the same, stepping around the conference table to face me head-on.

"Are you going to kill me?" My voice cracked a little. "Or are you going to actually listen to what I'm saying? I. Don't. Have. The. Money. Or the bullets. But I know you won't believe me, so I'm here hoping to make a deal."

I needed to make a decision here. *Shoot and flee? Flee then shoot? Wait and hope for a better opportunity to get a head start?*

He looked up at me and smiled. Let me tell you, a bull smiling is far from reassuring. "So, make me a deal. And I better like it, or you're going to die nice and slow."

Shoot and run? Run then shoot? I did neither—although I did pull my pistol out and aim it at his peen.

"Five thousand in payments. Five hundred per month in cash," I said. It would mean I'd need to take additional jobs south of L.A. and delay paying Bishop all I owed him, but Bishop would wait for payment and not kill me. I couldn't say the same about these demons.

He laughed. "Seventeen cases of bullets, and you want to pay us five grand? Over time with no penalties or interest?"

"I didn't take the salvage," I snapped. "I'm offering to pay you five grand that I don't fucking owe just to get you guys off my back. If you want the rest, find the cop who filed the report because she's the one with the cash and/or the bullets."

He shrugged. "That's your problem, not ours. Some cop set you up? Then you go take care of it. Either way, you still owe us fifty-two thousand dollars. And that number is going to increase daily."

The pistol shook in my hand. I didn't know what to do. I didn't fucking know what to do. I couldn't find the cop. Going through the appropriate channels was taking forever, and there was no guarantee that the police would resolve this.

I was backed into a corner, and I didn't know how to get out of it.

Walk your fine ass downtown into their office and start bull-shitting. Cut a deal.

Bishop was right. I sucked in a breath and tried to calm my nerves. "I made you an offer. You rejected it. Now it's your turn to counter offer."

He eyed me, gaze focused for a long second on the pistol. "Payments over time for the full fifty-two thousand with twenty percent interest per annum, or settle the amount due immediately for eighty percent of what's owed."

My blood pressure went through the roof. I didn't

fucking have eighty percent. I didn't even have thirty percent, because I'd never taken the salvage to begin with.

"Either option also comes with a hundred years of service to the tax office," he added.

A hundred years? A *hundred* years? A lifetime of servitude. This was the worst fucking deal ever. Pay in full the full retail value of the salvage plus interest and penalties *and* a lifetime working for these assholes, or somehow manage to find almost forty-two grand. And *still* owe them a lifetime of service.

It was insane, but it was better than dead. No. I shook my head. No, I couldn't think like that. The last month had worn me down, but I couldn't let myself agree to this shitty deal just because it seemed like these dicks held all the cards.

They didn't hold all the cards. I was smart. I was resourceful. I thought of a random cop who'd stood up for me, of Bags, of Hellkitty. And of Bishop. He might have acted from a sense of outrage that those Fixers had dared to snatch someone on his property, but I got the feeling there was more in his rescue of me last night. I had some powerful friends on my side. And I'd always been able to weasel myself out of trouble in the past. There was no reason to doubt I couldn't do it now, even if I was standing in front of a giant pierced minotaur-demon with a huge fucking cock.

He shrugged. "The last three weeks have shown us that you're particularly resourceful. Employing contract mercenaries or putting out bounties usually gets the job done, but there are times when it would be useful to have someone of your talents to call on. I've decided that no matter what the deal, there needs to be some sort of service to the tax office included."

Right there his words let me know there was still room to negotiate.

"This service you're talking about, it's not full time then?

By the job? A certain number of hours per week? And what sort of work are you talking about here?"

I don't know why I had an image of myself in a cubicle, typing away at the computer eight hours a day for one hundred years. Obviously, that wasn't the sort of work the tax office would be demanding of me.

He chuckled, a low and oddly sexy sound coming from a bull's mouth. "No, not full time. The type of work will vary, and when you have an assignment, you are expected to drop every other obligation and give us your undivided time and attention."

It was still better than dead. But one hundred years…

Walk your fine ass downtown into their office and start bull-shitting. Cut a deal.

"Fuck that shit. Ten grand. Payments over time, but no interest or penalties. I'll work for you, but once the tax debt is paid, my service ends." I threw it out there, still hoping I could track down this cop and beat the money or the bullets out of her. Or if some miracle occurred, and I could scrape together ten grand, I could deliver it here and the whole fucking nightmare would be over.

The demon grinned. "No, it doesn't end with payment in full. One hundred years. Payments will be allowed on a reduced debt of forty thousand. No interest charged—which is incredibly lenient of us. Or immediate settlement of the debt at seventy percent. It's a generous offer. One hundred years of service is not a lot to ask."

Says a demon that lives for fucking ever.

"I didn't take the salvage." I held up a finger. "But if I did, then the taxes are only due when the goods are pawned. You yourself said there's been no proof of a large-scale pawn. There's also no proof that I sold it off by the box. Technically, I don't owe shit."

"The report—"

"That report is a lie," I interrupted. "And taxes aren't due until it's sold. You suspended my license. You put the word out that any pawnbroker dealing with me, on or off the books, was going to get a not-so-friendly visit from you guys. If I've got the bullets, then I clearly haven't sold them. Which means I don't owe you shit."

It also meant they had no standing to put a bounty out on me or to pull my license. If these guys had been the human IRS, I would have filed a form or gotten a tax attorney or something.

There was no appeal to a mandate from the tax office.

Or was there? I remembered the book had said there was some hierarchy among demons. And from what I'd heard, they did follow some code of a sort with binding oaths and loyalties. Maybe there was a higher demon authority I could appeal to. Or maybe that would just get me killed quicker.

"The report is the proof. It's been three weeks. If you haven't sold the salvage yet, that isn't our problem. You took it. There's a report that says you took it. Thus, you owe taxes on it."

"There's nothing in the licensing regulations that says taxes need to be payed within a certain time of the salvage," I bluffed. "I only owe the taxes when I sell the haul. And it hasn't been sold. So, I'm not delinquent on my taxes, and you all shouldn't have a bounty out on me."

The minotaur-demon narrowed his eyes. "Section four nine five, subsection eight. 'Taxes are considered incurred at the moment of salvage, to be paid at the time of sale or within three days of salvage, whichever comes first.' Sometimes a Vulture collects something they want to keep. That doesn't mean taxes aren't owed or that they get an indefinite time to pay them."

Damn it. The fucker memorized the regulations. I'd tried to weasel out on a technicality. I'd tried to convince him I was set up. I had nothing left at this point—nothing I could think of on the fly, at least.

"Ten grand. Payments over time. No interest or penalties." I had no aces in the hole, nothing to bargain with, but I wasn't giving up yet.

"No." He sighed. "You're ballsy, I'll give you that. But let me tell you something, little human, life isn't fair, and demons don't play by the rules—even rules we've set up ourselves. Now, you've got one last chance to make me an *acceptable* offer. Make it good, because I'm starting to think slowly breaking every bone in your body until you tell me where you've hidden the money and the bullets would be a lot of fun."

Shit.

"Fifteen grand now—well, in the next forty-eight hours now—and the debt is considered paid," I told him. "In addition, you can request my service for one job within the next year. One. If I'd taken the salvage and pawned it, you would have only gotten twelve or thirteen grand, so I consider this a more than fair offer."

I thought for a quick second about an alternative, because my coming up with fifteen grand in the next two days was almost as farfetched as me coming up with fifty-two grand.

"Or, if I can't deliver the fifteen thousand within forty-eight hours, then I will owe twenty thousand, payable over time with thirteen percent interest per annum. In that scenario, I will give you my service for five jobs at any time during my life."

The bull-demon was silent, which gave me some hope that this might end up being resolved without me suffering any excruciating physical pain.

"I came in here voluntarily. I want to resolve this, even though I was set up. Considering you've been chasing me for weeks and are running out of mercenaries willing to take the job, this is a good offer. It's better than zero, which is what it's honestly looking like you're going to get if you just keep trying to hire Fixers to bring me in."

A puff of smoke curled from the demon's nostrils. "Don't get saucy, girl. You're standing right in front of me. I no longer need to hire Fixers to bring you in."

I held my breath at that, deciding that maybe I needed to shut the fuck up and let my offer stand.

"Fifteen thousand now and ten jobs for us in the next year, or twenty thousand over time with twenty percent interest and fifty jobs over your lifetime. That's my final offer."

I got the feeling that if I didn't take this offer, I wasn't walking out of here alive. It sucked, but it was better than being dead. And like the demon had said, life was unfair. I'd learned that fact long before the demons came. Sometimes you had to pay for a crime you didn't do. No sense crying about it.

"I need forty-eight hours to get the money. I don't walk around with fifteen thousand dollars in my wallet. At least give me time to pull the money together."

His nostrils widened and he puffed out a breath. "Forty-eight hours or the cash deal is off the table and the other option will be considered accepted and binding. You will make the payments, and you will provide whatever we ask on the jobs we assign you. We want our money, Eden Alvaro. And if you try to back out of this deal, we'll kill you. No more dicking around with mercenaries and bounties. No more putting pressure on you in hopes that you'll pay your debt. Deal or dead. Forty-eight hours."

Fucking asshole. I wanted to shoot him in the dick just for the hell of it, but that would probably only piss him off and remove this last opportunity to save my ass.

"Forty-eight hours," I promised. "Should I deliver the money here? To you?"

"You can drop the money off anytime and get a receipt. If I'm not here, then call me. I'll arrange to meet you later to sign the official paperwork on your employment." He flicked his fingers and extended a business card toward me. I was a little reluctant to take it because the guy was naked and magic or no magic, I didn't like the idea of where he might be storing these business cards.

Thankful that I had a little bottle of hand sanitizer in my backpack, I extended my left hand, putting my pistol back into my shoulder holster. With the tips of my index finger and thumb, I gingerly took the card and stepped back before glancing down.

Corundum. Office of Taxation, New Hell. And a phone number.

"Forty-eight hours, Eden Alvaro." His voice was soft but carried an undercurrent of steel. "I don't care which option you choose, but if you don't contact me within forty-eight hours with either the cash or acceptance of the other offer, then you're dead. No more offers. No more negotiation."

Yeah, I heard him the first time. I nodded, shoving the card in my pocket. The demon walked out, and I waited for a few seconds before leaving the conference room, not sure if someone needed to escort me or not.

I took the elevator down and saw Blister with her feet on the desk, examining her lime-green nails. She grinned at me and swung her feet down.

"Look at you, all alive and everything. Even got your arms and legs still attached."

"Surprised? Because I am." I walked up to the counter and adjusted my backpack.

"Nah. I called Corundum in because he likes humans,

likes to bargain and cut deals. He should have been a cross-roads demon. Dude missed his calling."

"Thanks." The bull-demon had been terrifying, but I realized it could have been much worse.

"Did you fuck him?" Her gaze roved down my body.

"Are you kidding me? No, I didn't fuck him." There was no orifice in my body that could comfortably accommodate that thing between the demon's legs. What a horrible way to die. Although surviving that might just be worse than death.

Blister shrugged. "Heard he's good. And like I said, he likes humans. He might have erased your debt if you'd given him a quick blowjob, then ridden the pony."

I'd do a lot of things to get out of paying a debt, but screwing that thing upstairs wasn't one of them.

"Next time, maybe." I gave her a quick salute and headed for the exit. "Thanks for your help, though."

"You owe me a drink," she called after me. "I made sure you got Corundum and not some asshole. You owe me at least a beer for that."

Demons. For crazy, violent beings that lied, cheated, and stole, they took this quid pro quo thing oddly to heart.

"Fine. One beer," I agreed, walking out the door.

I made it half a block before my adrenaline dropped and I realized what I'd done, what I'd promised—and I didn't mean the drink with Blister, either. Leaning against the side of a building, I choked back the vomit that rose in my throat. There was no time to be sick, no time to think about what I'd just done.

I had forty-eight hours to find fifteen grand. Because the other alternative wasn't something I wanted to accept.

CHAPTER 14

I couldn't believe I'd left the tax office in one piece, let alone with a deal. Yeah, it was a sucky deal, but it was still a deal. Either way, within forty-eight hours, I wouldn't need to worry about bounty hunters anymore.

No, I'd need to worry about paying off a twenty grand debt and working for the demons. There's no way I was going to come up with fifteen grand in the next two days, so option two was going to be my fate.

Thinking about it made me want to puke again, so I pushed it all aside and headed back north on the freeway.

Driving back into the Valley, I headed for Van Nuys and what used to be a swanky country club. Growing up in the Valley, I'd gone to school with a few people who'd ended up in gangs. I hadn't distanced myself from those people because I'd never really had a problem with gangs. Besides, gang or no gang, lots of those people were decent folk. A few of them I'd even dated, and at one point I'd flirted with the idea of joining the Gray Dogs myself. Normally, I subscribed to the Groucho Marx philosophy of not wanting to be a part of any group who'd have me, but Sebastian had been a pretty persuasive dude.

Ultimately, we'd gone our separate ways, and I'd remained unaffiliated.

Last I'd heard, Sebastian was working his way up the chain of command and was assisting with the gang's attempted expansion into Southside Militia territory. Our parting had been amicable, and he was one of the few Gray Dog members I knew well enough to ask about the unusual death of one of their men.

I pulled up to the entrance of the country club. Someone in the Gray Dogs must have liked golf, because the course was mowed and maintained. I squinted, looking across the expanse of perfectly manicured green and saw two golf carts on the fifth hole and several figures congregating around the vehicles while a man took his shot.

Sebastian hadn't golfed when I'd dated him, so instead of walking across the course, I headed for the building. I'd heard looters had trashed the place two years ago when the demons had knocked our society and rules onto its ass. I had no idea if the original owners had fled the area or been killed, but no one had protested when the Gray Dogs took over and claimed the entire club as their headquarters.

They'd seen me drive up, so I wasn't surprised when I was met by two gang members before I'd finished climbing the steps to the entrance.

"Weapons." The man held out his hand where the woman fixed me with a thousand-yard stare.

I surrendered my gun without protest. Gray Dogs might be a gang, but they had a code they lived by, and that code included safeguarding and respecting visitors' property. If I attacked anyone, they'd keep my gun, but otherwise I'd get it back when I was ready to leave.

The woman patted me down, handing over my knives

and multi-tool to the man. Then she looked through my backpack, taking out Navy SEAL Guy's HK as well as the anti-magic gun before returning the backpack to me.

"I'm here to see Sebastian, if he's in," I told them.

"Yeah, he's in." The woman lifted her eyebrows and looked me over.

"I'm an old friend of his from back in school. Eden Alvaro. Can you ask him if he has a moment to speak with me?"

The woman stiffened and exchanged a quick glance with the man. Muttering something under her breath in another language, she walked inside. The man turned to put my weapons in a metal box that had once been outside a doctor's office for laboratory sample pickup. Why someone had lifted it and brought it here, I had no idea.

"He's got a woman, you know," the man grunted. "You looking to stay, or is this just business?"

"Business. I'm only here to ask a few questions about a matter of mutual interest," I said carefully. "I'm not staying."

He grunted again. "Good. Otherwise, Isabella would lose her shit. She's gonna lose her shit anyway, but if you'd decided to stay, then someone would have died. Maybe you. Maybe Sebastian."

I grimaced, wondering how many people here knew of Sebastian's and my history. I wondered if Isabella knew. If so, this was going to be very awkward. I might not be getting my gun and knives back. Hell, I might not be leaving here in one piece.

Sadly, I didn't know any other Gray Dogs well enough to quiz them about the death of one of their members. Sebastian was it. I needed to do this. I owed Juke, and if that meant I might have to deal with a jealous girlfriend, then that's what I'd have to do.

I heard shouting from inside the building, clear through

the closed doors. Glass shattered nearby, and a man's voice promised violent retribution. Everything fell silent. I waited. The man next to me waited. Finally, his phone rang and he answered, replying with only a "Yeah," before pocketing the phone once more.

"Follow me."

I did, trying to ignore the shards of glass littering the foyer. The guard led me into a side room where Sebastian stood with his back to me, looking out a series of tall windows at the verdant golf course.

"Eden." His voice was cool but friendly. "It's been…what? Four or five years?"

"Four years. How are you, Sebastian?"

He turned to face me at the pleasantry, looking just as he had four years ago when I'd left and not returned.

"You're looking good," he observed, not answering my question. I wasn't looking good. My cargo pants had stains and dirt that no amount of laundry detergent would erase. My tank top was spotted with sweat. My hair was a snarled mess, held back in a low ponytail that was far from flattering. I had no makeup on. I was wearing a sports bra that squished me into a uni-boob. My boots were scuffed and caked with dried mud. Clearly Sebastian still carried fond memories of our long-ago relationship if he thought I was "looking good."

"Thanks. You, too." Hoping that would be the end of the awkward personal stuff, I pulled the folder out of my backpack and got down to business. "A Gray Dog member died a few weeks ago. Guy named Herbert Adams. Went by Dragon. His girlfriend found him on the couch, dead and boneless, when she came home."

Sebastian's lips thinned. "Fucking demons. If I find out which one did it, I'm going to pulverize *his* bones with a tire iron."

I wasn't sure if I was relieved it wasn't a bone-dissolving

creature or not. Although a demon who killed someone like this was probably just as bad.

"So, I'm guessing you have no idea which demon did it?" I asked. "Or how they did it? Or why they did it?"

He shook his head. "Dragon had a run-in with a couple of them last month when he was out partying. There's also a demon who was pushing to take over one of our businesses in Reseda. Any one of them might have killed him for revenge or to send a message. Pulverizing someone's bones. That's a shitty way to die. I'd rather get shot if you ask me."

I grimaced, thinking of how it might feel to die by having your bones dissolved. Did they have massive internal hemorrhaging? Slowly suffocate without anything to support their lungs? Lie there in a motionless puddle until all their organs shut down?

"Yeah, I'd rather die by a gunshot, too." I pulled the folder out of my backpack and slid out the photos that I hadn't bothered looking at before now. "Three other people died the same way, and I'm wondering if you knew any of them. Maybe there was a connection between them and Dragon that will help narrow down which demon did this." I spread the pictures on a table.

Sebastian moved next to me to look at them.

"The first one to die after Dragon was a woman who worked at the morgue." I pointed. "Then her sister. Then a pawnbroker."

Sebastian and I stood nearly touching as we looked down at the pictures. They were horribly gruesome, especially the sight of people's faces without the framework of their skulls. None of the dead had anything in common besides the fact that their flesh flattened like an empty sack without the support of bones, but I recognized something on the first picture that made me suck in a sharp breath.

Dragon had a necklace on his deflated body. It was a

heavy gold chain sporting a gaudy dragon pendant with ruby eyes, around what should have been his neck. It was the ugliest thing I'd ever seen, and I'd seen it before on a dead man—one who'd still had all his bones intact.

"That necklace." I pointed to the picture, trying to force down the burn of bile in the back of my throat. "Is that something the Gray Dogs are using as a symbol? As an identification of rank in the gang? Do other people have necklaces like that?"

Sebastian shook his head. "No, it was Dragon's personal jewelry. I don't know where or how he got it, but he loved that damned thing. Wore it twenty-four seven. He started wearing it about a week before he died."

I glanced at the other pictures, but none of them were wearing the necklace. Maybe it was just a coincidence. After all, the guy I'd robbed two days ago hadn't been boneless.

"I don't recognize any of these other people," Sebastian said. "But it's kinda hard to tell if I know them or not. Looking at a person with their skin wrapped around a skull is a bit different then seeing their face like a deflated balloon on the floor."

If I hadn't known Sebastian, I would have thought none of this gruesome stuff bothered him in the slightest. He was good at hiding emotions. It's one of the things that made him so successful in the Gray Dogs. Underneath it all, I knew Sebastian was just as repulsed and disturbed by the pictures as I was. And there was no hiding the fact that he was pissed at Dragon's death and had meant it when he'd promised a bloody vengeance.

"Hey. Wait a minute here." He leaned closer to the photos. "Isn't that the pawnbroker from ABC? Stinky, or Slinky, or something?"

"Yeah. Slinky Moore. Do you know him? Did he have any connection with Dragon?"

Sebastian shrugged. "We all know him. He lets us know if he gets something in the shop that we might be interested in. Dragon went in there sometimes to pick up the usual stuff. Buying some ammo, or a good knife, or a leaf blower for the course. That kinda thing. Damn. Can't believe the guy is dead."

"Think Dragon might have bought the necklace from him?" I had no idea what the hell a necklace had to do with a murdering demon, but I had a hunch, and I was going with it.

Sebastian held his hands outward. "No idea. Like I said, Dragon showed up with the necklace on about a month ago, strutting around like a damned peacock. He might have bought it at the pawnshop. He might have lifted it off someone he killed. Maybe his girlfriend gave it to him. I don't know." His eyes narrowed as he looked at me. "Do you think maybe he stole it from a demon, and that's why he got killed?"

I shrugged. "I honestly don't know. None of the others are wearing the necklace in these pictures, and these are crime scene photos from the police. They wouldn't have removed jewelry before taking the photos."

"No, but maybe Dragon *did* get the necklace from the pawnbroker. He's dead and boneless too…" Sebastian growled low in the back of his throat. "And who's to say someone didn't steal the necklace from the other dead people before the cops got there? Maybe there's a demon tracking down his stolen goods, killing anyone who ever touched the thing?"

Killing anyone who ever touched the thing.

I frowned, thinking of my conversation with HB and Bishop last night. Dragon had the necklace. Maybe the morgue woman stole it to sell. Maybe her sister went through her effects after she died and pawned it. Everyone who touched it died.

That didn't sound like a demon. A demon would've found the necklace, killed whoever had it, then took it back. I couldn't imagine one inept enough to take a week to find the new owner, then after killing them, leave the jewelry behind. No, it didn't sound like a demon killing at all. It sounded like a cursed object.

But maybe I'd been reading too many fairy tales, thinking too much about mages and magic.

"Dragon obviously died wearing the necklace. I guess his girlfriend didn't have a chance to remove it before the police carted him away? It probably went with Dragon's remains to the morgue, right?" I asked.

Sebastian's lip curled. "I can't see Nicky taking the necklace. It wasn't her kinda thing. And she was completely freaked out finding Dragon that way. I don't think she'd have the stomach to take it off his corpse—not when he was looking like that."

"I'm sure she was too distraught over seeing her boyfriend like an empty sack on their couch to think about taking anything of value off his body," I agreed.

"Yeah." He stared down at the pictures for a moment. "Nicky'd only been dating Dragon for a few months. I'm not even sure she knew he was a Gray Dog. When she found him, she called the police first, then called a friend of Dragon's after they took his body away. That's how we found out he'd died. I went with her to get the body, and the necklace wasn't in the packet of stuff they gave us with Dragon's wallet. Money was gone too, but you kinda expect that, you know?"

The necklace went to the morgue with the body. Then this Rene Schell woman with the morgue stole it, and probably the money as well, from the personal belongings packet.

She took it home, died a week later. Her sister, Amy Schell, died nine days later, followed by Slinky the next day. Did they put the necklace on? Was possessing it enough to trigger the curse? And how long did it take for someone to die? Judging by the dates on the photos, I was guessing a week.

It wasn't just some demon. This was a cursed object, and it was still out there, its next victim completely unaware that a horrible death awaited them in just a few days.

And I had a feeling I knew exactly who that next victim would be.

"I don't care if Dragon stole that necklace off a demon or not," Sebastian said. "No one kills one of ours and gets away with it. I'll find that fucker. I'll find that fucker and he'll pay."

"Yeah. You do that." If Sebastian was smart, this was all just him blowing off steam. If he wasn't smart, well, he was going to end up dead after trying to avenge Dragon. Sebastian was tough, but if he started going after demons, he was going to be dead.

"There was a hit two days ago," I said as I stuffed the pictures back into the envelope and into my backpack. "It was in Sherman Oaks near Hesby and Willis. I recognized the dead guy as a Gray Dog, but I didn't know his name. I think it was probably a Southside Militia thing over the territory dispute because it didn't look like a robbery."

It didn't look like a robbery because the dead guy still had a wad of cash in his pocket. Even though I was within my legal rights to rob the dead, I was sure Sebastian wouldn't be happy that I'd made off with that much money.

"Binks. Damned shame. He was a good guy." Sebastian shot me a perceptive glance. "And Binks had just made a pickup. He was carrying some green on him."

I'd taken that green and still had almost eighty dollars of it in my pocket. Not that Sebastian needed to know about any of that.

"I got run off the salvage by some other Vultures." It was only partially a lie. "I just remember the guy was wearing the same dragon-pendant necklace. It's distinctive. There's no way two of those necklaces are floating around the city."

Well, there might be a way, but I doubted someone was mass producing identical gaudy gold necklaces.

"Binks was Dragon's best friend," Sebastian admitted. "If it got stolen out of the morgue, then it probably wound up at ABC. Binks knew how attached Dragon was to the damned thing, and he makes daily stop-offs there. If he saw it there, I can just see the damned fool buying it to remember Dragon by."

Let him think a demon killed Dragon and the others. I could tell Juke my theory and just dump it all in her lap. Let her deal with it. Juke and the cops could hunt down the necklace. And if I was wrong, and it was a demon who'd done this? Well, a truly ugly necklace would be off the streets, and it wasn't like the cops were going to prosecute a demon anyway.

None of this was my business. Juke had asked me to talk to the Gray Dogs and get some info. I'd done that. The rest of it was her mess to deal with.

But I didn't like the idea that a possibly cursed necklace was out there in the Valley—*my* Valley. What if someone brought it into Bags's pawnshop? What if Telaney picked it up at a salvage job? What if one of the girls found it somewhere and brought it home? It didn't bother me that Karen and/or Chad were most likely the cursed necklace's next victims. They were assholes. I didn't care if they died with no bones.

Okay, I kinda *did* care. Not because I liked them, but because deep down inside, I didn't quite think they were assholes enough to die this way. Cursed. And not even cursed personally, but because they just happened to be doing their job and salvaged an ugly necklace. And Binks…if he hadn't gotten shot, would he have died as well because he'd been sentimental and wanted to honor a friend's memory? The idea pissed me off, and I hadn't even known Binks.

There were people who deserved to die and deserved to die horribly. Karen and Chad hadn't quite made that category. And it bothered me that the necklace might kill other, far more innocent people.

Damn it all. I had enough to do. I didn't have time to hunt down this fucking necklace—especially if it wasn't truly cursed.

But I was the queen of procrastination, so necklace hunting it was. At least until lunchtime, then I was going to need to put on my big girl panties and deal with my own problems.

CHAPTER 15

BC Pawn was smaller than Bags's shop and considerably darker inside. Judging from the displays, they dealt more in jewelry and estate antiques than the practical stuff Bags sold. I walked past cases of watches, engagement rings, and one that was filled entirely with crucifix pendants of varying sizes and styles.

A voice came from under the counter near the back of the shop. "I'll be there in a sec. Just stacking the silver."

I walked over there and bent down to look, curious exactly what sort of silver the man was stacking. They were spoons—thick, heavy silver spoons with ornate handles. We both stood at the same time and a middle-aged balding man smiled at me, round wire-rimmed glasses over light blue eyes.

"What can I help you with?" He took in my attire. "You've got something to salvage?"

"I'm trying to track down a necklace I think you might have sold three or four days ago." I held up a hand to stop his protest. "It was a legitimate buy and sale. I'm not claiming it was stolen or anything. I just want to know who brought it in for sale, who purchased it, and the dates of the transactions. That's it."

"Customer records are confidential unless you've got a warrant." The man's smile vanished. His hand slid out of view. I was willing to bet he was gripping a pistol right now. Trying to calm him down, I put my palms flat on the counter.

"They're all dead. The seller is dead. The buyer is dead. The pawnbroker who did the transactions is dead."

He paled and took a step back, pistol visible in his hand. "You…you killed Slinky?"

I held very still, both hands still on the counter. "No. I had nothing to do with it. I think he and the other people might have died because of a cursed object. I want to see if you had a necklace in here, if a woman named Amy Schell pawned it, and if a Gray Dog named Binks bought it."

"A necklace?" The guy kept the pistol trained on me. "You think a cursed necklace killed Slinky?"

"Maybe. It's the only thing that makes sense." I held up my hands. "If you confirm that it came through here, that an Amy Schell pawned it and Binks bought it, if you've got a picture or some way to confirm what it looks like, that would be helpful as well."

He eyed me, gun steady as it pointed at my chest. "You're a mage? I thought you were a Vulture."

"I *am* a Vulture. But there are reasons why this is important to me. I swear I'm not here to harm you. I just want to get information about the necklace. If it's cursed and killing people, then I need to track it down." I'd also need to find out who made it and try to determine how the curse worked and if there was a way to neutralize it, but that might be more than I could squeeze in today.

After a few tense seconds, the man nodded and lowered the pistol. "She was a friend of yours? The woman who sold it and died? This Amy Schell?"

"No, but if I'm right, this thing could end up killing a whole lot of people. Can you help me?"

He put the pistol back under the counter and walked over to a computer. "Do you have any idea what day it might have come through here? We get a lot of jewelry, and it would take me forever to search unless I have a date."

"I'm guessing three or four days ago, but it could have been any time in the last week." I thought of when Rene Schell, the woman from the morgue, had died. "Ten days ago, at the most."

I doubted her sister had run right down to the pawnshop the same day, but what did I know? Some families weren't the sort that mourned when one of their own died.

The guy looked up from the computer and sighed. "That's gonna take forever. You might want to come back tomorrow."

I didn't have until tomorrow. Karen and Chad might not have until tomorrow. Hell, I might be locked in some demon's dungeon by tomorrow.

"Maybe you'll remember it. It was this big, heavy gold chain with an equally big, gold dragon pendant on it. The dragon had rubies in its eyes. It was really ugly."

"Wait, I do remember that thing!" He typed something into the computer. "I told Slinky we should take it to one of those pay-by-the-weight places and have it melted down because no one was going to buy something that ugly. He insisted we keep it for a few months, thinking a gang member with more flash than taste might pick it up. He was right. Thing sold within the week. Here. Look."

He turned the computer screen around, and there it was —the same ugly necklace I'd seen two days ago around Binks's dead body, and the same one that was adorning Dragon's corpse in the gruesome photo Juke had given me.

"We processed the sale to us seven days ago from an Amy

Schell. Sold it three days ago to John Doe."

I wrinkled my nose. "John Doe?"

The man shrugged. "That's the name we use when buyers want discretion. Got a fake driver's license number we use and all. John Doe buys a lot of stuff from here."

"Any idea who this John Doe really was?" I asked.

He smiled. "A Gray Dog member known as Binks. He and Slinky did a lot of business together. I think they even shared a beer now and then. Slinky puts a little code down here in the memo section so we know who each John Doe is. You're a Vulture. You know how these things go. It's all to keep transactions away from the tax demons."

Yeah, I knew all about that. And I knew how it could come back to bite someone in the ass, even if it wasn't their illegal doings.

The necklace matched. From Dragon to the morgue. From the morgue employee's sister to the pawnshop. From the pawnshop to Binks. Demon-schemon. This was a cursed object, and I was willing to bet Dragon was the original target. Name like Dragon? Gaudy necklace with a Dragon on it? Someone gave it to him—someone who wanted him dead. And the rest of the people were collateral damage.

I wondered if the mage who created this or the person who'd commissioned it had any idea the necklace was still killing? If they knew, if they didn't care, then that person was just as bad as a demon.

"Do you know if your boss wore the necklace at all? Maybe put it on for a joke before sticking it back in the display cabinet?"

I needed to know if just touching the necklace triggered the curse or not. And if it had to be worn, how long did a person need to have it around their neck for the curse to take effect?

The next question would be how long after triggering the

curse did someone have before they went all boneless. I looked at the date Binks bought the thing and made the assumption he'd put it on right away—probably before he even left the store. He'd been shot three days later with all his bones still intact, so the curse had to take longer than that.

Then I looked at the date Morgue Girl's sister sold the necklace and remembered when she'd been found dead and boneless. Four days had passed between the two events. That meant once the spell was set, taking the necklace off and even selling it didn't negate the curse.

"We've got video," the man told me. "Hang on. I'll pull it up."

He scrolled to the appropriate day, and I watched the morgue attendant's sister come into the store, looking very different from her gruesome crime scene photo. After some chatting and some flirting, she walked away with cash and the pawnbroker fingered the necklace.

He cleaned it, tagged it, went to put it in the display case, then paused. Then, with an impulse that most likely cost him his life, he draped the necklace over his head and looked in the mirror. With a laugh, he took it off and put it in the case.

How many of the others had done the same thing? According to Sebastian, Dragon had really loved the stupid necklace, and Binks had actually worn it as well. But the gaudy hunk of gold probably wasn't something either two women or the pawnbroker would have hung around their necks for more than a few seconds of amusement.

Put it on for a heartbeat, and you'd be dead in five days. I felt cold at the realization.

"I touched it." The man paused the video with shaking hands. "I straightened the cabinet and remember moving it aside to clean the glass. Do you think...?"

"When?"

He glanced at a calendar hung behind him on a wall. "It

was before Slinky died. Seven days ago? Yeah, seven. I was cleaning the cases right after that thing came in."

Seven days. From the timeline, it seemed the others were dead within five. If I were a mage, I wouldn't want everyone who brushed up against the thing to get the curse. But then again, if I were a mage, I would have fixed the fucking thing so it didn't kill every single person who draped it over their head for a quick gag, either.

"I think you'd already be dead if just touching it activated the curse." I pointed to the frozen video on the screen. "Your boss put it on. I'm willing to bet the woman who sold it did the same, as a joke. Her sister probably did the same."

"And the guy who bought it is dead? That was only three or four days ago." The man went to the video for that day, and I watched Binks and the pawnbroker negotiate the sale. Sure enough, Binks put the necklace on before he'd even handed over the cash and probably never took it off.

"Yeah. He's dead, too." I didn't bother to tell him Binks had died in a shootout before the necklace had a chance to do its thing. Which was a far better way to die, by my reckoning.

I needed to track this thing down. I was certain Karen and Chad hadn't left any item of value on Binks's body. Besides, if the Gray Dog had been brought home still wearing the necklace, Sebastian would have let that slip. No, I was pretty sure Karen and Chad either still had it or had sold it.

Hopefully they were still alive, because I needed to find that necklace. But before I panicked Karen and Chad with the news that they were most likely going to be dead in a few days, I needed to try to find the mage who'd made this thing and hope he had a way to reverse the curse or some sort of antidote.

And there was only one person I knew who had some

connections in the magical community, who might know a mage skilled enough to apply a curse to an ugly necklace —Alfie.

* * *

"MANY HUMANS PRACTICE MAGIC. They don't all buy books from my store." Alfie lifted a shoulder. "I don't know them all, and I don't know the particularities of their magic."

The bookseller had transitioned from a helpful purveyor of information to tight-lipped the moment I'd mentioned the necklace. I wasn't sure if that was a cue to slip him a twenty, or if he needed added incentive to talk.

I set my backpack on the floor, pulled out the envelope, and spread the photos across his counter, hoping that would be enough incentive.

"Put those things away," he hissed, glancing around at the other customers.

"Take a good look, Alfie. That's what this thing does. Aren't you worried that it might end up in your store? In the hands of your family or friends?"

He scooped the photos into a pile and turned them face-down. "You think I'm without protective amulets and magical security? I sell more than just books here, and I know to be careful. I'm not scared of cursed objects."

Alfie dealt in information, and he'd always been happy to help me in the past. There had to be a reason this information wasn't for sale. His store carried spellbooks. I was guessing the mage was a customer, and that's why Alfie didn't want to rat him out.

I changed tactics.

"It's killing random people. The police are on the trail and where they might be willing to turn a blind eye on a Gray Dog being magically assassinated, they're going to go after this guy for the deaths of two women and a pawnbroker. One shot from an anti-magic gun, and they'll have this guy in cuffs. He'll be in jail without his spellbooks or ingredients, maybe in a special cell where his magic won't work."

Alfie glanced over to his cell phone, and I knew he was itching to call his customer and tell him to get out of town.

"Me, I don't care about arresting a mage and locking him up for life. I'm sure this was a terrible mistake, and that he never intended for those other people to die. If I can get the cursed item off the streets and secure some type of antidote to keep others from dying, then this whole thing gets swept under the rug."

Alfie frowned down at the photos. "Four people are dead."

"Demons," I announced. "The Gray Dogs are convinced these gruesome deaths were the work of a demon. Who else but a demon would kill someone by dissolving their bones? Who else but a demon would dare kill a Gray Dog, then merrily go around on a three-week spree doing the same thing to three other people?"

"The police won't arrest a demon." Alfie exhaled slowly. "They'll complain to the human politicians about it, but that'll be the end of it."

"Yep." I picked up the photos and put them back into the envelope and my backpack. "But if the killings keep on happening, and the police find out it's a cursed object and not a demon…"

Alfie reached under the counter and produced a business card. "Here. I didn't send you. You got this from someone else south of L.A. And you owe me a favor."

Not going to happen. "Nope. If anything, you owe *me* a favor. I'm going to keep your mage buddy out of jail."

Alfie laughed. "He's not that good of a friend. Okay. We're even on this one."

I took the card and headed to my bike, nervous about

what I hadn't encountered today. Where were the Fixers? The mercenaries?

I hadn't been attacked since last night, and that made me more uneasy than usual. Navy SEAL Guy had been on me like a damned glue trap yesterday. The cops would have released him within an hour or so of his arrest, and I'd expected him to have come at me by now. Had he believed me when I'd told him about the cop who'd set me up? Was he too busy tracking her down to bother about me right now? The idea gave me mixed feelings. As relieved as I'd be to have him off my ass, I didn't want him getting to the cop, and the loot, before I could.

And that didn't explain why I hadn't had any attempts by any other mercenaries today. I was pretty sure Bishop had killed the guys who'd ambushed me last night, but surely there would have been more tempted by the increased bounty. If those guys had the balls to try and grab me outside of Suerte, then surely they wouldn't have hesitated to ambush me outside of the Gray Dog's clubhouse or even here at the pawnshop. *Someone* should have made a move on me by now.

I rolled the card between my fingers, then looked down at the address. Mathias's Magics and Oddities. Encino. That was Gray Dogs territory and less than an hour away. I still needed to meet Telaney downtown tonight. Did I have time to do this?

I weighed the risks. If I put this off until tomorrow and the necklace killed Chad and Karen, I wouldn't be able to push this off as some crazed demon murder spree. Juke wasn't an idiot. She'd connect the dots, especially if either Chad or Karen were brought into the morgue with the jewelry still around their neck. If I was going to keep my word to Alfie and lie to the police about the cause of the deaths, then I needed to take care of this now.

CHAPTER 16

*M*athias's Magics and Oddities stood out compared to the adjacent shops. It didn't have bullet holes riddling its concrete façade or duct tape and plywood holding the windows together. That was probably because of the swooshy red and black tag painted beside the door that proclaimed the shop was under the protection of the Gray Dogs gang. Inside, the air smelled of freshly sanded wood, dried herbs, and buttered popcorn. A good-looking man sat on a stool by the back counter. His black hair was shaved around the sides and back, a short dark fuzz on top. What he lacked on his skull was more than made up for by the shiny curls of beard hanging at least three inches from his jaw and chin. The facial hair glistened with product and was so sharply edged it looked as if he'd trimmed it using a ruler. I'd seen women in Beverly Hills take less time on their hair than this man must spend on his beard.

"Can I help you?" Cheerful brown eyes met mine as the man slid a bowl of popcorn behind a rack of drying herbs.

"Are you Mathias?" The guy didn't exactly scream sorcerer at me, but what did I know?

"He's in the back." The man spun on his stool. "Matty! Customer for you!"

The man that appeared from the back room didn't exactly scream sorcerer, either. No robe. No busy eyebrows. No staff clenched in a gnarled hand. Mathias had long, light brown hair pulled back from a receding hairline into a low ponytail. He wore jeans and a wrinkled tan T-shirt. His blue eyes were kind, and the fingers he wiped on a rag were long and elegant.

"What can I do for you?" He smiled, a hint of a dimple creasing his right cheek.

"I need to know if you made this necklace." I slapped the crime scene photo of Dragon down on the table. Both men looked at it, neither one flinching at the gruesome image.

"I'm not a jeweler." Mathias pushed the photo away. "You've got the wrong store."

"I'm not looking for the jeweler that made the necklace. I'm looking for the mage that enchanted it."

The other man tensed, but Mathias just shrugged. "Tell me what it does, and I'll let you know if I can replicate the spell on something more aesthetically pleasing."

"*This* is what it does." I pushed the picture back toward him, then added the others one at a time on top. "And this. And this. And this. The only reason it didn't kill a fifth guy was because he got shot before the curse took effect."

His eyebrows came together as he picked up the photos and shuffled through them. "This…four people? That's… that's not right."

I should have been pissed that he'd been such a shitty mage he'd not realized the spell he was casting wasn't a one-time-only thing, but instead I was relieved. Mathias may be a murderer, but he wasn't shrugging the other deaths off. From the expression on his face, he was truly disturbed that people besides Dragon had died.

"Four people. And it's going to go on killing people if I can't find a way to stop the curse. I've got a good idea where the necklace is right now, or if they sold it. I might be able to quickly track it down. But that's not going to do any good if I don't know how the curse works and how to stop it from killing someone after the spell is activated."

Mathias hesitated. The other man shot him a worried glance and stepped closer.

"The police are looking into the deaths," I went on. "They have me asking around the Gray Dogs to see if any of them know who might be responsible." I watched as the two men tensed, not from my comment about the police, but about my mentioning the Gray Dogs. "Right now, the Gray Dogs believe a demon did it. The police might end up believing a demon did it as well. But that's not going to hold up if more people die like this."

I let the implications of what I'd said settle between us for a moment.

"I know you did it. And that stays with me unless other people die. Help me stop this thing. Help me save some lives here."

"Matty, we can't let innocent people die," the other man said. "People who just have bad taste in jewelry, or picked it up as a joke, or are just doing their business? Those are innocent people like you and me."

The mage seemed to be wrestling with something for a few seconds. I waited, and finally, he nodded. "No one else knows?"

"There's a pawnbroker who thinks the necklace might be cursed, and I may have to tell the people who have it now to get them to give it up, but that's it. No one will ever get your name from me, I swear it. And the police and the Gray Dogs will go on thinking this was some demon on a rampage."

"I'm the mage that enchanted the necklace," Mathias

finally admitted. "It was only supposed to work once, then just go back to being a plain old gaudy piece of jewelry. I didn't make the jewelry myself. It was something I picked up at a pawnshop. Maybe that's why the spell went awry. There might have been some alloy in the gold that screwed up the spell."

The other man put a hand on Mathias's shoulder. "It was the ugliest necklace I'd ever seen. But hey, dragon? For a guy named Dragon? Stupid idiot loved the thing. It was perfect for the job."

"So, you placed the curse on the necklace." I waited for Mathias's nod. "And this is what it was supposed to do? Dissolve someone's bones? That wasn't an accidental side effect or a mistake?"

Clearly, there was a whole lot I didn't understand about magic.

"Yeah, it was supposed to do that. I know it sounds horrible, but I needed to have it kill him in a way that wouldn't be traced back to the necklace or to me. I wanted something dramatic and kinda gross—something a demon might get blamed for," Mathias said.

Well, boneless dead certainly was gross, and the Gray Dogs *had* blamed a demon for the murder. It was a smart move. Outside of Sebastian's posturing, the gang wasn't going to try to hunt down a demon, especially one who could kill like this. And the cops wouldn't normally care about a gang murder. They probably never would have pursued it if it hadn't been for the other deaths.

"That asshole already *was* boneless," the bearded man said defensively. "The necklace just made him physically boneless. I thought it was brilliant."

"Israel." Mathias turned to the other man. "Can you go check on the kiln? And take that popcorn with you, please. I need to talk to this woman in private for a moment."

Israel's gaze darted back and forth between me and Mathias. He picked up the bowl of popcorn, then scowled at me before heading into the back room. I read that scowl loud and clear. If he returned and there was so much as a papercut on Mathias, I'd find myself with Israel's fist in my face.

Mathias watched him go with a fond expression, then, shaking his head, he turned back to me. "I don't know who hired you to find me—I'm assuming a relative of one of these other dead people. I swear to you that the curse wasn't supposed to do this. It was only supposed to kill once, and only the person wearing it. I made sure the target had put the necklace on before he left my store. If he'd taken it off and given it to someone else to wear, it shouldn't have mattered. Five days after he put it on, he was supposed to die. Anyone else who wore it would be fine, except for their questionable fashion sense."

"I'm not a private investigator. I'm a Vulture," I told Mathias. "And clearly something went wrong with the spell because these photos aren't just random boneless dead people. They each had contact with the necklace. I'm assuming they each put it on, but I can't rule out that the necklace isn't cursing people who have a certain amount of physical contact with it."

"That wasn't supposed to happen," he repeated. "It was just supposed to be the one guy. We pay good money to the Gray Dogs. Weekly. In return, they're supposed to ensure we don't get vandalized, and if someone robs us, that someone pays. Dragon was our contact, the guy in charge of protecting our store. We got robbed four months ago, and he declined to do anything about it. Basically, he was too scared to go after the guy, but we were still supposed to continue paying protection money to him and the gang."

"So, you murdered him?" It was a legitimate beef but killing over it seemed a bit extreme.

"It wasn't just that." Mathias glanced toward the back room. "Look, I don't normally produce things like this. Dragon wouldn't help us. He wouldn't provide a service we've been paying for two years now. A demon robbed us, and he wouldn't do a damned thing about it. We got into a shouting match. That night, three Gray Dogs jumped Israel coming out of the store and beat the crap out of him."

I winced, knowing where this was going.

"Dragon doubled what we have to pay for protection and threatened to kill Israel if we didn't pay the new amount. I spent months on that spell, then called a meeting with Dragon to calm him down and smooth things over. I gave him the necklace, saying it was a goodwill gesture, to thank him for all he's done for us and to keep him from knifing Israel." A hard gleam shone in the sorcerer's blue eyes. "No one harms my husband. No one. The bastard deserved what he got."

"And these people deserved what they got too?" I pointed to the other crime scene photos.

Mathias winced. "It was a one-time curse. It shouldn't have done that. They shouldn't have died."

"They *did*, though. Dragon ends up dead and boneless. This woman from the M.E.'s office stole the necklace, and she winds up the same way. Her sister goes through her effects and takes the necklace in to a local pawnbroker to sell. Less than a week later, they're both dead and boneless." I looked up at him. "There's more. The pawnbroker must have sold it to another Gray Dog member, but he got shot before the curse took effect, because I saw the body, still with all its bones, on the street two days ago. I got run off by two other Vultures before I could salvage the necklace. Lucky for me. Not lucky for the other two Vultures."

Mathias shook his head. "I swear I only spelled it for the

one death. I figured Dragon might pawn it or give it to someone, and I didn't want innocent people to die."

"Well, innocent people have died. And they'll continue to die unless you help me do something." I leaned over the counter. "I've got a good idea where the necklace might be, but I need your help in safely collecting and disposing of it and reversing the spell on anyone else who might have been cursed."

He ran a hand along the top of his head and sighed. "I'll pay a buyback fee if you retrieve it for me. It's ugly as sin and not worth more than the metal, but I'll pay a fair price for it."

"First, I have to find it. And before I find it, I need to know exactly how it works and if there's an antidote or not."

He nodded, then sat on the stool that Israel had vacated. "The curse is activated by someone putting it on—even for just a quick second. They'll die five days later. Doesn't matter if they still have the necklace or are still wearing it. Put it on, and it's a done deal. Cursed. And eventually dead. But I structured the spell to only hold *one* curse. Just one. If it's killed other people, then I'm not one hundred percent positive that the rest of the curse parameters held."

"So, it might be activated by touch? Skin to the object? Or if someone just carries it around in their pocket?"

He held out his hands. "It's not supposed to, but right now I can't guarantee that's not the case."

Great. "And an antidote?"

He hesitated.

"There are two Vultures in possession of the necklace. It's been two days since they salvaged it. I need an antidote, or they're going to die, and if they or anyone else dies, then all bets are off. The police are coming to haul you away—if the Gray Dogs don't get to you first. There will be a trail even a fool could follow. Every new person who dies means it's less believable that a demon did this—especially when the necklace is clearly an item that connects them all."

"Okay, okay." He got up and came around the counter. "I did create an antidote. I was afraid that Dragon would make Israel or me put it on first. That would have sucked, because not only would one of us have been cursed, but Dragon wouldn't have, since it was only supposed to kill one person. Turns out, Dragon wasn't that smart. He slapped that thing right around his neck and clearly didn't take it off. Probably showered with it on."

"Probably," I agreed, following him over to a wall of herbs and spices.

"The antidote is a simple herb. It has to be brewed fresh and drank right away for it to take effect." He pulled a plastic packet off a hook and handed it to me.

"Tea?" I stared in disbelief at the exact same stuff the girls, Bea, and I had enjoyed the other night.

"Herb-a-licious Teas is Israel's company." Mathias took a second packet down. "He blends everything himself and sells on consignment through small groceries and other shops. He used to make a good living at it before the demons came, back when the tourist trade was more happening."

"Israel is a mage, too?" And he was selling magic antidote tea at three bucks a packet? Wow, business really must be off.

"No." Mathias chuckled. "But there's magic in everyday items as well as everyday people, just waiting to be released. That's why mages use stones and herbs and wood. They're focus items. They release the magic we all hold inside of us, if we know how to properly use them."

"So, you magicked Israel's tea?" I was so confused over how all of this worked.

"I crafted the curse so it could be broken by a lavender tisane. Plain salt can contain and disrupt magical spells. Certain stones, woods, and herbs do the same, but they're more specific in what they counteract." He held the second packet out to me. "Plain old lavender tea will do, but this has a very soothing mixture of flavors. Israel's good at herbs and spice mixes. It's actually how we met."

Both packets went into one of my pants pockets. I believed Mathias. He didn't have any reason to lie. Even though the curse hadn't gone quite as he'd planned, I could tell he was a smart enough mage to have made plans to safeguard himself and his partner in case things went wrong.

"I need to know everything I can about the cursed object and how it works. Can I pick it up with a stick and put it into a bag? Like it was a rattlesnake? Or use gloves? Or hot dog tongs?"

Mathias slowly shook his head. "I don't know. Like I said, it's only *supposed* to trigger when someone puts the necklace on, but it also was only supposed to kill one person, so I'm not one hundred percent positive anymore."

Great. I hoped this tea worked. "And it works on everyone? Demons? Shifters? Elves? Humans with magical abilities?"

"I didn't specify humans only when I crafted the curse. Dragon seemed human, but you never know these days. He could have been a shifter, or part demon, or all demon and just really good at hiding it. I didn't want to take any chances."

There went my hope that my strange magical ability might shield me from the curse.

"Of course, demons regenerate." He held up both hands. "I don't know if they could regenerate fast enough to overcome the curse, or if being boneless would even kill a demon. I was pretty sure a shifter wouldn't be able to heal fast enough to live, but with demons, I wasn't positive."

I picked up the photos and put them back into my backpack. Glancing around the shop at the supplies and ready-made charms, I thought of the woman in Alfie's bookstore buying the grimoire. "Do you give lessons or anything? Take on apprentices?"

Mathias snorted. "Few people have sufficient natural magical ability to do more than a few easy charms or spells, and I don't have time to mess around with amateurs."

I hesitated. "But if someone had some ability? Such as minor telekinesis? An elemental affinity?"

"Then I'd tell them to get a basic spellbook and come see me when they've got at least six charms and two illusion spells under their belt."

I left, wondering how much Alfie would charge me for a basic spellbook. I probably wouldn't have enough spare cash for something like that, given my current circumstances, but the idea that I might be able to expand my magical abilities was tempting. How long would it take me to learn six charms and two illusion spells? Was my time better spent studying that or learning karate or something?

And who was I kidding? I didn't have time to study and learn magic. Maybe if I managed to pay off all the debts I owed, then I could play around with chalk sigils and a cauldron of herbs.

But until then, I'd just have to stick with the magic I knew.

CHAPTER 17

Finding Chad and Karen wasn't all that difficult. The husband-and-wife team typically worked together, but even on days where they split up to maximize their take, they still met for lunch. Every day. At the exact same place in Burbank.

I pulled into the parking lot of Salsa and Beer, went inside, and easily found Chad and Karen in the same back booth they always used, the usual chicken flautas with extra guac on their table. I made a mental note to grab some carnitas molcajete before I left, then approached the table with my hands held up, palms up.

Predictably, Karen and Chad both went for their guns. Other customers dived under their tables. The manager yanked a shotgun from behind the bar and shouted at us to take it outside.

I stopped, hands still out. "I'm not here to cause any trouble. I just need to talk to you both about that salvage a few days ago."

Karen waved her pistol at me. I started to sweat because, as usual, the woman was not practicing good trigger safety.

"You were trespassing." Chad grabbed his fork in the other hand and pointed it at me along with his pistol.

Normally, I would have been more worried about the fork, but Karen had managed to shoot me the other day. The way my luck was going, Chad would probably blow my head off by accident.

"That salvage was in our territory," Karen added. "Your license is suspended. You had no right to be poaching on our take."

Technically, there were no territories with Vultures, but she was right about my license.

"I'm not arguing about that. I just need to find that necklace the guy was wearing—the big gold one with the dragon pendant."

"You have no right to any of that salvage." Karen nearly knocked over her margarita waving her pistol around. "It was ours. All of it was ours."

"Put the guns down or I'm opening fire," the manager yelled. A few of the customers were crawling for the door, one of them holding a plate of enchiladas. I was tempted to just walk out myself and leave Karen and Chad to their fates.

"The necklace is cursed. It's killed four people, and it would have killed that guy if he hadn't gotten shot. I'm not here because I'm trying to steal your salvage; I'm here trying to save your sorry-ass lives."

Karen and Chad exchanged a glance, and their pistols lowered.

"You're lying." Chad's voice shook. "You just want the necklace. It's ugly, but it's probably worth a few hundred in scrap."

I let out a breath, relieved that they hadn't sold it yet. "I'm not lying. I've got photos the police gave me of the victims. I've got to get it off the street before it kills more people."

Karen frowned. "What do you care if other people die? What do you care if *we* die?"

That really was the question of the day. It wasn't just that I worried one of my friends or family might somehow come across the necklace and die horribly. I didn't want *any* innocent people to die. Hell, I didn't even want assholes like Chad and Karen to die. We now lived in a world where survival came first, and if that meant someone else had to die for me or my family to stay alive, then so be it. I'd always been okay with that philosophy even before the demons came. Innocent people died every day. Shit happened. It wasn't my responsibility to save these two Vultures or random people I didn't even know. I shouldn't care.

But I did. And that felt…weird.

"I'm taking some pictures out," I told them as I lowered my hands and slid the backpack down to the floor. In clear view, I unzipped the top, pulled the envelope out, and passed it to Chad. "This is what the necklace does to people."

Chad slid the photos out and gasped as he spread them across the table. Karen gagged and covered her mouth.

"That's what the curse does," I repeated as I pointed at the pictures. "Put the necklace on and five days later, that's your fate."

Karen's gag turned into a sob. "Put them away. Put the pictures away. I don't want to see them."

Chad somberly did as she asked, handing the envelope back to me. "Can it curse more than one person at a time? What if someone just touched it and didn't put it on?"

"I put it on, you asshole," Karen shouted at him. "Stop worrying about yourself and think about what's going to happen to me in…oh, God, in less than three days."

"Am I going to die too?" Chad ignored his wife. "Or am I okay? I just touched it taking it off the dead guy's neck, then Karen grabbed it. I only had it in my hands for a second."

These people were fucking horrible. Just horrible.

"Technically, it's only supposed to be activated if someone puts it on, but there's no guarantee even handling the necklace won't transfer the curse. And yes, it can curse several people at once. Two of the people that died had the curse only days apart from each other—and they died days apart from each other."

"Oh, God! Oh, God!" Karen wailed and burst into tears.

Chad, that dickwipe, didn't even make an attempt to console her.

"How do we know if we've been cursed?" Chad put his pistol on the table. "Are there certain symptoms? Would my hands feel funny? Numb? Tingly? I barely touched it."

Karen put her head in her hands. "I don't wanna die."

"Just don't do it in here," the manager said, still pointing the shotgun at us.

"I've got an antidote," I said, because Karen was on the edge of a panic attack. Not that I blamed her. I liked to think I was pretty tough, but the thought of dying that way would freak me out as well.

Both of them lunged forward. I jumped back, yanking my gun out of the shoulder harness. "I get the necklace first, then you get the antidote. For five hundred bucks," I added. Hey, I wasn't completely altruistic. They were assholes, and I did have to come up with fifteen grand in two days. Five hundred wasn't close to that, but at least it was a start.

"I'm not paying you five hundred bucks for some antidote." Chad scowled.

"Oh, yes you are," Karen snapped. "Deal. The necklace is yours as well as five hundred cash, as long as I get an antidote."

Perfect. I waited for a second, but neither of them produced the necklace. "So...where is it? The necklace, I mean."

Karen sniffed, wiping her eyes on a napkin. "It's in our house. Locked in our safe."

Chad turned to her. "I'm not taking her to our house. If she knows where we live, she'll come back and steal everything."

"I'm a Vulture, not a thief," I said, which was a lie. I'd stolen before, and I'd not hesitate to steal again, but I wasn't going to go breaking into people's houses to take stuff unless there was a good reason for it.

"Well, *I'm* not touching that thing again," Karen said. "And I'm pretty sure you're not, either. Someone's got to get it out of the safe. If neither of us is going to, then that leaves her."

Chad nodded. "Fine. She can follow us to the house. We'll change the locks afterward. And the combination on the safe."

It was normal to be paranoid, especially in these times, but this was ridiculous. I was surprised they didn't insist on blindfolding me and driving me there themselves, just so I wouldn't know the address.

I might as well have been blindfolded because Chad and Karen led me through a maze of streets all over the Valley. I'd talked the manager into throwing some tacos in a bag for me before we left. One of the downsides of having a motorcycle for transportation was that I couldn't really eat and drive. I hadn't eaten anything since the apple at Bishop's house, and my stomach was a knot of hunger at the thought of the tacos in my backpack. As soon as I wrapped stuff up with these two, I was going to shove them down as quick as I could, then head downtown to meet up with Telaney.

Finally, Chad and Karen pulled up to a cute hacienda-style home with rose-strewn wrought iron trellises and a four-foot reproduction of Michelangelo's *David* in the front yard. Judging from street signs I'd passed, we were west of Reseda. Maybe Canoga Park or Winnetka.

I parked my bike, waited for Chad and Karen to get out of their last-century BMW sedan, then followed them to the front door. Security cameras jutted out from the porch as well as each corner of the house. The static feel that I'd come to realize signaled the presence of magic hit me as I stepped over the cheery welcome mat and into the house.

Inside were more miniaturized Italian statues, white leather sofas, and a light gray rug that was striped with arrow-straight vacuum cleaner marks. Neither Chad nor Karen offered me a seat, so I stood awkwardly by a glass-topped hallway table, trying not to mess up the direction of the carpet pile.

Karen collapsed onto one of the sofas, staring at her hands as if she expected them to suddenly become limp and boneless. Chad swung aside a painting of a plump naked woman that was probably a reproduction of something famous. I found myself staring at the artwork of a reclining woman who held a bunch of flowers in one hand, the other hand covering her snatch. The expression on the model's face made her hand placement look less like an act of modesty and more like she'd been caught in the middle of masturbating and wasn't one bit embarrassed about it. In the background, a woman seemed to be digging around in a trunk while another looked on. Maybe they were trying to find a dildo for the main woman.

I was just wondering if it was a regular thing for servants to go fetch sex toys for their employers, when something beeped.

Chad's face appeared around from the back side of the painting. "I've got it open. You can come over here and take the necklace out. If you touch anything else, I'll shoot you."

"You can't shoot her until she gives us the antidote." Karen was twisting her hands together, feeling each one of her finger joints.

I ignored the implication that they were going to shoot me after I gave them the antidote and dug around in one of my pants pockets for a pair of surgical gloves I kept just in case a salvage job got really gross. Then I pulled out a small cloth bag. This was going to suck. I hoped Mathias hadn't lied to me about the antidote, because I was taking a huge risk here.

Chad stood back, and I rounded the painting. Behind the artwork was a good-sized wall safe with several shelves dividing the inside. One shelf held a metal box, the other had a stack of cash, and the bottom one held a tangle of jewelry. I heard the sound of a slide, of a round being chambered, and realized Chad wasn't joking about shooting me.

"I can't pull the necklace out without touching all this other crap," I argued.

Karen sucked in a sharp breath. "What if the curse transferred to the other jewelry? What if it's all cursed now?"

I doubted that was the case, or we'd be having boneless dead people in epidemic proportions. For weeks, the only people who'd died in this way had been linked to the necklace, not the shirts, coats, countertops, or other shit the necklace touched. But if Karen wanted me to take all the jewelry in this safe, just to err on the side of caution, I wasn't going to argue.

"No. The rest of the jewelry will be fine," Chad said before waving his pistol at me. "Just move the other stuff aside. I see anything go into that bag besides the cursed necklace, you're getting a bullet."

And with Chad's aim, there was no telling where that bullet might end up. Could be in the wall. Could be in my head.

With a careful index finger, I moved the jewelry around, pushing bracelets and earrings toward the back of the safe as I tried to untangle the mess of chains from each other. I finally ended up pulling them all out and sorting through them on the glass-topped table under Chad's watchful eye.

"There. One cursed necklace." I held it up, marveling once more at how amazingly ugly the thing was. I slid it into the bag, then stripped off my gloves and stuffed them into the bag as well, just in case.

It hadn't *felt* magic. Those tingly static sensations I got when I passed through magical security barriers were not present when I'd picked up the necklace. I wasn't sure if that was because this particular curse didn't work on me, or because it had been crafted with added stealth. That was something I'd need to figure out. This sucked. I liked reading, but studying had never been my thing. Here I needed to not only go through a giant book on demonology but find something akin to Magic 101. With nervous hands, I stuck the cloth bag into one of my pants pockets, then stepped away from the pile of other jewelry, pretty sure that if I picked it up to put it back in the safe, there was a good chance I'd get shot.

"Give me the antidote," Karen said, standing up and pulling her pistol out as well.

"Give me five hundred," I countered.

She waved the gun at her husband, and he pulled a wad of cash out of his pocket, counting out some bills.

"There. Three hundred. That's all I'm giving you," he said as he handed me the money.

This was getting old. "Look, assholes, I didn't have to come here and help you. I could have just waited for Karen to die and grabbed the necklace from whatever pawnshop or gold-for-cash place you took it to. Five hundred, or I'm walking."

I wasn't walking, but we'd agreed on five hundred, and it irked me that they were trying to talk me down at gunpoint.

"Let her have another two hundred," Karen screeched. "I'm not going to die over a few Benjamins."

"Fine." Chad counted out the rest of the money and handed it to me with a scowl. "Now give us the antidote. And if it's a fake, and Karen still dies, I'm hunting you down."

"Wait." Karen frowned, then glared at me. "What if she's lying? What if she made up the story of the curse just to get us to give her the necklace and some money?"

Idiots.

"Yeah, I'm really going to go to all this trouble for an ugly necklace worth a few hundred in scrap and five hundred bucks. I'm going to cook up an elaborate scheme complete with police photos of gruesome dead people—one of which is wearing the exact same necklace. Then I'm going to track you both down, take the chance that you might shoot me on sight, let you lead me into your home where no one would look for my body, just to get this piece-of-shit necklace and five hundred in cash." I gestured at their pistols. "There are a lot less dangerous ways to get money than this."

Chad considered my words, then nodded. "She's right. And we probably wouldn't have even gotten two hundred for that thing. Scrap prices have been crappy lately."

Karen sucked in a breath. "Then the antidote. I need the antidote."

I held up a hand and eased my backpack off my shoulders and onto the floor. "I have to get it out of here. Don't shoot me."

Holding my breath, I reached into a zippered section of the backpack and pulled one of the bags of tea out. Karen snatched it from my hand. I flinched as the muzzle of her pistol swept my body.

"Do we burn it, like a smudge stick?" she asked. "Smoke it in a pipe? Bathe in it?"

"Make it into a tea and drink it," I told her.

She looked at the label. "Herb-a-licious. Luscious Lavender. Is this a joke?"

"No, it's not a joke." I winced as she jabbed her pistol toward me. "I wouldn't joke with two people less than five feet away pointing guns at me. The mage who created this thing told me that lavender negates the curse."

"I read there's herbs and stuff in magic spells," Chad chimed in.

Karen glared at him. "You read that on the internet."

"Make the tea. Drink it. You'll be fine." I hoped she'd be fine, otherwise I'd have one more person gunning for me. And if Mathias had lied to me, then the police were going to be the least of his worries.

CHAPTER 18

I sat on Telaney's couch with my legs curled under me, counting money while she poured wine in some of the largest glasses I'd ever seen.

After being lectured about the state of my hair and my lack of a dress or makeup, Telaney had pulled a wad of black Lycra out of her backpack along with a hair tie and a makeup bag.

My friend was taller and thinner than me. The dress had fit…sorta. It had probably helped our salvaging that I looked like the dress had been painted on. Actually, it had probably helped more that Telaney's dress barely covered her ass. That woman's legs went for miles.

"What's the take?" She handed me a glass that held half the damned bottle.

"Twenty-eight hundred. And change."

She wrinkled her nose. "Damn. I was hoping there'd be more cash."

Me, too. We'd cut a deal where I got the cash, and she got the goods. She'd definitely got the better end of that bargain with a generator, two ARC welders, a big-ass diamond ring, and eight boxes of .45 bullets. The guy who helped us load the generator and welders into the back of Telaney's car had tried to pick her up. And failed.

I sighed and slid the cash into my backpack. Twenty-eight hundred. Plus the five hundred from Chad and Karen. That left only eleven thousand seven hundred left to go and under two days to find it.

Telaney sat across from me, stretching her long brown legs out in front of her. "I've got a few grand I can loan you. Maybe three or four if I can sell all that shit tomorrow."

I blinked back tears at her generosity. That would probably be everything she had, including her emergency slush fund. And I knew she wanted to keep that generator, not sell it.

"Thanks, but if I don't have the remaining amount, then three or four grand won't make any difference." I lifted my glass at her. "I appreciate it, but unless some miracle happens in the next day, I'm going to be kissing that demon's ass for the rest of my life. Or worse, if I miss a payment and have to beg for mercy."

I'd told my friend all about the visit to the tax office, and the bargain I'd made with that horned devil. She'd been sympathetic—more sympathetic than I'd ever imagined.

Telaney lifted her glass as well. "The offer's always open. In the meantime, you and I are having a girls' night in. Slumber party. Wine. Snacks. Neither of us is going to worry about the future."

I wished I could forget about the future. Taking a drink of my wine, I vowed to try—at least for tonight.

"Wow. This is good." I eyed the contents of my glass with respect.

"A salvage two months ago. Everyone else was running off with paintings and crap while I was raiding the wine cellar." Telaney's smile was smug. "Got two cases of red and one of white. Kept every damned bottle, too."

Hell, yeah. I took another sip, thinking that it had been ages since I'd had a decent wine. It had been ages since I'd had wine at all. Other than that half a beer I'd drunk at Suerte a few weeks ago, I couldn't remember the last alcoholic beverage I'd drunk.

"So." Telaney toyed with the stem of her wine glass. "When are you going to get your own place? There isn't anything available here right now, but I can keep an eye open in Los Feliz for you."

"I almost had a place in Los Feliz." I told Telaney about the house on Canyon Drive, about the weird brawl I'd had for the right to stay there, and how I'd luckily escaped without a mob trying to kill me.

"That sucks." She pulled another bottle of wine from a side table and set it between us. "You need your own place, Eden. That way you can date and live your own life."

"I'm happy with Bea and the girls." I was, but this last month I'd felt like my presence was putting them at risk. I loved my family, and that love gave someone else easy leverage over me. Maybe it would be better if I had my own place so it didn't seem like I was tied tightly enough to my family to make them a target.

"I know you love them, but you're a grown-ass woman." She waved a finger at me. "And a grown-ass woman deserves her own pad."

I finished off the contents of my wine glass. "Once I get this shit straightened out with the tax office. And pay off Bishop. Then maybe I can afford something of my own."

She shot me some serious side-eye. "So...Bishop?"

I felt my face heat up at the question she wasn't saying out loud. "Yeah. He's hot. He's dangerous. And if I pay him off, there's a chance he might actually sleep with me."

Telaney sighed, settling back into the cushions of the sofa. "Girl, you're in love with him."

"Lust," I corrected her.

"Love," she countered. "I know the difference. Trust me."

"So do I," I shot back. "He's got some scary unknown powers. He's grumpy. He looks like a surfer who's spent a lot of time at the gym. He's…"

He's there whenever I need him.

I eyed my empty wine glass and reached for the bottle, wondering if Telaney was right. I'd never really been in love before. There had been that brief intense relationship with Drew, but we'd been teenagers. Both of us were desperate to forge an emotional connection that we'd been deprived of our whole lives.

"Love." Telaney eyed her mostly full glass, then the one I was busy filling. "Girl, aren't you drunk?"

"No." I sat back with my wine and decided to be honest. "I metabolize alcohol in some weird way. I get buzzed. Sometimes I get a little tipsy. But in half a second, I'm sober as a judge." There had been that time I'd been pulled over after having three beers, and when the cops had breathalyzed me, I'd blown zero. Fucking zero. After three beers, it should have registered something, but they'd tried two different systems. It had registered zero both times. The second they'd pulled my car over, I'd gone stone cold sober.

"I think it might have something to do with my birth," I confessed, setting the wine bottle on the table between us. "I was a foundling baby. I had a lot of issues as an infant. They assumed I'd had Fetal Alcohol Syndrome. Maybe drugs, although I didn't seem to be going through withdrawal, and I didn't test positive for anything at the hospital."

Telaney's gaze met mine. "Eden…I'm so sorry."

I shrugged. "It is what it is. I avoided alcohol until I was about fifteen. Then I realized that it didn't affect me the same way it did other people. I still try to stick to beer and wine, just in case. I don't want…well, I don't want to take chances."

I didn't want to end up like my mother. She'd abandoned me. She'd left me naked in the fucking parking lot of a church. She'd probably been an alcoholic, but that would never excuse her actions in my mind.

"You're not your mother, Eden." Telaney took a drink of her wine. "Just like I'm not my father."

"He was that bad?" I whispered, not sure if I was jealous that she'd known her parents, or grateful that I hadn't gone through the pain she had.

"Yeah." She took another drink. "But Mom was amazing. I give thanks every day that she had the strength to leave him. We might have spent a few years in shelters, but that was better than living in fear every single day."

I'd never experienced that. Suddenly, I was grateful for all the foster parents who'd taken me in. I'd been a difficult child, but every one of them had done their best to care for me. From the moment those two women returning home from work had found me in the parking lot and called the police, I'd never been without food or shelter. And at thirteen when I'd been placed with Bea, she'd somehow gotten through all the defiance and self-isolation and reached my heart.

She'd taught me that I was worthy of love. And in return, I'd learned that I had it within me to love someone back. I was glad Telaney had experienced that with her own mother, just as I had with Bea.

My phone rang, and I glanced down, smiling at the name on the screen. Bags.

He was someone else I'd learned to love. He'd been a trusted work associate, then a friend, but now he was someone I'd trust with my life.

I waved to Telaney that I needed to take the call. "What's up?" I asked Bags.

"Got a tip you want to hear about. Are you somewhere you can talk?"

"Yeah, go ahead," I said. Telaney was another person I'd learned to trust. Even if she could piece together our conversation, I knew she'd keep my secrets.

"I put the word out with some of the other pawnbrokers that there might be an unlicensed individual trying to unload up to seventeen cases of bullets, and that there was a lot of scrutiny going on about this particular salvage."

That minotaur-demon had indicated as much. The tax office was keeping their eyes open for any hint that I—or whoever—was looking to move those bullets. And if Juke was looking into my claims, then the police would be watching as well. If that cop who'd set me up was smart, she would have sat on the stash until I'd been caught, and the heat had died down. Maybe she took a chance and moved a box or two here and there, but anything more would have gotten flagged.

But it had been three weeks. She had to be getting antsy about the whole thing. That was a lot of ammo to have just sitting around your apartment. It was bulky. It was heavy and not all that easy to grab and go if there was a problem. Getting the salvage converted into cash had to be a looming priority for her, especially if word had leaked through the police department that someone was looking into the matter. She had to be weighing the risks right now and thinking maybe it was time to unload this stuff and get the hell out of New Hell.

"Well, I got a bite. A pawnshop down in Torrance," Bags continued. "Old buddy of mine named Shavonne owns the place. She called a few minutes ago and said a couple came in looking to sell multiple cases of bullets. Indicated they were willing to deal as long as they could keep it under the table."

"How many cases?" I didn't dare hope it was the cop who'd set me up. It wasn't super rare for a Vulture to salvage a few cases of bullets, and I could believe a non-licensed person might have legitimately found or stole a few cases and be looking to unload them for cash without having to pay the tax man.

"At first, the couple were kinda vague-like about how much they actually had. Four, then six, then eight."

I caught my breath. "Eight's a lot."

It was, but this still might not be the woman I was looking for.

"Oh, it gets better. Shavonne said she didn't have the cash flow for that large of a deal but knew someone who did. She offered to broker the deal off-site for ten percent of the take. She also told them the buyer would take everything they had, and if they had access to more than eight cases, they'd deal with no questions asked."

That was believable. Gangs and militias were always on the lookout for ammo. If one of them was gearing up to snatch some territory, or knew they were going to have to defend themselves, they would absolutely put out a call among trusted pawnbrokers. And they would absolutely want the deal off the table. If anyone would be willing to face off against the tax demons, it would be a gang or militia.

Or Bishop. I'd pay good money to see him face off against that bull-demon from this afternoon. Or a whole room full of bull-demons.

"That's when they admitted they had seventeen cases in total they were looking to sell off the books. Shavonne told them she'd set up a meet-and-greet that included the sale of four cases, just to test the waters with the buyer before any larger deal went down. Then as soon as the couple left, she called me."

"I need to be in on this," I told him. "And I need to bring Juke in as well. I don't want anything happening without a police witness that I trust."

"I figured as much. Shavonne don't wanna be there, but she figures the couple will run if she's not, since it's supposed to be an intro and she's getting a cut. There needs to be a man as well to pose as the buyer, since that's what she told them. You and Juke will need to hold back somewhere, since if this is your cop, she'd probably recognize the both of you and know it's a setup."

"I'm sure Juke knows someone."

"If not, I'll do it," Bags said. "These two won't recognize me."

No, but Bags hardly looked the part. Not many of the gangs or militias tended to employ anyone over forty, but that might have changed. Besides, before the demons came, some of the big drug cartels had been run by guys north of sixty. But none of them would have personally appeared for an ammunition buy.

"I'll let you know," I promised, torn between my desire to keep Bags safely out of the way of what might end up being a firefight and wanting to respect that the guy knew how to handle himself in a bad situation.

"Meeting is tomorrow." He recited an address downtown. "Good luck, Eden. Let me know if you need my help. And you call me as soon as it's all over, got it? I need to know you're safe."

I smiled, my heart warmed because I felt the same way about him. "I promise."

"Did they find the cop? Are you in the clear?" Telaney asked excitedly as I put my phone down.

"Maybe. I'm pretty sure it's them. If not, then the detective I know will still grab them, and hopefully I'll score some points with the tax office." I toyed with my wine. "Even if it's them, I'm not off the hook. I made a deal, and the tax demons are still going to make me hold up my end of the deal, even if it's proven that I wasn't responsible for that salvage."

"That's fucking unfair," Telaney burst out.

I nodded. "Yeah. Life's unfair, though. I made a deal because I was in a tough spot and time was running out. Once I made that deal…well, it doesn't matter if the police reverse that record of my taking the salvage or even arrest that cop. It's an agreement, a contract."

Telaney grumbled something and leaned back against the couch cushions. "That's some world-class bullshit right there. If it doesn't make any difference, then why bother going tomorrow? Let your detective friend handle it and come do a job or two with me instead."

"Because I'm still hoping to get either the bullets or the cash." I took a sip of my wine. "That cop is my one hope to get enough money in the next forty-some hours to take the lesser of my agreed-upon deals with the tax demons. And if I can manage to find the entire seventeen cases? Or more than fifteen grand? Well, that's gonna make my family's life all that much easier."

It might even get them out of New Hell. I'd still owe Bishop, and favors to Desiree, and that bull-demon at the tax office, but once all that was done, maybe I could join Bea and the girls. And then we'd be free to live our lives.

"I want you to make your own life better, Eden." Telaney's eyes met mine. "You're a good person. You work so hard for your family. It's time for you to do something for you."

I thought about that for a second, thought about what I'd want if my family were safe, if the girls were going to school and both they and Bea had whatever they wanted to eat, hot showers every night, nice clothes and television and air conditioning because the damned electricity didn't turn off every six or seven hours. Where they didn't worry about Fixers breaking down the front door looking for me, or demons jacking off on the lawn and killing what little grass we had, or Hellkitty slicing through the screen and coming in through the window.

I'd have a place of my own. I'd keep salvaging, because I loved being a Vulture, but I wouldn't worry about trying to make ends meet with whatever I found. I'd come home and do my hair, put on makeup, slide into something sexy, and cook dinner for my man. Maybe he'd cook dinner for me.

Unbidden, the vision of that Canyon Drive house came to mind, Bishop across a candle-lit table from me, the lights of the city visible through the huge windows looking down on L.A.

"I will do something for me," I promised. "But I'd never be able to enjoy that unless my family was safe and comfortable. That's just how I roll."

She smiled and reached for the bottle of wine. "I know that's how you roll. And that's why I call you my friend."

CHAPTER 19

The banging had me up with my pistol in hand before I'd even registered that I was awake. Telaney had been moving seconds before me and was already at the door, one finger at her lips while the other hovered over the trigger of her 1911.

"Who is it?"

I had to cover my mouth and choke back a laugh at her saccharine sweet tone. Whoever was on the other side of the door was probably envisioning a fifties housewife wearing a crinoline skirt and preparing breakfast for her husband and two-point-five kids.

"I want to talk to Alvaro," a masculine voice shouted.

Hey. I recognized that voice. Navy SEAL Guy.

Telaney shot me a questioning glance, and I hesitated. Navy SEAL Guy didn't sound as if he were happy, but then again, he hadn't shot his way through one of the windows or kicked the door down. The man clearly knew I was here—which wasn't all that surprising, given the fact he seemed to track me down no matter where I was in the city.

"I'm coming out," I called back. "Let's not trash my friend's house, okay?"

"Fuck the house," Telaney told me. "If this bastard is going to try to bring you in, he's going to have to do it with half a dozen bullet holes in his head."

Which he might just be able to survive, given how quickly he'd recovered from Hellkitty's attack.

"I just want to talk," the man said. "I'll only start shooting if I need to defend myself."

This time, it was me sending Telaney the questioning look. She shrugged and started unlocking the door, keeping her pistol at the ready.

Navy SEAL Guy didn't appear to be any worse for wear after his probably brief stint in the police holding cell. He held up his hands, glancing from Telaney to me.

"Can I come in?"

"No." I kept my pistol steady. "Say what you need to say, then get out."

He nodded. "Fine. I believe what you said before. I found the cop that set you up. She and her partner are trying to unload the bullets through a pawnshop in Torrance."

"I already know all that." And I had no idea why he was coming to me with this information instead of going after the loot himself.

"I want in."

Telaney and I exchanged a puzzled glance.

"In the house?" I asked.

"No, in on the sting you're setting up. You've got something planned, and I want in. You *owe* me."

My mouth dropped open. "And just how the fuck do you think I owe you? Three times you've jumped me. You shot my friend at Bear State Pawn. You've tried to electrocute me and tranquilize me. You've cuffed me at gunpoint. I don't owe you shit. If anything, you owe me."

"You made me an offer yesterday. I'm here to accept."

I frowned, wondering what the hell he was talking about.

"You offered to split the loot—bullets or cash—if I worked with you to catch the cop who set you up," he explained.

I laughed. "Dude, that deal is off the table. I offered, and you refused. You were going to turn me in for the bounty, then go look for the cop solo. It's too late to accept now. I don't need you anymore."

He went to put his hands on his hips, only to jerk them up again when Telaney motioned at him with her pistol.

"You *do* need me. The tax office upped the bounty on you again. I've got first rights on an exclusive contract to take you in because of my record. If I accept, I'm the only one who's after you. If I don't, dozens of mercenaries are going to be on you like flies on shit." He grinned. "Think, Alvaro. I take the exclusive, and the heat's off. We'll work together to grab this cop, split the loot, and then go our separate ways. I don't make any attempts to bring you in for the bounty. I leave your family alone. Or you tell me no, and a mercenary is going to have you in cuffs and downtown before lunch."

Fucking demons. When I'd made the deal with Corundum, I'd assumed the contract on me would be pulled. I had forty-eight hours to bring him the money. Evidently that forty-eight hours wasn't considered a cease-fire as far as the bounty on my head went. Not only did I still have a contract out on me, the demons had upped the damned bounty.

I seriously needed to work on my negotiation skills. I hadn't closed up that loophole, and now it was biting me in my fine ass.

I let Telaney keep Navy SEAL Guy in line while I went into the kitchen to think and get a glass of water. Having a bunch of mercenaries nab me before this afternoon's sting went down would suck. Having a bunch of mercenaries blow my cover in the middle of the sting would suck. Teaming up with Navy SEAL Guy would suck as well. I hated that guy.

But if there was a time to keep my enemies close, this was it.

If some rogue mercenary tried to take me in, I could probably count on Navy SEAL Guy to help me out. He'd lose out on the bounty *and* lose out on half the take if I got nabbed out from under his nose. I'd need to watch him carefully. He'd absolutely try to double cross me if he got the chance—which meant I'd need to make sure he didn't get the chance.

I walked back into the living room. "Okay. You're in. It's all going down at noon today. You're going to pose as the buyer. Shavonne, the pawnbroker from Torrance, is brokering the deal between you and the cop and her partner. They're supposed to bring four cases to test the waters, with the promise that you'll buy everything they have if the deal goes smoothly."

He frowned. "Why only four cases? This is our one and only chance. They could have hidden the rest of the stash anywhere. If they don't bring everything for the deal, we'll lose our opportunity to get all seventeen cases."

"No one who's looking to buy serious quantities of ammo is going to go into that big of a deal with a stranger right off the bat," I explained. "She's a cop. You said it yourself that she's probably worked Vice in the past. She'll know how things are done. If we set this up for the whole batch, she'll be suspicious, and we'll either find ourselves at an ambush, or she'll back out."

"Then how the hell are we going to get the rest of the bullets? We're obviously not buying four cases from her. This afternoon is going to end with a bunch of dead people and us only with four cases of bullets." He snarled. "I'm not doing this just to split four cases. The bounty on you is worth more than that."

I shrugged. "We'll have to get creative. Make sure we don't kill her so we can let her lead us to the rest or search her house afterward. There are only so many places someone can hide seventeen cases of bullets. She's got to have them either in her home or her partner's, and I'm betting she's paranoid enough to want them right where she can keep an eye on them. Once we know who she is, finding out where she lives will be easy."

He glanced over at Telaney, then took a step backward, his hands still raised. "Fine. But if this goes to shit, or we can't find the rest of the stash, I'm keeping all four cases."

I nodded, knowing that if this went to shit, he'd also turn me in for the bounty. But what he didn't realize was that we wouldn't be the only two there with the pawnbroker. Juke would be there along with backup. She'd make sure this asshole didn't pull anything.

"Fine. We've got a deal." I grabbed a packet of sticky notes from a table and wrote down an address, giving the paper to Navy SEAL Guy. "Here. Meet me there at eleven, and we'll get set up and ready for the deal."

He looked down at the address, then nodded. "Screw me over, Alvaro, and you're a dead woman."

Yeah, yeah, yeah.

"And I want my stuff back." He glared at me.

I feigned innocence. "Stuff?"

"My pistol. I know I'm not getting the cash back, but I want my pistol. And…" He shifted his weight. "My rock."

"Rock?" Telaney snorted. "You took his engagement ring or something?"

"I already sold the pistol." I'd given it to Telaney last night, telling her to pawn it and keep half the cash for herself.

A muscle twitched in his jaw. "And the rock?"

I shot him an incredulous look. "Seriously? That blue rock? I tossed it. I'm not lugging around a worthless rock."

He paled. I swear the man looked like he was about ready to pass out. It was all I could do to keep from laughing. I had no idea how much that bit of magic had cost him, but I'm sure it was a good chunk of change. And from what Bishop had said, the teleportation thingy wouldn't work without the focus.

"You…bitch." His face contorted with the word.

I shrugged. "Does this mean our deal is off?"

He took a deep breath, visibly trying to calm down. "No. Just…do you have any idea where you threw the rock away?"

"In an empty lot a few blocks from where you tried to grab me. Why? It's just a plain old rock."

"It has sentimental value." Navy SEAL Guy looked down at the address again. "I'll meet you at eleven. This better end up with me in possession of eight and a half cases of bullets, Alvaro."

I nodded. "Oh, it will."

Telaney and I watched him go. My friend kept her pistol trained on him until he was out of sight.

Closing the door, she set the gun down and wiped her hands on her pajama pants. "You do know the police are probably going to grab those four cases when they arrest the cop, don't you?"

"I'm planning on grabbing them and running while the cops are busy with the arrest."

"And if that asshole grabs them first?"

I sighed. "Then the race will be on to find the rest of the bullets."

"And if the asshole gets them first as well?" Telaney grabbed the coffee pot and began to fill it with water.

"Then the race will be on for me to find the asshole and relieve him of his treasure." I grabbed two mugs from a cabinet. "I need to have fifteen grand to the tax office by four o'clock tomorrow. This is my only chance to get that much money by that deadline. I'm gonna make it happen."

"Even if it's over that asshole's dead body?" Telaney asked.

I thought about that a second. Navy SEAL Guy was a total dick. He'd turn me in for a bounty without a second thought. He'd kill me without a second thought. When he was cornered, he'd shot Bags without a second thought.

"Yeah. Even if it's over that asshole's dead body."

CHAPTER 20

I barely had time for a quick cup of coffee with Telaney before I needed to be heading back to the Valley and my meeting with Detective Juke.

As soon as I'd gotten off the phone with Bags last night, I'd called her and filled her in on what was going on. She'd been pissed—pissed that this was happening without enough time to truly plan out the operation and pissed that both me and a pawnbroker were going to be in the thick of things. If I had to hear one more time about how civilians had no place in a police operation, I was going to scream.

She was going to be even more pissed when she found out about Navy SEAL Guy.

I was totally in a "keep your enemies closer" mode here. The guy was a dick. I had no doubt he'd try to grab all the loot instead of the fifty percent we'd agreed upon, then he'd try to turn me in for the bounty as well. I didn't trust him—which is why I wanted him along on this little excursion.

Parking my bike in the pothole-strewn lot, I made my way back into Grits. Juke usually mixed it up a bit on our meeting places, but she must be on a food roll here. Luckily grits were just as good for breakfast as they were for lunch, and I ordered a small bacon and cheese with a Sunny Side Up egg on top. The server/cashier was just putting my bowl down when Juke came in.

We only had three hours until we assembled to get ready for the sting, but Juke still took the time to order some breakfast before she joined me at the table.

"Ugh. That's gross." She wrinkled her nose at my food.

"What? You're the one who chose this place."

"I mean the egg. It's raw. It's all slimy and stuff. How the hell can you eat that shit?"

I swirled the egg into my grits and took a big bite. "Mmm, good. Don't tell me you've never thrown a raw egg into the blender with your smoothie? Or drank eggnog?"

She shuddered.

"Besides, it *is* cooked." I took another bite. "Just not cooked all the way."

"That's still raw in my book." She pulled out a notepad. "I've got four officers coming in on this deal, including the guy from IA. My lieutenant is on board with the operation. If this bust doesn't go down, that raw egg is gonna be on my face."

"It's going down. Sitting on seventeen cases of bullets for three weeks has got to be killing this woman. It's not like you can hide that much ammo. It's probably stacked up in her living room or something. Plus, she's got to be getting nervous. She most likely knows I haven't been caught by the Fixers yet, and every day I'm free is one more day I might find her. She'll want to unload this stuff as fast as she can and get the hell out of there before she gets caught."

Juke nodded. "Here's how this is going to happen. You need to be out of sight, since there's a good chance she might recognize you. I'll stand in with the pawnbroker, and the rest of the officers will be acting as employees and guests in the hotel lobby. We're getting everyone out of there that we can in case this goes south, and bullets start flying."

"Actually." I squirmed in my chair. "There's someone else who needs to be front and center with you and the pawnbroker. Shavonne told the sellers that the buyer was a guy. I've got a mercenary who's going to pose as that buyer."

As predicted, Juke totally busted a gasket at the idea. Once she'd stopped shouting and waving her arms around, I let her know who Navy SEAL Guy was, and why he was ideal for this sort of thing.

"He's got magic. He's damned near impossible to kill. And honestly, if he gets killed, I'd throw a fucking party, so no loss there. He can talk the talk, and walk the walk, and he's motivated to keep this thing nonviolent. He won't want to kill your dirty cop or her partner."

Juke raised an eyebrow, ignoring the girl who put her grits down on the table in front of her. "Really? And why would this mercenary do that? What's his stake in this whole thing?"

"He wants the loot." I ate more of my grits, focusing on how good these things were for a few seconds. No wonder Juke kept wanting to meet here. Still not as good as Bea's, but definitely tasty.

"He wants the loot," Juke repeated with irony dripping from the words. "Imagine that. I'm sure you want the loot as well."

I swallowed, then patted my lips with a napkin. "Yeah. Honestly, I do. I went to the tax office yesterday and cut a deal. I need to come up with fifteen grand by tomorrow, or I'm going to be paying them for decades on time and doing work for them on the side. So yeah, I want loot. I want the loot to get my ass out of the sling."

Juke's eyebrows knitted together, and she ran a hand over

her bright red afro. "Eden...I'm so sorry. I got the okay to put a notation on the report last night. It's marked 'pending investigation.' They shouldn't be holding you responsible for this."

Fuck. If I'd just waited another day, then maybe I wouldn't have had to cut a deal after all. Then I thought of what Navy SEAL Guy had said this morning. Even with a deal, the demons still had a bounty out on me. A "pending investigation" note on the report probably wouldn't have changed anything. Hell, a deleted report might not have changed anything.

"You really agreed to pay the tax office fifteen grand?" Juke asked.

"More if I can't come up with the total amount by tomorrow. Plus, I still have to do some jobs for them." I shrugged. "I didn't have any other choice."

I really didn't feel all that casual about my situation, but I was done bitching about it. My energy would be better spent trying to come up with that fifteen grand. And if I didn't, well, option two was still better than dead.

"I can't guarantee you'll be able to keep the bullets they're bringing with them," she warned me. "And we'll get warrants to search their homes. If the bullets or money is there..."

The police would take it as well. I appreciated the heads-up. Juke was basically letting me know in her cop-speak that I needed to find a way to get this loot before the cops did—and before Navy SEAL Guy did.

We both ate, and I thought through the logistics. "I hope this is them. I mean, it's a possibility that there are other people out there trying to unload this amount of ammo. Someone else having exactly seventeen cases would be a weird coincidence, though."

"Oh, it's definitely the cop who set you up all right." She

pulled an eight-by-ten photo and slid it over to me. It was a grainy printout from a security camera, but I still recognized the woman—even without her SWAT gear on. "After I got off the phone with you last night, I called that pawnshop and had them send me this."

"It *is* her," I confirmed.

"It's not against the law to pawn stuff, and while an officer trying to sell several cases of ammunition is sketchy, she hasn't actually sold it yet," Juke pointed out. "We need this setup to work, or we won't have enough to arrest the pair of them."

"Even with the setup, *will* there be enough to arrest them?" As she'd said, pawning stuff wasn't against the law. Pawning multiple cases of ammunition without a Vulture license really only violated the tax code. While the demons there might be very interested in these two officers, in the eyes of human law enforcement, what they were doing amounted to a misdemeanor. Even if Juke could trace the ammunition back to the salvage and prove it was an illegal salvage and that the report had been falsified, the most that would probably happen would be these two losing their jobs.

They'd done so much harm to me and my family, and that was probably all that would happen to them. It made me furious, but I had to let it go. Fifteen grand. That was the deal I made, and I was determined to not lose sight of my one way out of this with as minimal pain and suffering as possible.

"It depends." Juke shrugged. "We'll arrest them. They'll be kicked off the force. The rest is up to the courts. But once we have them, we should definitely be able to delete that report saying you took the salvage."

Unfortunately, that wouldn't do any good at this point.

"Do you recognize them?" I asked her.

She nodded. "Yeah, although they're not from one of the

Valley districts. Chelsea Henneg has been an officer for three years, and Brett Bah, who has been an officer for six. Chelsea's partner was Conner Bah. He died just under a month ago—he's the one who supposedly filled out the report on you. Brian Bah is his brother. Both Henneg and Conner Bah work out of Hollenbeck. Henneg patrols El Sereno and Bah covered Lincoln Heights, so neither of them had any reason to be in North Hills that day. Brian Bah works in El Sereno. I'm assuming Henneg brought him in when Connor died. Either that, or the other Bah brother was in on it the whole time."

Chelsea Henneg. I finally knew her name. I finally knew where she patrolled. It would be easy to find out where she lived with that information. I'd do an internet search, and if that didn't reveal anything, I'd place a quick call to Alfie. If he couldn't come through for me, I'd turn to Bishop for help. Now that I had her name, knew who the heck she was, I could find her. I'd grab the four cases at noon, run them home, or to Bags's or Telaney's for safekeeping, then track this woman and the rest of the cases down.

This was another time when I was regretting my motorcycle. Hmm. I might need to call Bishop even if Alfie came through for me, just so I could use his truck to haul the stash.

"Did you ever talk to the Gray Dogs?" Juke asked. "Find anything out about those four boneless deaths?"

"Yeah. The Gray Dogs are convinced it was a demon." I felt the weight of the necklace, still in its bag in my pocket, and felt a twinge of guilt for the lie.

"All four?" Juke frowned. "Were they connected somehow? Did your contact recognize the morgue employee and her sister? And the pawnbroker?"

I shrugged. "He said they did a lot of business with that pawnbroker, so there's one connection. He didn't know the two women, though."

Juke ate a few bites of her grits, then narrowed her eyes. "I wonder if it had something to do with that necklace. Dragon had it on when they scooped him into the body bag and took him to the morgue, but it wasn't on the personal property report."

"Huh." Crap. I really didn't want Juke connecting the dots on this.

"Wouldn't be the first time something went missing off a body. I wonder if the morgue employee stole it? Maybe Dragon stole the necklace from a demon, then the demon went on a killing spree to track it down and take it back," Juke mused.

"Then why wouldn't the demon just take it off Dragon after he killed him?" I pointed out. "It's more likely that the morgue employee and her sister were involved in some scheme with Dragon and the pawnbroker, and that's why they were all killed."

I was so going to hell for this. Lying wasn't exactly a rare thing for me, but something felt really wrong about smirching the reputations of two innocent women. Well, one innocent woman. The morgue employee *had* stolen the necklace, so I shouldn't feel all that bad about making up a story about her being involved in criminal gang activity.

"True." Juke nudged her empty bowl aside. "Well, unless someone else turns up boneless and dead, I'm marking all four as a demon hit and closing the case. Hopefully, this demon is done killing for now, because no one up the chain of command is going to want to try to pursue a demon for murder."

I let out a slow breath and relaxed. Hopefully, Mathias was right about the tea, because if Karen's bones suddenly dissolved in the next two days, this whole thing would blow up in my face.

The detective pushed back her chair and stood. "I need to

get out of here. There's a lot I still need to do to get every-thing set up for this afternoon. Eleven o'clock, Alvaro. Don't be late."

"I won't," I promised her.

I wouldn't be late. In fact, I planned on being early.

CHAPTER 21

I wiped my sweaty palms down my pants and tried to see from my spot just inside the bar. Juke had insisted I stay out of the lobby. She'd insisted everyone stay out of the lobby except Shavonne, Navy SEAL Guy, and another cop who was mopping the same spot on the floor over and over. Juke was posing as a desk clerk with another cop by her side. Yet another was just outside the front door pretending to be a bellhop. I had no idea where the other officers were, but I was sure Juke had them stashed all over the place. Probably hiding behind the potted plants or something.

It was ten minutes past noon, and I was getting worried. Something was wrong. You didn't set up a very profitable meeting that was a gateway to a far more profitable meeting and show up late. Shavonne had positioned Navy SEAL Guy as a gang leader with cash and status. Being late was disrespectful; it would jeopardize the whole deal. Had Henneg found out about the setup and bailed? Had something happened to her in between her last call with Shavonne and noon? Was there some communication screw up, and we had the wrong place or time?

I heard the faint sound of someone's phone ringer. Shavonne dug into her pocket and answered, glancing over at Juke as she spoke.

What's going on? I texted the detective.

She ignored me. After some back and forth, Shavonne pocketed her phone, turned to Navy SEAL Guy, and informed him in a loud voice that the seller wanted to meet them on the roof.

I didn't wait for Juke to figure out how the hell she was going to get all her officers up to the roof unnoticed. Grabbing a tray off the bar and slapping a few shot glasses and a bottle of Jack on it, I walked straight for the elevator.

"Eden!" Juke barked out. It was my turn to ignore her. I got on the elevator, hit the button for the roof, and was heading up before she could round the check-in desk and get to the elevator bank.

I'd never been in the InterContinental, either as a hotel guest or to visit any of the high-priced restaurants and bars, but I'd secretly fantasized that maybe one day I'd be rich enough to drop a grand on a fancy dinner and drinks. Or maybe dress in my best and rub elbows with the one-percenters in the gorgeous rooftop bar that looked down seventy-three stories to the city below.

The roof. I couldn't imagine Henneg would want to meet on the real roof of the hotel where the air conditioning units and other shit were. First, I had no idea how to get up there. Second…well, there was no second. Quite a few of these downtown high-rises had helipads on their roofs like the nearby US Bank Towers, but this particular building's helipad was on the nineteenth floor, not on the "roof."

The elevator opened, and I sauntered out, heading straight to the bar with purpose. The space was long and rectangular with a bar to the left and a maze of privacy shields and cabana seating to the right. The eight-foot wall of heavy glass that surrounded the bar was shattered in some places and completely missing in others. No one had even bothered to rope off the damaged areas or put some sort of caution tape around. Guess they weren't too concerned about patrons plunging to their deaths. Actually, patrons plunging to their deaths was probably what broke the glass to begin with.

It was noon, which wasn't exactly clubbing time, but this was L.A. I counted at least six people, including the bartender, who shot me a quizzical glance as I walked behind the bar.

"So, we're not doing uniforms now?" She shook her head. "When did that memo come down?"

"This morning." I sat my tray down. "I'm relieving you for a break. Take twenty."

She laughed. "Well, that's a first. Thanks. Table four already paid their check and are just lingering. I just served table six. There's a couple back in the corner I haven't gotten to that just came in, and a woman at twelve who's been nursing a Bellini for the last half an hour."

"Got it." Seven people, give or take a few. Juke would have a fit that this was going down with a bunch of civilians around. I was worried too, because if Henneg switched locations at the last moment like this, it meant she was anxious. Anxious people were quick to pull the trigger. Juke wasn't the only one who didn't want a shootout seventy-three stories up in the air, with her cops and carefully-planned-out sting down below in the lobby.

Fuck it. The bitch might not even serve jail time, and there was a chance she'd wiggle out of the whole thing. My priority was getting the bullets and/or the money. There were only two ways out of this bar—the elevator and the staircase. Juke's team would be covering all the exits, and she'd probably be up here along with Shavonne and Navy SEAL Guy within minutes, so I needed to act fast.

Grabbing a bottle off the top shelf and a pair of glasses, I made my way around the bar. A couple got up from a nearby table and headed toward the elevator. That must be table four. Two tables over was a man typing on his phone, a full glass of wine beside his laptop. Bah. I recognized him even from the grainy pawnshop video still. I lowered my head, turning slightly as I walked past.

He was here to keep an eye on the elevator. Had he recognized me? He hadn't been there at the salvage, so there was a good chance he wasn't texting Henneg right now to let her know that Vulture she'd set up was here.

Hoping I wasn't about to be shot in the back, I walked over to the lounge cabanas, wincing at the hideous upholstery. The whole bar was ultra-modern with the shiny onyx bar and the drum-shaped bar stools, but the designer must have been on an acid trip when he'd put these things together. The bench seats were covered with a green furry fabric that looked like a cross between Astroturf and seventies shag carpeting.

A couple sat off to the side on a pair of the ugly benches. I handed the man the bottle, then gave the woman the glasses. "Here. On the house, but only if you leave right now. Come back in an hour or so, but you've got to leave."

"We just got here," the woman protested.

"Some demons are coming up for a meeting. Trust me, you don't want to be here."

"Demons?" The man got right to his feet. "Come on, Jen. Let's go back to our room."

She jumped up as well. "Thanks for the tip. And the booze," she told me as they practically ran toward the elevator.

That took care of the civilians. Bah was up front, and I was pretty sure the woman nursing the Bellini was Henneg. She *would* recognize me, so I ducked my head, taking a circuitous route back to the bar, trying to figure out exactly where she was sitting.

Juke was at the bar when I returned.

"I'll take a beer," she snarled at me.

"Bah's at five o'clock at the table. Henneg is probably to the left at the far end of the cabanas. I didn't want her to see me, so I didn't go that far," I whispered as I dug a bottle of beer out of the cooler.

"They're on their way up," she muttered as I handed her the beer. "I can't get more up here without making it obvious, but they're on standby."

The elevator door opened. Shavonne and Navy SEAL Guy walked out. The pawnbroker looked around while Navy SEAL Guy started loudly bitching about this being a waste of his time.

"Where the hell are they? I came here for a buy, and these clowns are playing some damned cloak-and-dagger games. I thought you said we had a deal."

"We do." Shavonne spotted Bah as he rose from his chair. "There he is."

Navy SEAL Guy strode forward, eyeing Bah, then looked over at the laptop on his table. "Where is it? The deal was four cases. There better not be some bullshit about going somewhere else. This was supposed to be a simple quick deal to test the waters, and let me tell you, buddy, I'm not liking these waters right now."

He was really laying it on thick, and I wasn't sure if that was a good thing or not. I glanced over at Juke, who was glaring at her beer. Yep. Navy SEAL Guy's overacting was gonna get us all killed.

"It's here," Bah snapped. "Four today and the rest as early as tonight. We need this stuff gone."

"Exactly how much is this 'rest'?" Navy SEAL Guy asked, practically salivating.

"Thirteen cases. Seventeen in total." Bah looked over at the bar as if he were just noticing that he had an audience. "You two. Get lost."

"I haven't finished my beer," Juke complained.

Bah's fingers brushed the pistol in his hip holster. "Drink it somewhere else."

This was not going to happen. I stayed behind the bar but moved a few steps up and touched my own pistol. "Whatever, dude. I've got one of those too. Everybody in this fucking city is carrying. I don't care what you're doing up here. Hell, I've probably seen worse. Just try not to break anything that isn't already broken."

"Time," Navy SEAL Guy interrupted. "You're wasting my time. I don't give a shit if they're here or not. I just want this deal done."

Bah glared at me for a few tense seconds. It was a total cop stare, and if this had been an actual arms deal, Navy SEAL Guy would already have shot him. Idiots. I was surrounded by idiots. Well, except for Juke. And Shavonne.

The pawnbroker had clearly participated in this sort of thing before because she was holding back, remaining silent, and keeping her eye on the stairwell exit. Juke was hunched over, eyes fixed on her beer, but she'd eased her pistol out during my little speech and was holding it out of sight against her thigh.

"You want the deal done? Then let's do it," a voice called out from my left.

I ducked my head, letting the strands of hair that had escaped my ponytail screen my face. Henneg walked up and tipped one of the fur-covered benches over, revealing four boxes underneath.

"Eight grand and they're yours," she announced.

Navy SEAL Guy laughed. "I'm not paying two bucks a bullet. I'll give you two grand for these and ten grand for the other thirteen cases."

"That's half of wholesale," Bah said. "How about a dollar a bullet. Cash. And we exchange the rest tonight."

"Okay, but open the cases. I want to make sure I'm not paying four grand for a bunch of rocks."

Navy SEAL Guy walked forward, placing himself between Juke and Henneg. Shavonne edged back and to the right, where she had the option of running for the stairwell or diving behind one of the furry benches. Henneg took six steps back, keeping the distance between her and Navy SEAL Guy, which put her back in Juke's view again, but far enough to the left that if the woman looked, she could clearly see Juke's pistol at her thigh.

She looked. Her hand went to her own pistol, then her gaze went from Juke's Glock to me.

"It's a trap," she shouted.

Everyone grabbed their guns. Since Juke already had hers out, she shot first, hitting to the left of Henneg and sending the other woman diving for cover. Shavonne dove to the floor behind a bench. Bah ducked behind the other side of the bar.

Navy SEAL Guy ran for the cases of bullets. Of course.

Bullets pinged off the black granite of the bar, sending chips of stone flying.

"Get in here," Juke shouted into a tiny mic on her shirt collar. The stairwell door flung open, and four cops in SWAT gear poured in, all yelling at us to stand down. Two years ago, we might have complied, but this was New Hell, so everyone just kept shooting.

I popped my head above the bar to get my bearings and saw Shavonne vanish through the door to the stairwell. Good. One less person to worry about. She was Bags's friend, and I would have done everything I could to try to keep her safe.

Henneg vaulted over a bench and rolled behind a thick rectangular marble planter. From the sound, Bah was already behind there. Navy SEAL Guy was trying to grab the bullet cases but couldn't manage to get all four cases in his arms. The cops fanned out, still yelling for everyone to stand down.

Juke dove around the bar, landing beside me. Her left shoulder was bleeding, but other than that, she looked fine. "We've got 'em trapped. There's no way they're going to stand there exposed while they wait for the elevator, and they'll need to get past us to get to the stairwell. Unless they sprout wings, they're not getting out of this building unless they're in handcuffs."

I didn't pay any attention to her because I was busy doing the math. Four cases. Around thirty-five pounds per case. Roughly one-fifty. That was fucking heavy, but Navy SEAL Guy was jacked and motivated. I had no doubt that if he managed to pick up all four of those cases, he'd be down the stairs and gone while we were still dealing with Henneg and Bah.

Fuck that. Staying low, I scooted past Juke, ignoring her hissed directive to stay put, and rounded the bar at the same time I saw either Henneg or Bah lob something over the top of the planter.

"Down!" one of the SWAT guys shouted. They all scattered, and I managed to jump behind a cabana just as the explosive detonated.

Shit flew everywhere. I covered my head and hugged the ground as chunks of metal, granite, wood, and green furry fabric pelted me. When the debris stopped flying, I looked up and saw three prone bodies, Bah peeking over the edge of the planter, and a bloody, dust-covered Navy SEAL Guy running for the stairwell.

Bah and I both took off. Henneg stood up to cover her partner. From the sound of the gunfire, Juke was still in play, as was one of the SWAT guys. Figuring they'd keep Henneg occupied, I poured on the speed, trying to reach Navy SEAL Guy before Bah did. Realizing he'd never get the stairwell door open before we were on him, Navy SEAL Guy changed directions and ran along the edge of the rooftop. I was four feet away from him, Bah only a few steps behind, when Navy SEAL Guy spun around and shot at me.

One of the bullet cases shifted, sliding out of his arms and to the ground where it burst open, spilling boxes and bullets across the floor. The shifting load must have thrown off Navy SEAL Guy's aim because he missed me. A shot sounded from behind and hit Navy SEAL Guy in the arm. He dropped the bullets, then dropped the gun as another shot hit him in the shoulder.

He fell, and I turned, ready to defend myself when Bah's foot hit me in the chest, sending me flying backward and nearly off the damned building. I grabbed at the jagged edges of the guard rail, barely keeping myself from falling through where heavy glass used to be to protect against this very thing.

Bah lunged at me. I tried to shoot him, but a fraction of a second before I pulled the trigger, he'd pushed my arm aside. A fist slammed into my face and then my stomach. I dropped the gun to use both hands to keep myself from going over the edge. Another punch in my stomach caused my hands to slip.

Navy SEAL Guy was down. Gunfire told me Juke was still dealing with Henneg. I was trapped between a man who held a weapon in one hand, and a very long fall. And there was nothing I could do to prevent what was about to happen. Another punch, and my hands slipped free.

My arms pinwheeled as I tried to keep my balance on the edge of the roof. Bah's eyes narrowed, a sly grin curving his mouth as he brought up a foot and kicked me over.

This is not how I expected to die.

My heart pounded, and I spun as I fell. There was nothing I could do, no way I could save myself. My minor telekinesis wasn't enough to keep me from going splat on the pavement, and electricity wouldn't do shit to help me. I was going to die. Crazy freefall, a painful bone-crunching impact, and hopefully an instant death. Panic spiked through me. My eyes teared up, and I wasn't sure if it was from fear or the wind velocity of my plummet to death.

Something hit me, knocking the wind from my lungs. With the impact, my direction abruptly changed, and for a split second, I wondered why the collision came sideways and not from the ground I was falling toward. My body was held immobile by the G-force of whatever had hit me. I felt us swirl and turn and fought down the urge to puke. I couldn't see. My eyes were teared up, and we were going too fast for me to focus or get any sense of my bearings at all. Suddenly we rocketed upward—or maybe it was downward —so fast that I couldn't force my diaphragm to allow me to inhale.

I couldn't breathe. I couldn't see. My lungs were burning, and my body ached from the impact. I welcomed the darkness that took my consciousness away.

CHAPTER 22

Everything hurt. It wasn't broken-bones hurt, but I definitely felt like someone had thrown me in a cement mixer with a bag of rocks and hit "tumble." Worse, I was soaking wet. Was I dead? If so, I was definitely in hell. Wet and aching felt like a worse infernal punishment than the fire and brimstone I'd heard about growing up.

But, according to the author of that demonology book, Hel was an actual place and not an afterlife. I doubted Desiree or the demons from the tax office would bother dragging me through the gates to Hel, and I couldn't imagine this as any sort of afterlife, so I opened my eyes.

It was daylight with a cloudless sky above me. The chit-chit noise and the water spraying over me clued me in that instead of an afterlife filled with torment, I was very much alive and lying on someone's lawn, being drenched by their sprinkler system.

Ugh. I wrinkled my nose, realizing that the homeowners used gray water for their lawns. Very environmentally friendly, but not something I wanted soaking me to the skin.

Getting to my feet, I looked over at the one-story stucco

I'd been sprawled out in front of. No cars in the driveway, so I didn't need to worry about someone opening the door with a shotgun and blasting me off their lawn. I turned around, my feet squishing on the grass. There were a few cars parked along the quiet residential street. The only sounds I heard were from the lawn sprinkler, and someone's dog barking a few blocks away.

Where the fuck was I? And more to the point, what the fuck had happened?

I should be dead. I should be splatted all over Wilshire Boulevard. That bastard Bah had tried to kill me and nearly succeeded.

Why hadn't they succeeded? I'd fallen. Then something had hit me from the side, like a truck running into me fifty or so stories up and carrying me forward with the momentum. But I doubted there was a truck flying around downtown, plowing into humans who were falling to their deaths from tall buildings.

I wasn't an idiot. There was a lot I ignored, because I believed in prioritizing issues, and things such as my weird healing, whether Bishop was a were-something, and if there was or wasn't a hell didn't come anywhere near the top of my list.

But this…

Had a demon swooped in to save me? They had wings. I'd seen them flying around downtown on occasion. A dragon wouldn't have any reason to save me—or any reason to save me and not eat me directly afterward—but I'd wonder the same thing about a demon. Desiree wanted me alive, but she would have stuck around and grilled me when I'd come to, not dumped me on a lawn who-knows-where in the city. Any demon saving me would have stayed and demanded their pound of flesh when I'd regained consciousness.

What—or who—would save me, then not stick around to ask for some sort of payment?

Flying. Whatever had saved me, it had been able to fly.

Super healing was pretty damned sweet, and I wouldn't say no if I suddenly developed teleportation skills but having wings would be epic. L.A. traffic? No problem. Overturned truck on the 5? Pfffft. Just fly over the damned thing.

Wings. I yanked off my shirt and checked the back for holes. Surely if I'd suddenly developed the ability to fly, the leathery things would have ripped right through my clothing. Seeing my shirt intact, I let out a long breath. Good. Flying sounded cool, but I was weird enough without suddenly being able to sprout wings. Besides, if I had wings, that would make me…well, something I didn't want to think about being.

"Why would a demon swoop in and save me?" I mused out loud, coming to only one conclusion—Desiree.

I had no idea if Desiree had wings or not. I wouldn't be surprised to hear she had. And she was the only demon who wanted me to stay alive enough to save me. All the others would probably opt to just watch the entertaining splat of my body on the pavement. But if Desiree saved me, then where was she? Why would she plop me down in someone's yard and leave? Why not haul me off to her lair where I could serve her for the rest of my life? Or at least stick around until I woke up so she could mock me and remind me of my fate as her lackey?

I wrung out the lower part of my soaked shirt and made my way to the sidewalk away from the sprinklers. Something scratched the skin around my waistband, and I dug my hand there and pulled something out.

A feather. It wasn't just any old bird feather, either. It was rounded, soft and downy, with a small quill positioned more in the center than would have been typical in a flight feather.

I'd seen these types of feathers before on chickens and other birds, but I'd never seen one this big. The thing was bigger than my hand. Frowning, I tried to imagine how fucking big this bird had been and only came up with "bigger than an ostrich."

I knew what it was before the sunlight sent a prism of reflected light across the sidewalk. Peach and gold, silver and orange. Sunrise and sunset right in the palm of my hand.

An angel.

I shivered, and it wasn't because I was soaking wet in ninety-degree heat. I'd never seen an angel other than on the news broadcasts two years ago when they'd come here to battle the demons, but I knew this feather couldn't belong to any other creature.

An angel had saved my life. What did that mean? Why would one of them bother? And what the hell was an angel doing flying around a demon-controlled downtown Los Angeles in a place now known as New Hell? It hadn't stuck around, so I was assuming New Hell might not be a safe place for a solitary angel.

An angel saved me. What sort of debt had I incurred because of that?

* * *

WHILE I'D BEEN GETTING an extreme baptism by some guy's lawn sprinklers, Juke had been blowing up my phone with calls and frantic texts, wanting to know if I was alive and where the fuck I was. Figuring this conversation would be easier via a call, I dialed her cell.

"Eden? Eden! Sweet Baby Jesus, are you okay? Are you in the hospital? Wait, is this one of Eden's sisters calling to tell me she's dead?"

"I'm alive. Wet, but alive. And strangely unhurt." I

marveled at that again. There were times I'd bitched about my magical gifts and wished for something more useful, something more reliable. I wasn't going to claim my super healing was all that reliable yet, but damn, it was one hell of an ability to have.

"I think I lost ten years of my life when Bah kicked you off the side of the building," she confessed. "We got the pair of them. As soon as they were cuffed and we had backup, I went down, expecting to find you pancaked on the asphalt in front of the hotel."

My stomach turned as I remembered the freefall, the vertigo of spinning in air, the terror and the certainty that I was only seconds from death.

"What happened?" I asked.

She barked out a laugh. "You tell me. Were you packing a parachute or something? Hundreds of layers of bubble wrap under your clothes? Nine lives like a cat?"

My mind immediately detoured to Hellkitty. Did it have nine lives? I sure hoped the fuck not.

"All I remember was falling, convinced I was going to die, and feeling the most terrified I've ever been in my life, then something hit me. It wasn't the pavement something, either. It was like I got T-boned by a truck. Something plowed into me from the side—something fast." I scratched my head, picking a blade of grass from the soaked locks.

"A demon?" Juke's whispered voice echoed my initial thoughts.

"No. I don't think it was a demon." I stuck the feather back in my pocket. Why the hell was an angel flying around New Hell? Wouldn't the demons have gone nuts if there was an angel downtown? And was it some weird serendipity that it had just happened to be flying by the very building I was falling off of?

Maybe it wasn't an angel. Maybe it was some freakishly

huge bird. Durfts, Hellkitty, and other creatures had come here from hell. Who's to say some giant bird with a savior complex wasn't among them?

"Hell if I know what happened, Alvaro. Just glad you're still among the living."

Me, too. "So, what happened? You all arrested Henneg and Bah. Are they still in jail? Out on bail?"

I needed to know if two more people would be gunning for me. I also needed to know how much time I had to find the rest of the bullets before they were out on bail and skipping town.

"They're still awaiting arraignment. Their lawyers will probably claim they didn't know we were cops, and that they're only guilty of trying to fence bullets from a crime scene without a license, so I expect they'll be out on bail by nightfall." There was an awkward silence that let me know I wasn't going to like her answer. "We've already searched their residences and didn't find the rest of the bullets, so we can only get them on the four cases."

Fuck. "And those four cases are locked away in evidence, right?"

"About a case was retained from the scene. The rest was not there after we subdued Henneg and Bah. Although we all saw four cases, I'm sure their lawyer will push that there was only one."

Her voice sounded...odd. I'd initially thought Navy SEAL Guy had grabbed the rest, but something about her tone made me wonder if Juke hadn't pulled a fast one.

"The other three cases are probably at a pawnshop by now," she continued. "Probably Bear State Pawn. Bummer we couldn't recover it all."

Bear State Pawn was Bags's store. I let out a long breath and smiled. "Yeah. Bummer."

"Your backpack and gun are with Bags, by the way. At his

pawnshop. I took them there just in case you were still okay. I tried to take them to your house, but the address you gave me was some sketchy bar up in the hills, so I figured if you were alive, then Bags would get your stuff to you, and if you were dead, he'd know where to find your family."

"Thank you." Tears stung my eyes. She'd stolen evidence for me. She'd collected my stuff and made sure it was safe. Any doubts I had about Sarah Juke were gone.

Three cases. That plus what I'd gotten at the job with Telaney last night would put me around eight thousand. That was far from the fifteen thousand I needed, but it was a start.

"Is Shavonne okay? And your team?" I grimaced. "I'm assuming they took Navy SEAL Guy out in a body bag." Or maybe not. He'd survived Hellkitty; he should be able to shake off a gunshot wound to the chest.

"Shavonne took the stairs to the sixty-third floor, then hopped on the elevator down. She's fine. Three of my team were injured, but they'll make it. The guy you'd set up as the buyer was nowhere to be found. We saw some blood over near where you'd gone off the ledge, but he wasn't on the rooftop."

I frowned. "How the hell did he get off the roof? And why did he leave the bullets behind?"

Navy SEAL Guy had teleported before, but I had the blue stone. Unless there was a second focus for the spell, he shouldn't have been able to teleport. That left the elevator and the stairwell—both of which would have involved him walking through a hail of bullets and in clear view of Juke.

Had he gone off the side of the building? Clearly, he hadn't been splatted on the street below, but maybe he'd been saved by the same whatever that had saved me?

Or maybe it was him with the feathery wings who'd shrugged off his wounds, dove over the side of the building, and rescued me from a certain death?

Nahhhhhh. No fucking way would that asshole ever abandon four cases of bullets to save my sorry ass. I wasn't ruling out that he had wings, but I didn't think he'd used them for anything besides getting himself out of trouble.

"The good news is that we pulled the report. Retracted it. You're no longer on the hook for that money," Juke said.

I snorted, because I was still on the hook for that money. But that wasn't Juke's fault. I'd made a deal in a moment of desperation, and report or no report, I was still going to be expected to abide by a deal I'd already agreed to.

"Thank you. I appreciate it," I told her. It wasn't her fault I'd run out of time and gone to the tax office. She'd gone out of her way to help me. She'd believed me when I hadn't expected any cop would. She'd stolen evidence and left it for me, knowing full well that I might still be on the hook for that money, whether the report was retracted or not.

"No problem. I just wish we'd found the rest of the bullets. Henneg had to have hidden them somewhere, but she's not going to talk. At least, she's not going to talk unless all the charges are dropped and she gets reinstated, or some shit like that."

"Fuck that," I told her. That bitch needed to pay. I'd find the bullets on my own without the police needing to work out a deal.

I'd find them on my own, and I knew exactly who I needed to help me.

* * *

BY THE TIME I'd hitchhiked my way back to the InterContinental hotel, I'd dried off. The management wasn't particularly thrilled about my plopping down in one of their lobby chairs to wait, but after I bought an overpriced beer with a soggy ten, they let me stay.

I was just finishing my beer when Bishop walked into the lobby like he owned the place, Bob trotting by his side. No one said a word about the dog, or weredog, or whatever. I waved him over to where I was sitting. When I'd called asking him to pick up Bob and come meet me for a job, I'd also asked him to swing by Bags's store and pick up my gear.

As Bob went to sniff a plant, Bishop came over and handed me my backpack.

I pulled out my Glock, checked the magazine, and put it in my shoulder holster. I'd felt anxious without the gun. And without my backpack. That insanely expensive demonology book was in there along with a lot of my supplies. Glancing through for a quick inventory, I noticed two full magazines and a wad of cash. Bags. I loved that guy.

He'd given me four grand for the three cases of bullets Juke had "redirected" to him. That put me at seventy-three hundred. Quite a bit shy of the fifteen grand I needed by tomorrow afternoon, but I had hopes I'd be able to make up the difference in time.

"Thanks for running by the pawnshop to pick this stuff up for me." I'd been embarrassed to ask, but Bishop would be driving right through Burbank, where I'd have needed to make an extra round trip if I'd gone myself.

He grunted in response.

"We need to go up to the roof," I told him. "Do you think Bob can sort the scents out? I've got something that used to belong to the guy I'm looking for to pull an initial scent from, but I've handled it and had it in my pocket since yesterday. Would the smell of the guy be too old by that point?"

"Depends on what it is. Sweaty shirt? The scent will still be there. Coin he carried around in a pocket that he rarely touched and that's been through the washer? Maybe not."

"It's a rock. That stone I showed you and HB back at

Suerte. The lapis that you said was a focus for Kirk's Marble or something."

"Kirby's Marble." Bishop waved for Bob to come with us. "It should still have enough of a scent, but we'll see."

We took the elevator up, the three of us watching the numbers light up as we made our way to the seventy-third floor. When the doors opened, I noticed that the hotel staff had gotten right to work cleaning up the mess we'd left behind this afternoon. There were still bullet holes all over the place, but the broken benches and tables, and other debris had been cleaned up.

"We're closed until six." A man looked over from the bar at us.

"Just looking around," I told him. "We'll be out of your hair in a second."

He nodded. "Be careful around the edges. Bunch of demons busted up the glass safety walls last night. One good breeze and you're going over."

I shivered, remembering very well how that felt. It all flashed into my memory—the terror, the rush of wind, the brief glimpse of the cars below as I tumbled downward.

Bishop put his hand on my lower back. Warmth spread through me—warmth and calm and a weird soothing feeling that felt...blue.

I've got you.

They weren't exactly words in my head, but some strange non-verbal communication. Safe. I was safe. I didn't need a winged-whatever to save me because Bishop was here. Bishop wouldn't let me fall.

I shook my head and stepped away from his hand. It was one thing to feel safe around someone, but I was developing a very unhealthy attachment for this guy. I trusted him but trusting someone and relying on them to protect and save you were two different things. Right now, Bishop and I only had a professional relationship.

"We're on the clock here," Bishop said, reminding me that I was paying for this and where he and I both stood in relation to each other.

I pulled the stone out of my pocket and showed it to Bob.

Bob huffed, then walked over to me. He sniffed the rock then froze, hackles rising as a low growl rumbled from his chest.

Bishop's eyebrows shot up. "Let me see that thing."

I handed it over to him and watched as he turned the stone around in his hand.

"Demon," he mused.

What? "Nooo. The stone belongs to Navy SEAL Guy—one of the bounty hunters that's after me. It doesn't belong to a demon…unless you're saying a demon spelled it?"

He shook his head. "Human mages do the spellwork to create a Kirby's Marble. I mean the owner of this stone is a demon. I can feel a very faint trace of his energy signature on the stone. And Bob smelled demon, not human."

My mouth fell open. "Navy SEAL Guy is a *demon?*"

That…that wasn't possible. The demons I'd seen on TV during the wars and here and there in the Valley were *demons*. Horns. Wings. Lizard-bodies. A weird mishmash of animal and human forms. Reptile eyes. Forked tongues. Dicks that shot out vegetation killing sperm. Yeah, Desiree and Blister looked like humans, but they still were a bit off. They didn't look like the kind of normal people I'd meet in the grocery store or in the park and not even give a second look. They didn't look like Navy SEAL Guy.

Fuck. If Navy SEAL Guy was a demon, then anyone on the street could be one, too. I remembered how Alfie was kind of odd and wondered if he was a demon. Was Juke secretly a demon? Telaney? The cook at the grits place?

Me? I nearly puked at the thought. No one had ever found my parents. I didn't know who they were. I had a lot of the same magical abilities as Navy SEAL Guy. But I couldn't be a demon. Surely, I'd remember if I weren't human.

"He could be part-demon," Bishop said, as if that were any less terrifying. "They call them hybrids. Demon father and, in this instance, human mother. If the father is an angel and the mother is human, then they're called Nephilim. Demon hybrids usually don't have much in the way of non-human abilities, though. It's mostly the temperament that carries through to the offspring. So, I'm thinking he's a low-level demon. Or he could be a young demon—three or four hundred years old maybe."

Oh, like *that* was any less terrifying.

"He's a demon." I still didn't want to believe that. "But he does magic. He can electrocute stuff, like a stun gun but using his hands."

Bishop handed the stone back to me. "All demons can do that. It's one of their first abilities. I'm pretty sure even Lows can create and wield electrical energy."

Sick. I was going to be sick.

"And super healing? Wounds gone by the next day or sometimes in a few hours?" Navy SEAL Guy had recovered from Hellkitty's attack, but at this point my questions were less about him and more about…well, me.

"A hybrid would have some minor accelerated healing ability. A Low demon would be able to heal most injuries if they had time. Higher-level demons…well, there are a lot of factors involved, but in most circumstances, they can repair any physical damage in an instant."

Okay. So, I couldn't heal instantly, but I seemed to have progressed beyond the hybrid ability. Did that make me a Low? I thought about Blister, the Low at the tax office, and shivered.

"But how about telekinesis? Swatting balls and stuff away before they get to you. That sort of thing."

He shrugged. "That's an unusual skill for a demon unless they're very high level or an Ancient."

Oh, lovely. Was I a half-demon freak? A full-demon super-freak? A Low? What the fuck was I? And what was an Ancient? If Navy SEAL Guy was a demon, then surely I was one, too.

That wasn't something I wanted to even contemplate—now or ever.

But wouldn't I know if I were a demon? My only memories were of being human. I couldn't be a demon if I had no recollection of being in Hel, or having a half-lizard body, or something. No, I had to be something else—a human freak, not a demon freak.

"Are you sure?" I tried not to hyperventilate, just as panicked over this as I had been going over the side of the building. "Are you sure he's a demon and not...something else?"

Bishop nodded. "I'm sure. Bob's sure. Demons are beings of spirit, so they have to manifest a corporeal form. Their physical body always carries a trace of their energy."

I suddenly remembered how weird Navy SEAL Guy's blood had felt when I'd touched that dried bit. Was it this spirit-being energy I'd sensed? If so, then the disturbing ability to sense the otherness in his blood pointed even more toward some demonic parentage in my own genetic makeup.

"Well, their physical body *usually* carries a trace of their energy," Bishop huffed. "There are a few demons skilled in locking their spirit-selves so deeply into the cells of their physical bodies that it's almost impossible to tell them from a human."

Was that me? Or maybe not? Was I a demon? A part demon? Some mutant human? Did it even matter?

"Have you ever met one?" I asked hesitantly. "A demon that you couldn't tell was a demon?"

He shot me a wry smile. "How would I know if they were *that* skilled? Although eventually demons always give themselves away."

I stared at him, trying to read into what he was saying. Did he think I was a demon? Did he know? Had I somehow given myself away, or had I been unknowingly leaving my energy signature all over the place?

No. I refused to believe it. I wasn't a demon. I wasn't some spirit-being wearing a human form like a suit. I *was* human. I was just a different sort of human. And Navy SEAL Guy…well, I didn't give a flying fuck what he was. I just needed to track him down and get the rest of the bullets or cash before my deadline at the tax office.

"Can Bob track him?" I held up the rock before putting it back in my pocket. "Demon or not, I need to find him."

Bishop turned to Bob and raised his eyebrows. Bob shuddered, then put his nose to the ground and got to work. We followed him around the rooftop bar, down the stairs for six floors, then down the elevator and outside to the street. I left my bike in the parking garage where it had been since this afternoon, and we took Bishop's truck through downtown and into Koreatown to a nice studio apartment on Berendo Street. I picked the lock but kept my gun in my holster. It was clear from the bored expression on Bob's face and Bishop's relaxed stance that Navy SEAL Guy had come and gone.

Still, I wanted to take a peek. I went inside to see that someone had already tossed the house. Sofa cushions were on the floor, the upholstery unzipped, and foam squares yanked from the fabric. Kitchen cabinets had been emptied. Closets stood open with clothes and shoes in a heap on the floor. Even the mattress and box spring had been upended and sliced open.

Cops didn't neatly fold your T-shirts and stack them in the drawers after they searched your dresser, but there was a careless sort of organization to the discarded piles they left behind. There was a methodical search, and there was a I-don't-give-a-flying-fuck search. This was the latter. I picked up a picture, recognizing the man who posed next to a yacht that was clearly out of his price range. This was Bah's place.

"Let's move on," I told Bishop.

I doubted that Bah would have been storing the cases of bullets in his apartment. First, it was clear to me that Henneg was running the show, and I doubted she would have trusted anyone with such a valuable commodity. Secondly, this was a studio apartment. There was barely room for the sofa and the bed in here, let alone thirteen cases of bullets. They would have been pretty much in plain sight in a closet or under the bed—where either the cops or Navy SEAL Guy would have easily found them.

Where Navy SEAL Guy went next would tell me if he had the bullets or not. Bishop and I followed Bob who led with his nose, and we once more got into the truck, this time driving into West Hollywood.

Bishop finally pulled up at a townhome on Gardner Street. Bah's tiny studio apartment in Koreatown probably ran him twelve to thirteen hundred a month in rent. He was a young cop, in his twenties, and the apartment was exactly what I'd expected he could afford on his salary, even after demons had taken over the city.

This townhome in West Hollywood was not what I'd expected a cop in her twenties with three years on the force to afford. It had probably cost close to eight hundred thousand two years ago and probably still would fetch five or six even now.

"Squatters' rights?" I mused out loud, wondering if it was

against department policy for a cop to obtain housing in that still mildly illegal and certainly unethical manner.

As we made our way to the entrance, the adjoining town-home's front door opened, and a bald head popped out to watch us. The guy had dark-rimmed glasses and a long black goatee. When he saw Bob, he relaxed and stepped all the way out onto the stoop.

"Is she selling the place? Did something happen to her? The police were here earlier, but she's a cop so I didn't think much about it. Then some man came by about a half an hour ago. You just missed him. Looked like he was military or something." He followed this speech up with kissy noises that I realized were directed at Bob.

Half an hour. We were catching up to Navy SEAL Guy. I was torn between telling Bob to keep tracking and going inside Henneg's house to see if I could find anything. I was pretty sure if the police hadn't found the bullets here, then neither had Navy SEAL Guy. Yeah, there were a whole lot more places to hide seventeen cases of ammo in a nice town-home like this, but neither would have left with just a cursory search.

I didn't even need to pick the lock, which was a good thing since nosy, dog-friendly neighbor dude had come over to join us. Bob curled his lip at the neighbor who was still making kissy noises and extending his hand.

"Nice doggy," Bishop warned Bob.

The weredog sniffed, cringing as the neighbor patted his head. I bit back a smile, pushed the door open, and gasped.

"Wow. What happened?" the neighbor asked as he continued to pet a very annoyed Bob.

"You tell us," Bishop said. "You live right next door. You must have heard something."

The neighbor gave up petting Bob and pushed past me to

walk inside. Clearly this was more interesting than the "doggy."

Following the neighbor inside, I stood in the center of the modern, open floorplan to take it all in. I nudged a broken table with my toe. There was glass everywhere. The couch had been sliced to ribbons and the stuffing tossed to the side. Kitchen cabinet doors stood open, their contents scattered across the counters and the floor. Flour and sugar containers had been opened and dumped out. This wasn't the cops. This was done by someone who was pissed off and frustrated. This was done by someone who had lost every last bit of his patience back at the apartment in Koreatown.

"It was that military guy," the neighbor confirmed. "The cops made some noise—thumping around and moving furniture. The other guy came, and I could hear glass breaking and stuff being thrown against the walls." He shrugged. "The woman who lives here is a cop. I figured she'd deal with it when she got home. As long as the guy didn't come over and start trashing my place, I wasn't going to get involved."

I rolled my eyes, because I got the feeling this guy got involved in everything that went on in his neighborhood, especially in this adjoining townhouse.

Climbing the stairs, I motioned for the neighbor to come with me. He reluctantly left Bob, who was sniffing around with Bishop supervising, and followed.

"When did she buy this place?" I asked as I peeked into the first bedroom, then moved on to the master.

"Six? Seven years ago? Although it wasn't her that bought it, it was Daddy Warbucks." He chuckled. "You're probably too young to know who that is. Basically, her parents had money. They got this place for her while she was still in college. Must be nice, huh?"

Yeah. Must be nice.

"I bought mine right around the same time, so I know

they paid close to seven hundred thousand for it. Can you imagine shelling out that kind of money for a college kid?" He shook his head. "Here I am sweating blood to cover my mortgage and she's diddy-bopping around with her college friends, letting her parents write the checks."

"Huh." I looked into the master bedroom, wincing at the destruction before heading up another set of stairs.

"Of all the people I figured to become a cop, it wasn't her. When she didn't get into law school, I assumed she'd lean on her parents for a position at one of the fortune five hundreds or something, not go patrol the streets and arrest junkies and thieves."

"Mmm." The third floor held a small laundry and a door out to a rooftop terrace that she shared with her neighbor. A row of potted plants delineated the boundary between the two spaces. On my side was a sisal rug, a couch with all-weather upholstery, and a gas grill.

"Maybe it was the adrenaline thing. She sky-dived, rock-climbed, and surfed. Wow, did she surf. After work, on the weekends and days off. She was always hauling that surfboard off to the shore, strapped on top of her Beamer."

It certainly took balls to do what she'd done, taking that salvage, setting me up, hoping the tax demons didn't get wise before she sold the lot of it. Money certainly hadn't motivated her from the sound of things. I remembered some of the girls from high school who'd shoplifted even though they came from families who could easily afford anything they stole. I'd shoplifted too, but because I either needed the item, or as a giant "fuck you" to the mega-store corporations. They'd stolen for the rush, often tossing whatever they'd lifted right outside the store's front doors.

The thought that Henneg had caused me and my family all this agony over an adrenaline-fueled lark infuriated me.

I went back down to the master bedroom, just in case my

eyes might spot something Navy SEAL Guy might have missed. It looked like a bomb had exploded in here, but I tried to notice everything, learning more about Chelsea Henneg.

"I think she's gay." The neighbor said this casually, as if he were proclaiming what kind of coffee she liked. "Or maybe bi. There'd be a guy or two in here. Another cop. The dude from the sushi place. But lots of women. They all stayed the night, but I got the feeling she might have been more into the women."

No surprise there. Tons of my friends were gay or bi. Hell, Bea'd had a wife back before she'd taken me in. She still talked fondly about Kendra, and we still got a Christmas card every year from Bea's ex and her new wife. They lived in New Hampshire or someplace like that. Heck, I was occasionally attracted to a woman or two.

"Is she dead?" the neighbor asked. "In trouble? In jail?"

"The latter," I told him as I learned more about the woman who'd ruined my life.

Henneg wore dime-store makeup and limited it to mascara, tinted moisturizer, and an assortment of flavored Chapstick. She had a dozen pairs of identical gray sweatpants. She had a thing for pastel colored seashells and a fondness for scented candles. There was a surfboard broken in half and tossed on the floor of her bedroom that looked as if it had never even seen the ocean. The crumpled picture torn from a wooden frame showed two blonde women on the Santa Monica Pier, arms around each other, sand dotting their bikinis. There were surfing magazines scattered across the bathroom floor. The torn page that remained taped to the mirror showed a woman next to a white Jeep, a surfboard in hand as she gazed out to a sunlit ocean. Dozens of smashed picture frames held photos of people on the beach, and one of an elderly woman in front of a little house. I frowned, picking it up and removing the photo from the smashed frame. This place…it looked familiar.

"Well, that's a shame because she was a good neighbor. Even sent me over a basket of fruit when my Snippy-whippy died. I know she didn't like my little Yorkie, but it was awfully nice of her to send me that basket and a sympathy card."

I sniffed, thinking Henneg had probably killed the dog. Why did this house look so familiar? I stuffed the photo in my pants pocket and continued to search.

"Hope she comes back or sells the place." The neighbor shuddered. "Otherwise, someone will pull a squatters' rights grab, and I'll end up with some murderer or drug dealer for a neighbor."

I hated to tell the guy, but the woman who'd lived here was probably far worse than he'd get in a squatters' rights grab.

The broken surfboard was new, but I doubted anyone this into the sport had only one board. Where was her old, faithful surfboard? Wetsuit? Swimsuits? Other gear?

Actually, the bedroom and bathroom had seemed oddly sparse, as if half the belongings had been removed.

What wasn't here was just as revealing as what was. I headed downstairs, the neighbor following along and talking about a time Henneg had gotten drunk and passed out on the rooftop terrace buck naked.

"We've got a problem," Bishop told me as I walked into the destruction that had been Henneg's living room. "The scent ends here. I don't know if the guy managed to buy another focus for the Kirby's Marble spell, or he used some other magical device, but he left here without a scent trail to follow."

"He didn't find the bullets here. Henneg has the bullets. If she didn't hide them in her house, then she hid them somewhere else—somewhere she could trust that they'd be safe." I pulled the picture out of my pocket. "Do you recognize this place? I think it's somewhere near Hermosa Beach."

"Oh, her grandmother lived at Hermosa Beach," the neighbor chimed in. "She'd had that place since the sixties. Oceanfront property. Probably worth over a mil now, even though I don't think the old lady updated the house since she bought it. Chelsea used to go there all the time to surf and hang out. She died a few months ago—the grandmother, that is. Chelsea inherited the place. I half expected her to sell and move there as much as she loved surfing."

Bishop and I exchanged a glance, then I turned to the neighbor. "You wouldn't happen to have the address of this grandmother's house, would you?"

ermosa Beach covered roughly two miles, capped by the marina at one end and Manhattan Beach at the other. Bishop gave me a ride, since my bike was all the way back at the hotel. Bob rode in the bed of the truck. I wasn't sure if the weredog had come along with Bishop or had also parked back at the hotel, but he was mighty displeased at having to come along now that his sniffing duties were no longer needed. Actually, I think he was probably still pissed about Bishop letting the neighbor guy pet him, but oh, well.

We parked by a tourist spot where a good number of shops were still open and in business. The pier was dotted with people fishing off the edge, staring through binoculars out into the ocean, or getting their daily steps in. We wove around the amateur yogis and volleyball players as we made our way north to the address the neighbor-guy had given us. Half a dozen surfers floated past the break, waiting for the perfect wave. I turned my back to the ocean and looked toward The Strand and at the huge modern houses with their eight-million-dollar beach-front views. As I scanned the row of craftsman-style and contemporary dwellings, one stood out.

"There." I pointed to the house, not even needing to read the number to know it was the right place.

When location was everything, buyers often razed the existing house and built to suit. This meant all the homes in the block had been erected within the last twenty years at the most—all except one.

The adorable gray and white one-story house had most likely been built in the thirties and had been lovingly maintained. It was tiny, surrounded by houses three times its size and height. Instead of trying to force a yard to survive against sand and wind, the owner had instead bricked in the patch in front of the house and filled it with Adirondack chairs surrounding a sunken fire pit. Clay pots filled with flowers added splashes of color to the patio area. I pulled the picture out of my pocket and looked past the smiling grandmotherly face to the house in the background.

"I'll send Bob around to see if anyone's home," Bishop said. The weredog trotted forward without any further commands, circling through the front yard, sniffing and cocking his hind leg to pee on some geraniums before heading around back.

I watched, looking for any movement behind the curtained windows, any sign that someone might be inside. When Bob came around and gave us the dog equivalent of a thumbs-up, I snuck closer, walking casually up to the front door as if I were asking to borrow a cup of sugar. Two cameras were pointed to the entrance. I didn't bother to knock, expecting my image on the cameras to bring someone running and shooting. There wasn't even a shadow across the peephole.

I didn't know how this particular security system worked, but I assumed the cameras were connected to a phone app that would alert the residents of a visitor even if they weren't home. If so, Henneg either didn't have her phone on her to get the notification or wasn't bothering to question my presence through the speakers.

Two cameras. And sensors along the door jamb. Putting a tentative hand on the door, I braced for a shock—or something else—but no electricity coursed through me. No knives shot out from the bushes into my back, either.

"He beat us here," Bishop told me. "Bob smelled him around the back door. He also smelled the woman who owned the previous house. She's been here recently."

I froze with my hand on the doorknob. "How recently?"

"Less than half an hour."

I swore, a cold chill of premonition shivering through me as I opened the unlocked door.

Blood decorated the lavender and cream walls. Stuffing protruded from bullet holes in the couch cushions. A body sprawled on the floor next to the couch. I didn't bother to check it for signs of life.

Two suitcases were stacked to my left, opened with contents dumped onto the floor. There was a clean area of the carpet beside the suitcases, blood splatter telling me that a box had once sat there—a box about the size of a case of bullets.

I walked over to look down at the dead body. "So, Navy SEAL Guy gets here, kills Bah, and takes the bullets. Why isn't Henneg dead?"

Bishop looked over at Bob, and they exchanged some wordless communication. "The man he was tracking and the woman were here at the same time. They left together."

I pondered that a moment. "So, he gets here, finds both Henneg and Bah out on bail and ready to skip town. There's a shootout—"

"There wasn't a shootout," Bishop interrupted. "This was

a hit. A violent hit, but still a hit. The only bullets are those in the couch and in this dead guy."

I swirled that around in my brain. "Navy SEAL Guy arrives and finds Bah. Shoots and kills him and goes to take the bullets. But Henneg arrives, and he doesn't kill her. He leaves with her." I walked over to the clean square of carpet. "Because not all the bullets were here? He killed Bah too quickly and realized only a few cases were here, so he's making Henneg lead him to the rest of the stash?"

Bishop shrugged. "That, or he's in league with her."

I frowned. "No. Not unless she just teamed up with him in the last hour or so. If he'd known Henneg before today, then he wouldn't have bothered to show up at Telaney's this morning to cut a deal with me."

"Bob can try to track him from here or track the woman. Depending on how the mage structured the spell, he might not be able to teleport more than one person via Kirby's Marble. Last I heard, it was one per focus."

"And I've got one of his focuses." I took the stone from my pocket. "I could see him maybe having a second one as a spare, but three?"

"That's a lot of money for three focus items," Bishop agreed. "So, he's probably not traveling by magic if she's with him."

I turned the stone over in my hand. "How does this work? Is there a magic word? Some sort of incantation?"

"I assume the spell is triggered through intent." Bishop raised his eyebrows. "You're not thinking of using it? It could take you anywhere."

"I'm guessing it's going to take me somewhere in the Valley, judging from the time gap from the last time I saw Navy SEAL Guy use it and when he showed up to grab me again." I looked up at Bishop. "Can you and Bob track Henneg, then text me if you catch up with either her or Navy

SEAL Guy? We're just following along behind him here. I'm going to see if I can't get ahead of the action."

He nodded. "What if the pair of them split up? Who do you want us to follow?"

I thought for a second. "Navy SEAL Guy. If he vanishes, I want to know."

Actually, if he vanished, I probably would know because he'd be right in front of me. I was assuming he'd gotten another focus and that would transport him to the same place I was about to go using this rock.

He'd killed Bah, grabbed Henneg, and would probably kill her once she led him to the bullets. Then I assumed he'd use this magical device to teleport himself and the bullets back home—or wherever this thing went.

And I'd be there waiting.

If Navy SEAL Guy didn't teleport back, then I was relying on Bishop and Bob to track him down and tell me where they were. Then…well, I didn't know what I'd do then. Call an Uber to drive me there or something? I'd figure it out later.

"Once I come out at the other end of this spell, I'll try to figure out exactly where I am and text you the location," I told Bishop, a bit worried that I might be getting in over my head. Navy SEAL Guy had taken me down every time he'd seen me. If it hadn't been for the help of others, he would have dragged me in for the bounty days ago.

"I'll know where you are," Bishop said.

I blinked at him in surprise. "But there's the magic. You said you and Bob couldn't track through the magic."

"That's others. I'll know where you are," Bishop repeated.

I just stared at him, wondering exactly what he meant by that.

"It will take me a half an hour at the most to home in on

your location once you arrive. If we reach a dead end on these two, I'll drop Bob at the hotel, then come to meet you."

"It will take you an hour or two to get to me, depending on traffic," I mused. If things really went south and I desperately needed Bishop, he'd arrive too late.

A ghost of a smile flickered at the corner of his mouth. "No. It won't. If things really go south and you're dying, I can get there faster. I'll be on time. I'll always be on time."

I caught my breath, remembering how he just appeared sometimes without a sound, as if he'd teleported there. But he'd said teleportation wasn't a common ability. Mages could craft a spell to mimic it. Some angels and demons could do it, but only very high-level ones.

What was Bishop? Was he a demon? Or…an angel?

"Okay." I looked down at the stone, then back up at Bishop. "See you later."

"See you later, Trouble."

I smiled at the nickname, rubbed the stone between my fingers, and told it to take me away.

CHAPTER 24

The Hermosa Beach house vanished, and I appeared in a living room, immediately doubling over with nausea and vertigo.

Screaming. A gunshot. Stumbling sideways, I fell over a couch, bounced off a footstool, then puked all over a blue and white striped rug. The room hadn't even stopped spinning when I felt something slam me in the stomach, sending me rolling across the vomit and the rug.

Wherever I'd ended up, I wasn't the only person here. And whoever else was in the room with me wasn't happy to have me pop from the ether into their little party. I tried to focus my vision, to get back to my feet, but the room tilted and dipped. Someone kicked me again, then yanked my arms behind my back and cuffed them.

Fuck. Cops carried handcuffs. And so had Navy SEAL Guy.

I dry heaved and tried to roll away from whoever was attacking me only to come up hard against a wall. Rough hands hauled me into a seated position. Even with my blurred vision, I recognized Navy SEAL Guy.

"You bitch." He gripped my shoulders and shook me. "You kept the rock. You kept it, and you know what it is and how to use it."

"What the hell?" a female voice shouted. "She appeared from nowhere. Is she a mage? An elf? Are my handcuffs going to hold her?"

My head lolled as I turned it, but I managed to see enough to confirm that the woman was Henneg. They'd gotten here before me. I was sure I had at least ten or fifteen minutes head start on them, but they must have gotten the bullets faster than I'd expected.

"It's a spelled talisman for teleportation," Navy SEAL Guy told her. "It's *my* talisman. She stole it from me, then used it."

"Just shoot her," Henneg said. "She's like a damned piece of gum on my shoe. I can't seem to get rid of her."

I held my breath at that, then remembered I was worth more alive than dead.

"Bounty," I managed to get out. "Alive and you get the bounty."

"That got cancelled yesterday. The tax office pulled it pending resolution of your debt or some shit like that." Navy SEAL Guy laughed. "Yes, I lied this morning when I told you I'd been offered an exclusive contract to bring you in. There was no contract. And there was no one else after you once that bounty got pulled."

Fucking dick.

"Then shoot her," Henneg repeated. "I'm not sharing the money with her."

Navy SEAL Guy stood, pulling the pistol from his hip holster. *Now would be a really good time to show up, Bishop,* I thought. He'd said he'd be here if I was going to die, and clearly this was a time when it definitely looked like I was going to die.

"I'm not sharing the money with her," Navy SEAL Guy said. "But I'm not sharing it with you, either."

He turned and shot in one fluid motion, hitting Henneg in the stomach. She bent over, eyes wide, then slid to the floor, leaving a smear of blood on the wall behind her. Navy SEAL Guy walked over and pulled her pistol out of the holster, tossing it away.

I stared at her, gasping on the floor, then looked at Navy SEAL Guy, wondering if I would be next.

"Still got a problem getting rid of this without paying taxes. I don't have a relationship with any of the pawnbrokers in the city, so there's a good chance they won't even buy the stuff, let alone pay me off the books for it."

He stuck the gun back into the holster, and I took a breath.

"This whole thing's falling apart," he complained to me. "First the bounty on you gets pulled, then the cops take those four cases from the botched hotel deal. I spend all afternoon running all over the city searching for the loot. Then bingo! I find it and shoot her partner, only to have this bitch walk in on me and put a gun to my head."

I shrugged, not seeing the big deal. He'd survived Hellkitty, and that wound had to be worse than a gunshot.

"I can fix most anything, but I've got the feeling having my brains blown out is not something I'm gonna walk away from," he said.

"You're a demon, aren't you?" I cleared my throat, happy that the nausea and vertigo had gone away.

"Am I?" He held out his hands. "I was hoping you could tell me. I never knew my real parents. They abandoned me as an infant. Maybe they were demons. Hell if I know."

I sucked in a breath, because his story was just like mine. A foundling infant. Parents unknown. Odd magical abilities.

But even if he was a demon, it didn't mean I was.

"Why didn't you shoot me?" It was a stupid thing to ask, reminding him that he'd neglected to kill me. Yet.

He shrugged. "I want to know how you survived. I saw you go over the edge of that building. It was seventy-three stories down, and I know you didn't have a parachute. And I wanted to know what you were, because clearly we're the same. Do you have wings or something? Man, I'd sure like it if one day I sprouted wings. That's how the regeneration thing came on, you know. One day I got shot, and the thing closed up while I watched."

"Yeah. I got wings," I lied. "You'll probably get them in a few years."

"Epic." He walked over to me and yanked my backpack off my shoulders. After a somewhat painful struggle as he tried to remove it with my hands cuffed behind me, he undid the straps.

"Let's see what you've got for me." He walked over to the sofa and started going through the contents of my pack. "You stole from me. Now I'll steal from you."

I winced as he tossed the expensive demonology book aside, clearly uninterested in that. He pocketed my knives, what cash I had in the backpack, then pulled a velvet bag out of a side section.

"Whatcha got here, Alvaro?" He untied the bag and dumped a thick gold necklace with a gaudy dragon pendant into his palm. "Holy shit. This is the ugliest piece of jewelry I've ever seen." With a laugh, he draped the necklace over his head. "Look at me. I'm a rapper. Shit, I might just keep this thing."

"It's cursed." I smiled. "Whoever puts that necklace on, dies. All their bones evaporate, and they die a puddle of flesh on the floor."

His laughter abruptly ceased. "Don't fuck with me,

Alvaro. You can die quickly, or you can die slowly, so I suggest you not fuck with me."

I nodded toward the backpack. "There's an envelope in there. Look in it. Four crime scene photos—each of them someone this cursed necklace killed. It was safe in that special, magical bag, but now that you've touched it, now that you've put it on, you're cursed."

I was embellishing a bit, but he didn't have to know that.

Navy SEAL Guy ripped the envelope open and pulled the pictures out, paling as he looked at them.

"The first guy's wearing it," I told him. "He kept it on, so he didn't die for a few days. The others removed it and…well, I'd suggest you not remove it."

"You're lying." His voice shook. "That's not…this necklace didn't do that."

"You've bought magical items before. You've got a stone that allows you to teleport to a set location. How is it such a stretch to believe a mage that has the power to create a tele-portation device could also curse an object to kill someone in a horrible way?"

"Bitch. Bitch." He threw the pictures down and came for me, hauling me up against the wall and banging me against it a few times. "I should kill you for this."

"Then you'd never find out the antidote."

He stopped banging me against the wall. "Give me the antidote, and I'll let you live. I'm not splitting the loot with you, but I won't kill you—at least not tonight."

"If I give you the antidote, you won't kill me or attempt to kill me for the next forty-eight hours. You will let me leave this place without further harm, on my own volition and not under any threat from you."

He shot me a puzzled look. "Uh, okay?"

"Swear it. Swear it on all the souls you bought or took or own." I had no idea why I'd added that little bit, except

Nevarra's kidnapper had insisted on such a thing when I'd made a promise to him, so I felt it must be important.

"Uh, I swear on my soul, or on others' souls, that I won't kill you or attempt to kill you for the next two days, and I'll let you leave here without further harm, on your own and not under any threat from me. Okay? Is that good enough? Where the fuck is the antidote?"

"In my backpack is a bag of tea. It says Herb-a-licious on the label. Brew it and drink it. The mage that cursed the necklace put the antidote in the tea." That wasn't exactly how it worked, but I didn't have time to go into a lengthy recitation of what Mathias had told me about the magical properties of lavender.

He ran to my backpack, tossing things onto the floor until he found the bag. "How do I know if it works or not?"

"You drink it, you take the necklace off, and you don't die."

Maybe the tea worked. Maybe it didn't. I hadn't heard anything about Karen dying, so I assumed Mathias had been right about it.

He shot me a narrow-eyed glance. "And if I do die?"

I shrugged as best as I could with my hands cuffed behind my back. "I'm stuck here handcuffed with a dying woman across the room. You'll probably regenerate your bones before I manage to get out of here."

"That's right," he breathed. "I can heal. I won't die. Curse or no curse, I'll be fine."

"No, you won't be fine," I reminded him, just in case he decided the deal was off the table. "You're going to suffer as your bones dissolve. Then you'll be a pile of goo on your floor until who knows how long. And I can't guarantee that you won't keep dying over and over again. The curse isn't broken until you drink the tea."

He nodded, then glared at me. "If this doesn't work, as

soon as I grow my bones back, I'm putting the necklace on you."

"It works."

"Swear on that soul stuff," he demanded.

"I swear that the mage who created the cursed necklace told me this was the antidote. I swear it on all the souls stuff." I glared back. "There. Happy?"

He spun around without replying, taking the bag of tea into the kitchen. As soon as he was out of sight, I yanked on the cuffs, trying to get them off. I couldn't get my gun out of the holster with my hands like this. I could probably manage to pick up Henneg's gun from where Navy SEAL Guy had thrown it, but trying to shoot him from behind my back with my hands secured at my waist would be tricky.

A noise in the corner caught my attention. I turned and saw Henneg, holding her gut wound with one hand, the other hand outstretched toward me. She opened her fingers, and there on her bloody palm lay a set of keys.

I ran to her, kneeling down and turning around. It took her a few tries, but finally I felt the cuffs slide off.

"Kill him," she hissed at me.

I intended to do just that. Rubbing my wrists, I pulled my pistol from the holster and hugged the wall as I made my way around the edges of the living room. With a quick prayer, I swung into the kitchen and unloaded my magazine right into the back of Navy SEAL Guy's head.

It made a horrible mess. I was pretty sure he wasn't healing half a dozen bullets to the brain, but just in case, I pulled his gun from its holster and emptied that magazine into his skull as well.

Bishop showed up just as I was unloading a third set of bullets into the guy.

"Trouble…what the hell are you doing?"

"Making sure. This fucker's like a zombie, and I want to make sure he's really dead."

"I can assure you that he's really dead. Even a zombie isn't coming back from that."

I dropped Navy SEAL Guy's gun on the counter, slid another magazine into mine, and returned it to my shoulder holster. "Took you long enough to get here. I almost died."

Bishop rolled his eyes. "You didn't almost die."

"I *did* almost die. They had me cuffed, and this asshole was going to shoot me."

"He didn't shoot you," Bishop countered.

"He almost did. And if you had waited to show up until he'd already shot me, you would have been too late." I gestured to the body on the floor with a splattered mess where his head once was. "That could have been me. I could have been dead with my brains all over the carpet in the living room by the time you showed up. You were supposed to be here instantly if I was going to die."

"You weren't going to die. Trust me." He smiled at me, and my heart did a few brief gymnastics. "But I'm here now, and I brought the truck. I'm assuming you need help transporting thirteen cases of ammunition to a pawnshop?"

"Well, I'm hardly going to walk down the street carrying it for twenty miles." Yes, my tone was more than a little bit snappish, but I was still upset over the almost-dying thing.

"Then get everything you want from this house and let's get going."

"Henneg's out in the living room. He shot her." I bit my lip, knowing that I couldn't just leave the woman here to die even after all she'd done to me. Yes, she'd uncuffed me, but one good deed didn't erase all the shitty things she'd done that harmed me, my family, and probably countless other people.

But as much as I hated her, I couldn't walk away and let

her die slowly and painfully. I had to see if I could keep her from dying. So she could stand trial for her crimes, you know. Yeah, that was it.

"I saw her. You want to take her body out back and use it for target practice or something? Maybe shoot a dozen bullets in her skull as well?"

"Body? Did she die? She was alive when I shot Navy SEAL Guy. She helped uncuff me so I could kill him."

"Well, she's dead now." He tilted his head and regarded me. "Were you seriously going to try to get her to a hospital or something? In the bed of my truck?"

It sounded ridiculous, but yes. That's what I'd been planning to do. Wait. I could super-heal. Navy SEAL Guy could super-heal. I was sure Bishop could super-heal better than either of us could.

"Can you fix her wound? Bring her back to life?"

His eyebrows shot up. "Are you kidding? No, I can't do that."

Bishop denied being able to do a lot of things I knew very well he could do, so I wasn't about to take that as his final answer.

"Please." I stepped closer and put a hand on his chest. "For me? Can you bring her back to life for me? I'd be very…grateful."

He laughed. "No, Trouble. Even though the prospect of having sex with you in a kitchen covered with blood, tissue, and brain matter is quite enticing, I can't perform resurrections. Dead is dead."

Well, I tried. And honestly, that was probably more than I owed Henneg anyway.

Bishop loaded the cases of bullets into the truck, then waited outside while I did a quick sweep of the house for anything of value and gathered my belongings into my backpack. Just before leaving, I plugged a few more bullets into

Navy SEAL Guy's head, just in case. Then I pulled the necklace off him and returned it, bloody and gory, to its bag.

Bags was waiting for me with cash in hand when we got to the pawnshop.

I came out to find Bishop's truck still outside the pawnshop.

"Get in. I'll take you to the tax office," he told me.

"It's after five. They'll be closed."

I was definitely nervous with all this cash. It had been hard enough to squeeze seventy-three hundred bucks in the inside pocket of my pants. There was no way I could manage to put the other thirteen grand in there, so it was divided up into pockets of my pants and my backpack. I was literally stuffed with money. And it worried me. What if someone robbed me? I wanted to pay off the tax demons and get this over and done with, but it was probably going to have to wait until tomorrow morning.

"The admin offices are closed, but there's always someone there for payments and after-hours work."

It made sense. Someone had to be around if a Fixer brought in a bounty late at night.

We drove downtown, the lights on the high-rises reminding me of better days before the demons ripped so many of these buildings apart. Bishop was right; there was a Low at the tax office who took my money and wrote me out a receipt as well as e-mailing a paid invoice to my phone. We swung by the InterContinental to get my bike, and Bishop surprised me by loading it into the bed of his truck and driving me home instead of just dropping me off in the garage.

I still had fifty-three hundred in my pants pockets. As we drove, I thought of all the things we could do with that. It would be a good start on savings to get us out of New Hell and established over the border. Or we could put solar panels on the house, put in some sort of water management system.

By the time Bishop had pulled up to the front of my house, I'd made my decision. Pulling the money out, I handed it to him.

"Here. I'll swing by tomorrow sometime and get a receipt."

I honestly didn't know how much I owed him at this point. I wasn't sure I wanted to know. As much as I hated handing this money over, he'd helped me. He'd earned it—him and Bob.

Bishop counted out the money, then handed me five hundred back. "Here. You're going to need this."

How many solar panels would five hundred dollars buy? I wondered. Probably not many, but I took the cash just in case. It would be good to have a little bit of a buffer, and I appreciated that Bishop didn't seem anxious to have this debt between us settled.

We got out. As Bishop unloaded my bike, I noticed a strange car in the driveway. A Prius. Newish. Very clean. Had Doctor Mwangi gotten a new car?

"Who's that?" I wondered.

Bishop parked my bike and looked over at the car. "Kevin Wong."

I did a double take. Who the hell was Kevin Wong? And Bishop knew him? I walked over to stand next to him. Both of us looked at the car, then in some weird synchronicity, we turned to face each other.

"Thank you," I told him. "For tonight. For...everything." I wasn't sure what I was thanking him for, so I made it a kind of blanket gratitude statement. Being my backup. Helping me track down the bad guys. Chauffeuring me all over the city tonight.

Maybe swooping in like Superman and saving me from splatting onto the pavement outside the InterContinental.

What was *he*? And what the hell was I? Was Bishop my feathered, winged savior? I didn't really want to think about that or about what sort of being had feathered wings, could teleport, and could mind-whammy people. The answer to that question was even more frightening than the one I was about to ask.

"Do you think…am I a demon?" I looked up into Bishop's blue eyes, afraid of what I might see there.

It took him a while to answer. "It doesn't matter what I think. It doesn't matter what other people call you," he said gruffly. "The only thing that matters is what you are."

I got the impression he wasn't just talking about me. Reaching out, I touched his arm, feeling that electrifying zing that went through me every time my skin connected with his. Not electric like my magic. Not electric like static. It was as if something beyond our bodies was connecting, something deep inside the both of us.

"I'm not a demon," I whispered. "I don't know what I am, but I'm not a demon."

He bent down and placed a kiss on my forehead. "You're Eden." He smiled. "And you're most definitely Trouble. Those are the only labels you need."

And with that, he got into his truck and drove away. I watched him go, still feeling his lips against my forehead. It hadn't been a kiss-kiss. It hadn't been sexy. But it was intimate. Like a benediction. Like a charm.

The exact opposite of that horrible necklace that I still had in my backpack. Ugh, I needed to get rid of it first thing in the morning. Hopefully Mathias's shop was open early. I could swing by his place, meet Juke for breakfast to give her an abbreviated version of what happened tonight, then check in with Bags and a few other people about any potential Vulture jobs.

Then I'd go to Suerte to see Bishop.

Going inside, I was surprised to see Bea and the girls in the living room, entertaining our visitor with glasses of iced tea and a large bowl of potato chips. Kevin Wong stood as I walked into the room. I came to an abrupt stop, recognizing him immediately.

This was the leader from the Canyon Drive neighborhood, the guy in the gray suit.

"I don't want any trouble." I shot an uneasy glance toward Bea and the girls. "Can we step outside and talk? I'm willing to come to some sort of agreement with you, to make things right between us."

Kevin nodded. "Yes, let's go outside." He turned to Bea and extended his hand. "It was very nice to meet you and your other daughters. Thank you for the tea. And the chips."

Bea stood. "Any friend of Eden's is always welcome. Please come back again, Kevin."

Friend? *Friend?*

We stepped outside. I led him over to his car, trying to put some distance between us and the house, just in case things went sideways. In spite of the whole friend thing, I didn't know what Wong was doing here or what to expect from him.

"First, I want to apologize for the other day," he jumped right in.

I waved that away. "It's okay. It was a fair fight. Dennis went a little far at the end, and I had to defend myself. Let's just call it good and forget the whole thing."

"No, I mean we never should have challenged you like that. I take full responsibility for the actions of my people. We just assumed you were a squatter moving in. If we had known…" He ran a hand through his hair, and it fell perfectly back into place. "But we should have known. I should have known, and I accept responsibility for that."

I had no idea what the fuck this guy was going on about. "It's all good. Seriously. No harm, no foul. We're totally good here." I stuck my hand out. He eyed it for a few seconds, then reluctantly shook it, releasing my fingers as quickly as possible. I was surprised he didn't wipe his hand on his pants afterward.

Instead, he put his hand into his pants pocket, pulled out a set of keys, and extended them toward me.

"I'm glad to hear it. I'm so grateful for your understanding and forgiveness. If you need assistance in moving furniture or other items, don't hesitate to call on any of us. Once you're settled in, please let us know your schedule. We would be honored to host a welcome party to introduce you to everyone. You honor us with your presence in our neighborhood, Ksatrei."

I took the keys and watched him drive away, not sure what the hell had just happened. Were these keys to the house? Welcome party? Bishop knew him. Had he somehow intervened in this? But how had he known?

And who the fuck was Ksatrei?

I sat on the curb, trying to sort through everything that had just happened—actually, everything that had happened today. Navy SEAL Guy was dead, hopefully. Henneg and Bah were dead. The fake salvage report had been removed. The tax demons were paid, and there was no further bounty on my head. My family was safe.

And I evidently had a house.

There was still the debt I owed Bishop. And that promise to Desiree. And the assistance I owed the tax demons. Still, life was good. I looked down at the keys in my hand and grinned. Life was really good.

Something warm and furry brushed up against my arm. I

started, then held very still as a little gray kitten crawled into my lap, kneading my pants with sharp claws before curling into a little purring ball.

Shit. I stared at the little monster for a few seconds, then slowly reached a hand out and touched its soft fur. The kitten's bright green eyes looked up at me, then he blinked them closed and snuggled in to sleep in my lap.

I was trapped out here, sitting on the curb with a kitten from Hel in my lap. It was going to be a long night.

* * *

READY FOR MORE? Ventura Hellway, book 3 in the California Demon Series, release July 27th.

Cornucopia

Unholy Pleasures

City of Lust

* * *

<u>Imp World Novels</u>

No Man's Land

Stolen Souls

Three Wishes

Northern Lights

Far From Center

Penance

* * *

<u>Northern Wolves</u>

Juneau to Kenai

Rogue

Winter Fae

Bad Seed

* * *

<u>The Templar Series</u>

Dead Rising

Last Breath

Bare Bones

Famine's Feast

Royal Blood

Dark Crossroads

* * *

<u>Accidental Witches Series</u>

Brimstone and Broomsticks

Warmongers and Wands

Death and Divination

Hell and Hexes

Minions and Magic

Fiends and Familiars

Devils and the Dead (2021)

* * *

<u>White Lightning Series</u>

Wooden Nickels

Bum's Rush

Clip Joint

Jake Walk

Trouble Boys

Packing Heat (TBD)

ACKNOWLEDGMENTS

Sending a big shout-out to Melissa Marr who read my very clunky first draft, and saw the diamond in the rough. Her suggestions made this book really shine!

Thank you to my friends and family who were my sounding boards and helped me connect with resources as I did my research.

I really appreciate the help of Adam Richardson from the Writer's Detective Bureau who gave me a cop's view on how the police might work in a dystopian LA.

Also, big thanks to my copyeditors Kimberly Cannon and Erin Zarro whose eagle eyes catch the typos and keep my comma problem in line, and to Damonza for once again providing me with an amazing cover design.

Debra lives in a little house in the woods of Maryland with her sons and two slobbery bloodhounds. On a good day, she jogs and horseback rides, hopefully managing to keep the horse between herself and the ground. Her only known super power is 'Identify Roadkill'.

For more information:
www.debradunbar.com

www.ingramcontent.com/pod-product-compliance
Lightning Source LLC
Chambersburg PA
CBHW021303190726
48288CB00003B/671